PRAISE FOR

Longlisted for the 2019 Internation

BLACK
FOAM

BLACK FOAM

a novel

HAJI JABIR

translated by Sawad Hussain & Marcia Lynx Qualey

AMAZON **CROSSING**

Previously published as رغوة سوداء by Dar al-Tanweer in Lebanon in 2018. Translated from Arabic by Sawad Hussain and Marcia Lynx Qualey. First published in English by Amazon Crossing in 2023.

Published by Amazon Crossing, Seattle

www.apub.com

Amazon, the Amazon logo, and Amazon Crossing are trademarks of Amazon.com, Inc., or its affiliates.

ISBN-13: 9781542034029 (hardcover)
ISBN-13: 9781542034036 (paperback)
ISBN-13: 9781542034012 (digital)

Cover design by Jarrod Taylor
Cover image: ©Remy Roosien / EyeEm / Getty Images

Printed in the United States of America
First edition

To Walid Mohammed:
It's still there, the bell that you hung to ring
whenever we look in the mirror.
But we barely recognize ourselves now.

The sole survivor of a slaughter comes to
worship the dagger.
—Atef Khairy

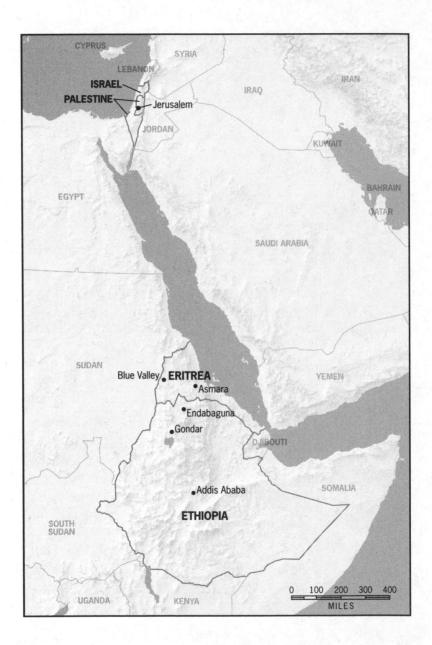

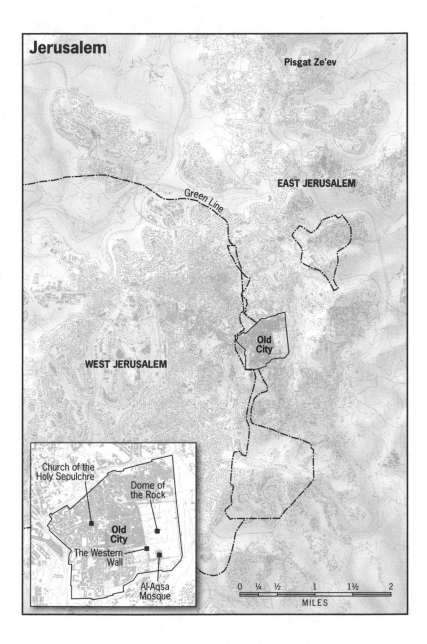

(1)

It seemed like any other Saturday in Addis Ababa.

It *looked* like any other December day. The sky was bleak, the weather verged on chilly, and the city's taverns were getting ready to welcome the crowds of customers, who had no intention of letting the weekend pass without pouring out their exhaustion at the bar: Stella, Heineken, Guinness, Corona, Harar—and, for the hardworking class, St. George. A soccer team that had snapped up the brew's name had instantly rocketed to stardom before even achieving a thing.

It could have been an ordinary day, if not for what was happening at that very moment elsewhere in the city.

Five buses, one after the other, were being escorted by two police cars as they sped through a light drizzle, moving from the meeting point in Meskel Square in central Addis to the suburb of Bole, where the airport was located. Onlookers lined up on both sides of the mud-spattered asphalt road for six kilometers: curious, resentful, sad. Only a few were waving, although they saw nothing but their own fragmented reflections in the buses' tinted windows.

Inside the buses were men, women, and children, all united in their delight at having been chosen, tinged by a feeling of loss—of their earlier life, their friends, and Mother Ethiopia. But it was a sentiment so fragile that it could be dispelled by a Martha Kidani song that a passenger in the fourth bus began to timidly sing. Everyone joined in enthusiastically, keeping the beat by clapping and drumming on the windows:

At last, the day has come:
It's come, it's come, the day has come.

It's come beautiful and tall, and unafraid of fate
It's come to wipe away our sweat:
It's come, it's come, the day has come.

It's come to say goodbye to yesterday
And to stay with us forever:
It's come, it's come, the day has come.

The man sitting by the window in seat 37 was the only one who didn't join in.

His head was covered up by a white scarf with blue knotted tassels, and he held a hand to his face, shadowing the rest of his features. He did his best to ignore the thickset man asleep beside him, the man's heavy head resting on his shoulder.

Unlike those around him and on the other buses, this man looked back, thinking about everything that had happened up until this moment, hoping against hope that this journey would end with his sole desire:

Salvation!

(2)

Last night, in vain, the man tried to fall asleep.

The kids around him were crying, and loud music drifted in from outside the stadium, pounding against his ears with its obnoxious beat.

He was desperate for sleep, and he was running from himself and the loud ringing. People around him knocked up against him, yanking him back to the reality of this unroofed stadium near Meskel Square, packed with those newly arrived from Gondar. The stadium was a pit stop on the way to their final destination, which they would head off to tomorrow.

Their journey had gone on for hours and hours before they arrived at the capital from the northern hinterlands. The Tata bus convoy had driven over paved roads and dirt tracks as it hugged the curves of a tiny, winding tributary of the Blue Nile. The bus swayed, but the view outside the window stayed the same: mud huts, animals milling around and people doing the same, their heads half-shaved, their eyes looking without interest before they went back to staring blankly into the distance.

The farewell scene at the camp stuck in his mind.

◆   ◆   ◆

The crowd had been ready to pounce on the buses that stood near the Gondar camp entrance. They had gotten tired of listening to an elderly rabbi reading methodically from a stack of papers clasped in his veined hands. When he fell silent for a moment, as though looking for a lost word, people thought he was finished—or they pretended to so they could be done waiting. They pushed toward the doors, leaving the rabbi stunned before he folded up the papers and stuffed them into a pocket.

He had been rooted to the spot, waiting for Saba to appear. He couldn't leave without saying goodbye.

He hadn't been waiting long before he caught sight of her, searching for him. He waved and she ran over, spreading her arms wide. He wanted to tell her so many things or at least to thank her, but in the end, he chose silence. She didn't say anything either. He felt her hot breath on his neck. Her voice rose in a sob. Still, he was silent. He didn't reciprocate her feelings of anguish. He was cold and stiff, although inside he was collapsing, and he wanted to howl like a wounded wolf. But he didn't. He couldn't.

When she'd calmed down a little, she took his hands in hers and looked in his eyes. Her wet eyes spoke volumes. She slipped some money into his pocket. He tried to refuse. But, as always, her insistence was stronger.

He boarded the bus and settled in at the back. She stayed where she was—where he'd just been. She waved at him, and this time, she was smiling. He gave her a faint smile, but it soon faded as the buses drove off, passing through the main gate.

Crowds thronged outside the gate, and when they saw the buses, they grew even louder. The police tried to restrain the angry crowd blocking the convoy. Some of the passengers had opened their windows, and the voices from outside reached them clearly:

"Take us with you!"

"We're Jews too!"

"God damn those of you who bribed your way on!"

Someone stepped on his hand while stumbling past, jolting him out of his Gondar memories and bringing him back to the noise of the stadium. He turned to the large clock hanging above him. Its hour hand was creeping lazily toward the eight. Suddenly he got up, seized by the idea of wandering around and losing himself in the Addis night. To be swallowed up in the crowd, to no longer know where he was!

He found Meskel Square bustling with sex workers, street dancers, and Christmas trees decorated in colorful, twinkling lights. He remembered Saba telling him how much Ethiopians loved to sing. He'd thought she was exaggerating when she said they couldn't live without it, that singing was their mother tongue.

He left the square and turned right, walking past the street's bars and cafés, ignoring the girls calling out to him to come into their shops. Sometimes, he averted his eyes; for others, he pretended not to understand their Amharic, which he'd mastered in the army. Like so many people, he knew how skilled these girls were at ambushing passersby and stripping them of their possessions without facing an ounce of resistance. He didn't dare test himself against their magic.

Addis was *alive*, unlike what he'd been hearing for so many years. The Ethiopians weren't preparing for war, as he'd thought. It was shocking how the river of life flowed here, unchecked, while their opponents in Eritrea had paused everything to wait for the first bullet. Here, there was no waiting. Everything just kept moving.

He walked through a crowded area to another street that seemed quieter. He slowed his pace and took in the names of the bars: **GREAT ABYSSINIA. THE EMPEROR. VICTORY.**

So the enemy hadn't totally set aside preparations for war. Instead, they'd made it a part of daily life. The bar **EDEL** caught his attention. He was struck by the name; it meant "destiny" in Amharic. He got closer, emboldened by the lack of a woman at the door to pressure passersby. Inside, a few customers were listening to live music. Hesitantly, he crossed the threshold and was swallowed up by the darkness inside. Only the space around the musicians was lit. He was greeted by a smiling brown waitress, who asked how many people were in his party. He remembered stories about these people's magic, and he thought about turning back, but the singer onstage had already ensnared him.

"Just one."

The waitress led him to an even darker corner at the back, with a view of the whole restaurant. As he walked, he saw the women's gazes shift in his direction, and a little vanity crept over him.

It was more crowded than he had expected. He sat down and turned toward the singer, who swayed in front of three musicians. It wasn't her version of Bob Marley's song, which he liked, that caught his attention. It was her short hair, her round glasses, and her large breasts, all of which took him back to his long days on the front lines in Komochtato. The waitress came back with the bottle of St. George that he'd ordered. A napkin fell out of her grasp, and he grabbed it first, telling her he'd keep it. Before she could get over her surprise, he leaned in and asked the singer's name.

"Deborah."

He smiled when he saw the singer really did look like her name. She truly was beelike, like her name suggested, stinging his soul with her graceful, swaying movements.

A young man walked into the bar. The women all turned to look at him, too, which dispelled any sense he'd had of being special.

The song ended, and Deborah bowed to the crowd's applause. He didn't join in. He was content to slug down half the bottle as he gazed at her, taking in her short black dress, which left her back bare; her wavy hair; and her broad smile. She looked as flattered by the applause as a child would be, her hand lifting to cover her mouth.

The noise fell away, and Deborah went back to singing. This time, it was a local song. But her presence kept distracting him from the song. He wondered which of the three men behind her was her lover. Was it the fat one blowing on the saxophone, who couldn't take his eyes off her and who kept exchanging smiles with her? Or was it the one sweating as he energetically beat the drums—the one who seemed deep inside himself, far from the scene? Or why wouldn't it be the cocky and handsome guitarist, whose gaze kept shifting between her and his fellow musicians?

It didn't matter. Deborah took a step forward, raising a hand to shield her face from the spotlight's glare. She was looking at him. He felt her studying his features, and a faint tremor ran through his body. Without knowing why, he decided to get up and leave in the middle of the song—maybe because he'd absorbed enough of her to keep going through the rest of the night. He downed the rest of the beer, put his money on the table, and stood up. As he walked out, Deborah followed him with her eyes. He could see her reflection in the glass in front of him. He was filled with a vain pride, and this time he left before anyone could come in and dispel the feeling.

(3)

The buses stopped in front of the entrance to Terminal 2, the terminal for international flights.

The passengers stayed on the bus, just as they were, for about an hour, until a group of rabbis flanked by guards in civilian clothes walked past the buses, one by one.

The man in seat 37 on the fourth bus watched everything from where he sat—or as much as the rain-streaked windows allowed. Clearly, he didn't want anyone else to notice how uneasy he felt—an unease exacerbated by the stocky man snoring loudly beside him.

Time passed, heavy and oppressive. He wanted to silence all the tongues that filled the bus with chatter and his head with anxiety, but something else took care of it: the doors to the fourth bus opened, chasing away the clamor of the women and their children. The sudden silence caused the man next to him to wake up in a panic.

"Shalom."

"Shalom aleichem," the passengers responded, making a show of answering this greeting from one of the three rabbis. He smiled in surprise at their mastery of the Hebrew greeting and added, "God bless Gondar." But as soon as he'd added these words, in the same language, it was apparent that no one understood what he was saying.

The rabbi's sermon lasted for ten minutes, interrupted by the translation. He seemed to be repeating what the local men of religion had said in Meskel Square—and before that, in Gondar—but with a feigned fervor.

"You are now hours away from fulfilling your dream of return to the Promised Land, to the land of milk and honey, to Great Israel, where suffering ends in submission to the will of the Elokim. Your group, 'the Dove's Wings,' is part of a blessed campaign, wrapped in the prayers of everyone over there, to end the diaspora of Beta Israel and return to the first homeland. The tribulations that you have so patiently borne before reaching Gondar, with the patience of believers, have ended forevermore. This was only a trial from Elokim to test the devotion of your hearts to the Holy Land. It was a trial that has hung around your necks since the great displacement of the Tribe of Dan before . . ." The rabbi stopped, noticing the dwindling enthusiasm with which his speech was being received. Suddenly filled with doubt, he asked, "Do you know what the Tribe of Dan should mean to you?"

His question was met with grunts as people fumbled for the right answer. Then heads turned to the back, confidently, the rabbi's eyes following them, until they settled on seat 37 next to the window. But the man who sat in that seat avoided their gazes, lowering his eyes and pulling his scarf down over his face.

"What! Don't you know that you were descended from the Tribe of Dan, and that it was your ancestors who were exiled from the Holy Land, and your ancestors who became lost? What did they teach you in Gondar?"

After a brief pause, the rabbi swallowed his anger and continued with his sermon, although he struggled to recover his initial tone. "This anguish plagued all of our souls, but Elokim has gathered up your diaspora once again in Gondar, where the journey to your final destination began. Aliya, aliya, may Elokim bless all the olim hadashim who are here."

The rabbi paused again, ready to test their knowledge. This time, the passengers were quick to speak, attempting to wash off the stain of ignorance that clung to them. They told him that they knew the aliya was the ascension to Israel, and that he had called down blessings for each ascendant among them.

As the rabbi wrapped up his talk, he felt some satisfaction, and so he began to share the good news about the sort of life that awaited them in Israel. The passengers scrambled up to kiss his hand, but he hurried out, his two companions in tow, and the doors closed behind them.

On the plane to Israel, the man who had sat beside the window in seat 37 of the fourth bus was still uneasy. It had nothing to do now with the stocky man, who had disappeared into the crowds at the departure hall. Nor was the man bothered that there weren't any seats on the plane, which was like the belly of a huge whale, swallowing a month's supply of people and bags, leaving the available air at a bare minimum. It wasn't because of the panic caused by puffs of white smoke billowing up from the sides of the plane, which the other passengers thought were signs of a fire, although it turned out to be just cold air, saving them from suffocation. It wasn't because of the rabbis' disappearances, either, as they'd chosen to travel on a different plane. No. It was because of what he had faced at the last checkpoint, just before boarding the plane.

◆　◆　◆

The rabbis left, and time passed before the bus doors were opened again. After that, the group was led to an inner hall, where they spent the night, waiting until shortly before dawn to check in. People got in line behind a security guard, who led them to the hall with the Ethiopian Airlines desk.

"Tezegaju . . . waraqat . . . waraqat."

The long line followed an airport employee's directions, getting their papers ready before they reached the checkpoint.

With a trembling hand, the man who had been sitting beside the window in seat 37 of the fourth bus pulled a sheet of paper from his pants pocket. It had all his personal information, including his fingerprints, and was stamped with the Tigray Region's government seal,

11

along with the seal of the American Association of Ethiopian Jews and the Jewish Agency for Migration. He felt the seals, then ran his finger over his name and reread this language, which was filled with a certainty about his identity that he couldn't feel. He did this ten times or maybe more, until he'd memorized everything on his paper, although his anxiety still didn't ease.

As much as he wanted to walk through the final gate, his feet resisted stepping into the space left by the person in front of him, as if expecting a trap that would lure them to injury. His eyes darted from side to side, peering through the tiny slit left open by the white scarf pulled tightly around his face. He didn't meet the gazes of the guards around him. It felt like he was standing on a small stage lit by a burning spotlight, while everyone else took their places as his audience. He tried to distract himself from his uneasiness by patting the head of a child next to him, which was shaved except for one patch of hair at the front of the child's head. But instead, he found himself pulling on the child's hair with a sharpness that made the boy cry out and attracted the hard stares of people around him.

Finally, it was his turn.

An Israeli officer grabbed the paper, his gaze darting sharply between the photo and the man's face as the man responded to the officer's command to completely remove the white scarf. The man was in his late thirties, on the short side with square shoulders. Dark skinned, with close-cropped, thinning curly hair. He had a small, jutting forehead, and his broad nose took up most of his face. The inspection took seconds. It seemed like an impossible eternity.

"This isn't one of us. He's not a Jew!"

The shout came from an old woman as she went through the gate, pointing in his direction. She let out a cruel laugh, revealing a lonely pair of teeth in the middle of her upper jaw. It didn't take long for him to recognize her. He struggled to remain calm as he felt the suspicious gazes of the officer and airline staff.

"What's your name?"

The officer, seemingly under the influence of the old woman, had chosen to examine him all over again. Even though the question was straightforward, it felt hazy and complicated, and it took him a while to untangle it. He answered in disjointed syllables, struggling to pull them together:

"Dawit."

(4)

The moment the black Cherokee stopped in front of the camp's entrance, the guards rushed to open the gate, which was freshly painted with a six-pointed star. They saluted the woman who sat behind the wheel with exaggerated humility, and she lowered her window. With their heads bowed and open palms outstretched, they approached her. She placed money in their hands and drove inside.

The man who sat beside her kept his eyes on the guards. They pressed their lips to what had been given to them, gratefully, before slipping it into their pockets and closing the large gate. His presence went unnoticed.

"Don't forget even one word of what we agreed."

He nodded, anxiously rubbing his sweaty palms. The whole way from the hotel to the camp, Saba had repeated her instructions until she was sure he knew them by heart.

"You've finally returned after you and your father, Elias, were separated fifteen years ago, on the way from Mekele to Gondar." She paused to emphasize how crucial it was that he pronounce these names correctly.

"Your father was still grieving the loss of your mother, Rachel. He'd only just turned his head for a minute, and the smugglers kidnapped you. You spent the whole time as a slave, held by a man who had you care for his farm, and you couldn't leave until he died. You'd heard from your father, over and over, about his frequent visits to the Abyssinia Hotel to sell ghee to a friend, which is why you came to find me." She paused for a moment, as if searching for a stray idea, before she went on. "That's enough. As for the rest, I'll take care of it."

The car passed a shelter that had been readied for prayers, then continued down a winding, rutted dirt road with jutting rocks scattered on either side. The Cherokee's violent shaking and the howls of the skinny dog running alongside the car shattered Dawit's attempts to hold himself together. His gaze flitted everywhere as he tried to quickly familiarize himself with the landscape: withered trees, stinking pools of water, broken-down thatch houses with cracked mud-brick steps. Children playing football, two leafless trees acting as the goalposts. Women padding through the streets barefoot in short, off-white smocks and tight robes, their babies bound to their backs.

The car stopped at a reed shed that sat on wooden supports, surrounded on all four sides by foot-high sandbags. Saba cut the engine and turned to Dawit, testing his readiness. He gave her a reassuring smile. Two men came out to welcome Saba, inviting her inside. Dawit noticed, for the second time, how he became invisible in her presence. It didn't bother him. No—he hoped it would stay like that until his wish came true.

Inside, he sat deliberately on the mud-brick bench next to his companion. In front of them were five men, all wearing loose white robes. One by one, the eyes of these men turned toward Dawit, who remained rooted. The weight of their gazes took his breath away. He felt no relief until Saba spoke.

"This is your son, the one I told you about. Dawit is the son of Rachel and Elias, and God has restored him to you after a long absence so that he could fulfill his true destiny, and so the breeze of relief can cool his parents' souls in the Kingdom of Heaven. It has been confirmed beyond a shadow of a doubt that this is the one you seek."

Saba continued in a confident tone, reeling off evidence based on her long relationship with Elias, Dawit's father, who had come to sell ghee and so spent some days at her Abyssinia Hotel. He had told her all

16

about what he was doing and how his family in Mekele were, until she felt she knew all the corners of his life. Although Elias had spent his final days in this very camp in Gondar, where Dawit was now sitting, no one really knew him as deeply as Saba had. As she spoke, Dawit observed the effect her speech had on her listeners out of the corner of his eye, watching how their gazes shifted between her and him.

◆ ◆ ◆

Saba's enthusiasm reminded him of their first meeting, when he had just arrived in Gondar, exhausted, after walking all the way from Endabaguna.

He'd headed straight for the camp and tried to enter but to no avail, so he went on wandering, and his thirst nearly finished him off. He found himself in front of the bleak-looking Abyssinia Hotel. His sore feet could barely hold him up, his forehead was smeared with a wound's coagulated blood, and his shabby clothes were held up by a strap, from which hung an empty water bottle.

As he passed the timeworn two-story brown building, he found a woman at the entrance. She was in her fifties with light-brown skin, her hair braided in delicate strands that fell to her shoulders and brushed the left side of her lips, which were covered in warts of varying sizes. She didn't notice him at first, since she was sitting behind a wooden table, busy turning the pages of a large blue notebook. He stared at her, broken, and waited for her attention. When she lifted her head, she was unsurprised by his presence, as if she had always seen him. He wanted to speak, but he hesitated when she went right back to her blue notebook with the same indifference as when she'd raised her head to look at him. A blur of time passed before she came to a page that she signed. Then she closed the notebook and called out for a worker to bring him something from the kitchen.

Now, Saba wrapped up her talk inside the old men's shed and sat quiet, waiting for their response. Silence. All eyes were on Dawit. The eldest placed one skinny foot over the other, his torso tilting forward as he rubbed an amulet that hung from a large ivory necklace around his neck. He examined Dawit's face, although his features were barely visible since his eyes were trained on the ground.

Then the man spoke: "It is good that Elokim has restored our missing son, and after we had lost all hope. And we are overjoyed that this has come from your hands, you who have done our community so many favors. We have no doubt that you have verified the matter. Still, we need to speak to our son in private."

Saba grew uneasy, and Dawit raised his head for the first time. He stole a quick look at the man before turning to Saba, as if begging her not to leave him alone. She looked at him, firmly pressed his palm, and left. The man didn't wait for Dawit to recover his composure.

"Tell us about your mother."

Dawit cleared his throat, making way for the words that were suffocating him, before he spoke.

His mother, Rachel, had died of tuberculosis shortly before their last trip to Gondar; she'd been helping his father prepare the ghee he used to sell from door to door. Dawit dwelled on her affection for him and her relationships with the neighbors. This last part he improvised without thinking, since he thought it must apply to all mothers. Then he remembered one last thing that Saba had told him:

"My mother was loyal to her Jewish faith, even though she took pains to hide it from the neighbors."

The group's elder went back to clutching his amulet, but this time his movements were full of a tension that moved *into* Dawit, who went back to taking quick, panting breaths.

"May Elokim bless the mother who guards her faith in her heart, and may Elokim bless her offspring."

The ones who were seated murmured, "Amen."

Upon hearing this, Dawit raised his head, but the man pressed further, seemingly reminded of another question.

"What a steadfast woman. But this means that, for all those years, she was deprived of her Jewish name . . . by the way, what was her name, according to our law?"

Dawit felt slapped by the question. He turned, looking for Saba to come rescue him. He broke out in a sweat as he dug through his mind, trying to find a way to escape this impossible request. The questioner smiled mischievously as he watched his words tighten around the young man's neck like a hungry snake. When the man was sure Dawit had no answer, he asked for one of his men to call Saba; then he leaned over to his companions and spoke with them in a language Dawit could not understand. They nodded in agreement.

Saba entered; her eyes were flooded with anxiety. Dawit was crouched down, his head buried between his knees in a stupor as he recalled the long, exhausting journey that he didn't want to end at this seemingly impenetrable wall. He was about to cry out in sorrow, pain, and fury, but instead he remained still. She sat next to him, her gaze shifting between him and the men, awaiting their decision.

"May Elokim bless you, Madame Saba. The return of our son Dawit is a favor Beta Israel will not forget. We will pray, as we always do, for Elokim to shield you with his compassion. Finally, Elias will rest in the Kingdom of Heaven, and his wife . . . Rachel will do the same." The man emphasized Rachel's name as he turned to Dawit with the same sly malice, as if telling him how close he had been to the answer and yet so far.

Dawit lifted his head, not believing that he'd been accepted into the camp, as Saba hugged him with affectionate congratulations.

She had been anything but warm on the first day they met, when he'd come back to her after wolfing down the food her staff had brought from the kitchen.

He'd been hoping she would go one step further by giving him a job, but she rebuffed him firmly with a sarcastic reply, saying that if she'd employed everyone who came asking, then all of Gondar would work in her hotel.

He left the Abyssinia Hotel empty handed, save for a promise of finding food whenever hunger struck him. That wasn't enough, since without the ten thousand birr he'd lost, he would never get into the camp in Gondar and reaching his final destination would be out of the question.

He roamed the streets with no particular destination. How small he felt before the colossal historic castles on the hills. Groups of European tourists overtook him without paying him any attention. He seemed to be in harmony with the sharp contradictions of this ancient city, as if the city had to remain poor and isolated so that the rich could continue to come through at their leisure.

A herd of sheep passed him, driven by a shepherd. He walked up to the shepherd, asking for work, but the shepherd ignored him and continued on his way. He was in a race against time, and his empty pockets portended the loss of everything.

He decided to see the camp once more, even though he hadn't forgotten what had happened when he'd tried to enter the first time. The first time, he had walked alongside the barbed wire resting on tightly packed stones that hid what was behind them until he reached the main gate. He had stood facing the gate for barely a second when a guard carrying a long stick came out, gruffly ordering him to leave. He begged to be allowed in, to meet an official about an important matter, but the guard refused. But before turning his back completely, the guard directed him to the Abyssinia Hotel: "If you're looking for food, then you'll find what you need there. Madame Saba doesn't turn away those who ask for help."

This second time, he made sure the camp guards didn't catch sight of him. He kept close to the gate, peering through the gaps in the tightly packed rocks. He spotted a crowd in an open-air shed, performing what looked like a communal prayer. They were standing, their torsos rocking back and forth, their faces barely visible under the white scarves with blue fringes, as a man walked among them carrying a huge open volume and two thin sticks with paper rolled around them. At first, because of the distance, he couldn't hear the hymns, but when the clapping started, the rhythm reached him, clear and even. Then a car drove past, snapping him out of the ritual prayers he'd been following. It was her—the owner of the hotel who had rejected him just now. He followed her with his gaze as she stopped at the gate. He moved a little closer and saw the guards greet her reverently before she drove inside. In that moment, he realized his fate rested in the hands of this woman who was disappearing from view, down a sandy, winding, and poorly paved road.

He was now riding in that very car with the same woman, Saba, who was swaying to Ester's voice as it pulsed out of the radio:

Why is that star still there, my darling?
Why didn't it disappear like the others?
Does this question ever cross your mind, as it crosses mine?
That star was the only witness to our love,
And the witness of a love is also beloved.

They were now driving around the camp's grounds, searching for a place for him to live. He told Saba what had happened in the shed during her brief absence, and she burst out with a cackle that surprised him. She turned to him, and his confused expression was met with even louder laughter, as she tipped her head toward the steering wheel before she turned down Ester's voice.

"He got you because you didn't know that the name Rachel, here, is a name for both Christians *and* Jews. Anyhow, it's not important." She fell silent, as if she wanted to pique his interest, before adding, "Everything that happened in that shed had already been arranged."

At his shock, Saba hastened to clarify as she fought back her mirth. "I agreed with the leader of their group about everything. His only condition was that I not tell you, so that everything seemed natural, since he didn't want the rumor to spread that they were letting people into the camp in exchange for ten thousand birr. That's why, for my part, I oversold it a bit, as you saw. Now, please keep all of this a secret so you don't ruin it."

She stopped the car beside a man who was gesturing toward a small straw house that seemed adequate. Saba got out to inspect the place, while Dawit sat in the car, exasperated, remembering how that talk in the shed had shattered his nerves. He closed his eyes and rested his head against the back of the seat as conflicting emotions crashed over him. He was exhausted by the hardships that had beset him and the anxiety that had dogged him—it was as if, with every step, he was pulling his feet out of thick mud. Just once he wanted to walk an easy path. He didn't want to have everything handed to him—just to walk a path that wouldn't burden his body and soul with exhaustion.

He meditated on this until Saba pulled him out of it, calling, "Don't you want to come see your new home?"

(5)

The airplane, crowded with people and their dreams, landed in Israel midmorning.

It had barely touched down when the passengers started jostling for the front, everyone racing to save a place for themselves, their bags, and the children that clung to them or rode on their shoulders. No one listened to the cabin crew's instructions: please stay seated until the airplane has come to a complete stop. No one paid any attention to how ridiculous this request was on a plane without seats. They surged forward, almost crushing Dawit, who had backed up until he was alone at the rear. As the plane taxied slowly along the runway, he looked out of the window at a round building with four arms branching out. At the center was the Israeli flag and next to it in enormous white letters: **BEN GURION AIRPORT.**

The plane came to a complete stop, and chaos erupted as passengers banged on the door. A long time passed, but nothing happened. Apprehension began to creep over them, and it turned into a protest with even more people pounding at the door, until someone broke out into loud song, and the noise died down. Those in front stared at the singer and then went back to banging. But the man went on singing, and others joined in, until the whole place shook with song. Singing was not only the language of joy but also the language of the anger that swelled in their chests and was written on their faces.

Here's the day we're waiting for,
The moment we've been waiting for,
Ha'aliya.
Yesterday has no place here.
Tomorrow has no place here,
Ha'aliya.
Next year, Yerushalayim, is already here,
Ha'aliya.
It's the day we carry inside us,
For all times . . .

Finally, a door opened, and people swallowed their voices. But they were stunned to see it wasn't the door where passengers had gathered but the door facing Dawit at the back of the plane. Two air stewards strode up and gestured for him to step out. He felt flustered. As much as he'd wanted this moment, he also feared it. At the very least, he didn't want to be the first to go. But his journey had ended.

It took only a moment for the other passengers to notice what was going on, and the stampede turned in the other direction. Dawit seized his chance to retreat. Passengers hurried down the stairs, falling in prayer as soon as they set foot on the ground. He saw a man too busy to prostrate himself, compelling both his children to kiss the concrete. A woman rushed to kneel, then remembered her bulging canvas bag. She squeezed it beneath her, hugging it as she flung herself down in prayer. Others raised their foreheads before they'd even touched the ground, then continued running to the buses parked in front of them.

Slowly, Dawit walked down the stairs. He lowered one foot, and then followed with the other, placing it on the same step. Even so, he wanted to stop for a moment. He was panting with fatigue, as if he'd been leaping *up* the stairs. By the time he got to the ground, the buses were filled with passengers. They were all watching him, hurrying him along with their stares. He got down on his knees and turned toward them before he bowed his head and kissed the ground. He didn't know how long he stayed like that. But the heat that grazed his forehead brought him back to his long journey.

Specifically, to Gondar.

◆ ◆ ◆

His first day at the camp had an explosive start.

He'd stepped out to inspect the place but this time as a resident. Now, he was an authentic part of it and not just some passing intruder. He liked the feeling.

"Get out of here, fraud!"

He drew back in a panic as he tried to avoid the foul-smelling water thrown in his direction by an elderly neighbor lady in shabby, dirty clothes. He dashed off as the old woman crowed with a mean, mocking laugh that showed off a lonely pair of teeth in her upper jaw.

After that, he felt a little less pleased to be here. Was this what Saba had warned him about yesterday before she left? She said it wouldn't be easy, and he'd have to be patient until it was time for him to leave. He was an outcast here: Most of the people in Beta Israel were Ethiopian Falasha, like this elderly lady, but others were Ethiopians trying to join the camp to find their own form of salvation. They were unwelcome. Then there were Eritreans, like him, who were hated by both the Ethiopian Falasha *and* the Ethiopians. He was at the bottom of the food chain. Saba told him to not attract attention and to avoid people except during lessons and worship. She had checked out his residence and slipped money into his hand. He tried to refuse, but she insisted, telling him she'd come back to visit him whenever she found time, to make up for the strict rules that prevented residents from wandering outside the camp.

Saba had been showering him with favors from the moment he'd nearly died, one dark night, while putting out a fire that had broken out in one of her hotel buildings. Dawit had been working for a shepherd, carrying firewood and guarding the sheep against wolves, in exchange for a place to sleep. That night, as it happened, he had just left the straw hut he shared with the shepherd and gone back to wandering with no particular destination, consumed with how to collect the money he needed. Then he spotted flames rising up from the direction of the Abyssinia Hotel. At first, he'd thought it must be one of those open-air barbecues Western tourists were in the habit of having, but then he heard screams of panic. This was the story he'd repeat whenever anyone was listening.

He would tell them how he dashed straight there, only to find flames lighting up the hotel's back courtyard. He'd tell them how several workers were trying to put out the fire that was raging. Without hesitation, he'd taken the lead among those advancing on the fire to put it out. With his bare hands, he'd scooped up sand and flung it at the flames. He tried again and again, but it wasn't doing any good. After that, he started looking for another way, only to find a fire extinguisher lying among the trees nearby. This seemed odd, but later the hotel owner considered it evidence that the fire had been set on purpose. Whoever started the fire must have gotten rid of the two extinguishers before they lit the blaze.

He opened the nozzle, sending a spray of white powder toward the window, which had erupted with flames. It was going to be useless unless he got closer and kept up the spray at full force. The heat from the flames seared his face. But he didn't retreat, afraid that the fire would spread, and then he'd lose control of it completely. Faced with the tremendous heat that was quickly draining his energy to the point of exhaustion, he almost gave up. But then, at just that moment, others joined him, also carrying fire extinguishers, and they started to help. The flames retreated, leaving only a few slender threads of smoke rising from the charred rubble. Then, at last, it died away for good.

This was what the bystanders saw, to their great excitement and admiration. And it was what others heard, even if they'd missed

Gondar's big event. Yet there was another facet to what happened that night that made Dawit feel guilty, even as Saba expressed her deep gratitude. But that feeling soon dissolved, replaced by excuses that eased his conscience. He simply had no other way of achieving his goal, since Saba had continually refused to hire him. And even though she'd fed him, she had done it only with extra food—food that she would have just thrown away.

In the first few days he'd been in the city, time had suffocated him. He couldn't find any work that might help him earn the ten thousand birr he needed to enter the camp. Then finally he stumbled on this ruse, the results of which surpassed his wildest expectations.

He'd kept an eye on the Abyssinia Hotel ever since he'd realized the extent of its owner's influence with the camp's leaders. He counted the hotel's exits, the number of employees, the timing of their shifts. He noted that it was quietest after midnight, and that's when there were the fewest workers. He snuck into the back courtyard, which overlooked a warehouse full of cleaning supplies. The window was easy to open, which made the job much easier. He grabbed the two fire extinguishers that hung on a wall and tossed them out among the trees. Then, once he felt sure his movements hadn't attracted any attention, he stuffed a kerosene-moistened cloth into an empty water bottle and slowly walked toward the warehouse, circling it warily. A sharp voice startled him, and he dashed back to his hiding place, before he realized it was just a frightened cat.

It took a moment before he regained his courage and stepped back toward the window. When he got there, it felt as if he were testing his resolve one last time. He waited a moment. Then he closed his eyes, drew a deep breath, and let it out slowly, squeezing the bottle of kerosene. Then he made up his mind. He lit the tip of the cloth, which hung out of the mouth of the bottle, threw it into the warehouse, and quickly backed off, anxiously watching the shadows of the growing flames as they flickered across his face.

The hotel's guests noticed, and they began to shout. Once people had gathered, Dawit realized his moment had come. He stepped in front of them, throwing dirt on the flames, the tongues of which stretched out through the warehouse window. Others echoed his futile efforts. At last, Saba arrived, wrapped in a robe, her expression full of horror. Dawit pretended to be looking for another way to put out the fire, until he reappeared with one of the fire extinguishers and began spraying it hard at the window. People retreated and watched him advance on the fire, without sparing a thought for himself, until another group with fire extinguishers followed him in. Finally, they managed to get the fire under control. It had destroyed the entire warehouse, but it had not yet reached the guests' rooms.

Dawit sat down on the ground, coughing and exhausted, his face and arms coated with a layer of scalding soot. Saba ran to him, kissed him, and showered him with gratitude. She offered him water and ordered him to rest, telling him the doctor was on his way. Then, once it was all over, she invited him to spend the night at the hotel.

The next day, after taking his medicine, he spent the whole day lying in a comfortable bed and wearing a blue-striped shirt the hotel owner had given him. A basket of fruit graced the table in front of him between meals, and Saba was constantly asking him whether there was anything else he wanted, her repeated thanks mingling with remorse over what had passed between them before. It was as if Saba had completely transformed. Gone were the half-hearted expressions with which she used to greet him. They'd been replaced with others that expressed an anxious, motherly love.

She'd become like a chatty grandmother, telling him first about herself and then about the hotel and its employees. She told him how, two decades earlier, she'd come to Gondar with her husband, who had bought this broken-down building, restored it, and turned it into the most important hotel in the city. Business had gone really well under her husband's management, and it had gone on that way even after his passing a few years ago. She explained that she was Amhara, while people in Gondar were mostly Tigrayans. She turned to Dawit to see if he understood what she was hinting at, and then she realized she had to explain further:

"People here have more respect for our kind. Maybe it's because of our numbers, or maybe it's because we ruled for so long. Or, I don't know. Maybe it's something else."

Dawit struggled to suppress his reaction, since he knew full well that the weak wouldn't continue to show respect unless it was to the liking of the powerful. At the same time, he was surprised she was being so frank with him, considering the tumultuous past shared by the Tigrayans and Amhara.

When she'd finished her story, she wanted to hear from him. And so he began, reluctantly, to tell his long story. Not exactly as it happened, but more like he wanted it to appear, since, to his mind, this was his chance at salvation. He mixed in just enough truth among the necessary lies. He told her that David was a name he'd left behind, a name to which he didn't want to return. He told her that he was an Eritrean civilian who had left his wretched country for the Endabaguna refugee camp in Tigray after he'd sold everything he owned to pay the traffickers. She listened to his story with a skeptical expression, and then she apologized and asked him to go on. He insisted on knowing what she was thinking, so she told him that she'd known he was an Eritrean *soldier* from the first moment she'd met him. It was his accent—she had met many men who spoke Amharic with his accent. All of them had learned it in the Eritrean military.

Dawit swallowed his surprise and nodded. He knew Saba's new-found trust in him was why she was being so honest, but now he was afraid she knew more than she was saying. He felt exposed. He went back to his story, telling her that he wanted a normal life, a safe one.

This had been his biggest hope when he fled Eritrea for the Endabaguna refugee camp in Tigray, but he'd been surprised when the refugee camp had become another hell—especially after he was unable to pay what he owed the smugglers, who had followed him and demanded the second half of their money. It had turned into a threat on his life. He'd escaped them and fled to Gondar, planning to gather up the money needed to join the Falasha refugee camp. From there, he hoped to travel to Israel before his pursuers could catch up with him.

He paused for a moment before admitting that he wanted to pay a bribe to be let in. He was afraid it wouldn't sit right with her, but he decided to move decisively toward his goal, since she had been so frank with him. He was counting on her immense sense of gratitude and her willingness to help. And, as it happened, Saba brushed aside the points in his story where he'd feared she might stop. But then she paused on another matter. "Do you think money is the only thing that stands between you and the Falasha camp?"

His attention sharpened, and he looked into Saba's eyes, as if asking her to explain.

"The camp's front gate separates two worlds. Inside, they have a different language, a religion you don't know anything about, and people who aren't like the ones you know. You don't even know that you're offending them by calling them Falasha. That's what they were called before they returned to their religion, when they were exiles who embraced Islam, Christianity, or paganism.

"What they call *themselves* is Beta Israel."

Dawit's head drooped, and he was seized by heartache. But now Saba came back, opening a window of hope: "If you spend enough time with me, I *might* be able to teach you what you need to know to enter the camp. And that will give you a chance to collect the money you need too."

Dawit asked how long it would take, saying he was afraid of the smugglers.

Her response was swift. "That's going to depend on you. But as long as you're here, you'll be under my protection. No one will lay a hand on you."

He wished that Saba wasn't the only person in Gondar who was kind to him. *Still*, he thought, as he edged past the old woman and wiped off the foul-smelling water dripping off his clothes, *one senile old woman isn't going to add much to my troubles.*

He went down to the registry office at the center of the camp. The employee greeted him with a smile and asked for his name. Then he narrowed his broad smile into a grimace when he heard the answer "Dawit Elias."

With mechanical movements, the employee gave Dawit his many papers, instructing him on where to place his fingerprints, all the while giving him a cutting glare. He took Dawit's photo, then told him about the dates for his Hebrew and religion classes. Dawit was about to leave when the employee called out indifferently as he shuffled the papers on his desk: "How much did you pay to be here?"

Dawit was caught off guard. How had his big secret gotten all the way to the registrar?

Two men stepped into the office, and the employee greeted them. Then, in a tone of forced kindness, he asked Dawit to stick to his scheduled lessons so he could make up for what he'd missed. He added: "But before you start, you'll need to pass by the synagogue. The rabbis are there, waiting for you."

Dawit left the office, anxious about the circulation of what he'd thought was a secret. He was afraid the elders would think that *he* had been the one to spread the news. He would never be able to prove it wasn't true. With heavy steps, he took his papers and went to the temple.

A low wall surrounded the white building that looked run down, even though it had recently been painted. In the outer courtyard, there were several religious leaders. He walked toward the door but then stopped at the threshold. He tried to calm down, remembering the hours he'd spent with Saba preparing for what he would find here. He remembered what she'd told him: people in the camp were seen as returning to Judaism after their previous lives had driven them to other religions. They had to go through mandatory purification rituals. After that, they were taught the minimum level of Jewish law to prepare them for their journey to the Promised Land.

At last, he went inside. The sandy courtyard stopped at the edge of this white building, decorated with handmade plaster menorahs, the tops of which were painted yellow. Below, there were three entrances, and he stood in front of them in confusion. A woman emerged from one, wrapped in a robe that completely covered her. She glanced at him before stepping into a side room. There were two entrances remaining. He almost walked into one before a voice came from behind him:

"Mikveh?"

Dawit nodded. The religious leader examined the newcomer's face and the papers he was carrying, then said, "Purification is through the other door." Then he left him alone in the compound. Inside, Dawit was met by a rabbi who took a stamped paper from the registry office and told him to stay put. The place looked like a public bath, and the smell of disinfectant drifted out through its many doors, as did waves of humidity and the echoing sound of water slapping against tile.

"Dawit Elias."

Dawit followed the call to its source. The rabbi ordered him to bathe, brush his teeth, and trim his nails. When he finished, he followed the man into another of the rooms, where he found a two-meter-wide mud-brick basin. It was filled to the brim with hot, steamy water and surrounded by four other men of religion. Three of them quickly slipped behind a curtain. This screened them off from the purification while leaving them in contact with their fourth companion. Dawit had barely taken in what was happening before the rabbi asked him to take off his clothes, as well as any earrings or rings he might be wearing. Dawit had expected this. He'd expected to be bare chested, but then the man pointed to his pants too. He pulled them off quickly and then moved to enter the basin, but the rabbi asked him to remove the last item of clothing that covered his body. Dawit hesitated a moment, realizing his ignorance, and then finally obeyed, taking off his underpants but holding a hand between his thighs to cover himself. He felt a fresh desire to plunge under the water, to cover his nakedness, but the religious leader stopped him and ordered him to lift his hand. It was clear he wanted to see what Dawit was trying to hide. After closing his eyes, Dawit slowly raised his hand.

"Good . . . he's already circumcised."

The leader said this sarcastically, turning toward the others behind the curtain before one of them mumbled in sympathy: "It's all fine. What's important is that he has finally returned to his faith."

He got what looked like a signal to enter the basin, so he hurried to cover his nakedness. The rabbi seemed eager to see every part of his body submerged, and he asked him to go all the way under. Dawit, who was in a hurry to get out, thought it was enough to pull his neck down and touch his chin to the water, but the man gave his head a shove, holding him completely underwater as he recited the scripture in a rapidly rising tone, emphasizing the final consonants:

"Sh'ma, Yis'ra'eil: Adonai Eloheinu Adonai echad . . . V'ahav'ta eit Adonai Elohekha b'khol l'vav'kha uv'khol naf'sh'kha uv'khol m'odekha. And you shall bind these words as a sign upon your hand, and they shall be as frontlets between your eyes. Hear, O Israel."

When he'd held his breath for as long as he could, Dawit pushed his way up, lifting his head and coughing, water spilling from his nose and mouth. The rabbis chuckled before the reciter hurriedly finished his prayer, coming to the end of the mikveh, which promised the beginning of Dawit's return to the religion of his ancestors after all those years of wandering.

◆　◆　◆

All of this came back to him in flashes, until his forehead was numb to the heat coming off the airport tarmac, and he realized how long he'd been prostrate. But this wasn't the only reason he'd come back to himself—he also felt a foot, nudging him. He raised his forehead to find an irritated rabbi looming above him, out of patience.

(6)

He'd barely found a place for his feet on the last bus when the doors creaked slightly and shut behind him.

He read fury in the eyes of the people around him, who had waited too long for him to get there. One of them muttered a few words, from which Dawit guessed he'd overdone it. Another reacted to the comment by purposefully laughing in Dawit's face. Dawit chose to ignore it all, turning his back to the driver and facing the bus's wide glass side. The rabbi who had ordered him up off the ground had settled into the back seat of a black car. As soon as the car moved, the buses on the tarmac at Ben Gurion Airport followed.

Slowly, their convoy moved over the cracked gray pavement, sending vibrations running through the body of the bus and the pole Dawit was gripping.

He stared at the ever-widening distance between him and the plane that had brought him here from Ethiopia. He didn't know what he felt about the meters that now separated him from a past that, just hours before, had been his only possible life. Slowly, the bus came to a halt; passengers knocked into each other. When Dawit glanced over his shoulder at the windshield, he saw all the buses had stopped, waiting for a plane that had landed to pass by. After that, the buses started up again, trudging along at the same pace. How strange that he needed to turn back in order to know where he was going.

The buses stopped in front of a hall labeled Number 24. Security guards and rabbis were waiting for them. Passengers shifted toward the door, and Dawit found himself wedged between the glass and the press of bodies, unable to escape.

The bus doors opened all at once. People were shoving so hard against him, it took effort not to fall over as he got in line, following airport security's orders. He felt better holding back a little, taking advantage of the others shoving ahead of him in line. But he tried to do it without seeming too obvious. He glanced behind him and saw a woman with two children. He offered her his place, and she stepped forward, thanking him profusely. He thought he shouldn't go *so* far back that he attracted people's attention, but he had to stop again and let people go past when he spotted his old neighbor, the one with the lonely two front teeth. She pushed past him, trying to secure a place up front.

Here, he was following Saba's instructions. She had always told him to ignore the old woman until he achieved his goal: a safe and secure life.

◆ ◆ ◆

But the old woman wasn't the only one out to catch him. For a while, it felt like all of Gondar knew his secret and that they took pleasure in wounding him whenever possible. And so even as time passed and he got used to the camp, he kept hurrying everywhere he went. He would throw frightened looks over his shoulder, thanks to an incident in his very first week.

On that day, he'd been on his way to a Hebrew lesson. Early for class, he strolled. He came across some boys playing soccer and stopped to watch, smiling at the moves of a skilled player. Noticing him, they stopped playing and pointed. He said hello, his smile widening, and was surprised when they picked up stones and charged at him. He wasn't sure what they meant to do until one of them threw a rock right at him. He ran as fast as he could, stones flying all around him. One of them hit him on the shoulder, but he didn't stop. When he was out of range, the boys fell back, laughing. But Dawit didn't stop running until they were completely out of sight. He was still catching his breath when a man appeared beside him, wrapped in a threadbare robe and giving him a smug smile that soon turned into a suppressed laugh. Dawit was furious. He walked up to ask what was going on, but the man shoved him roughly and called him a thief.

Dawit knocked on the classroom door as he fixed himself up.

He was a little late, since he had ended up running in the opposite direction, away from the place where he'd be studying. He had had to sneak back the long way so that the boys wouldn't catch sight of him. When he passed them, he glanced at them from the corner of his eye and was relieved to find they were absorbed in the game.

The teacher gestured at him, and he went to his spot, feeling all eyes in the class on him. As soon as he sat down on the scuffed wooden chair, the teacher continued with the lesson, and eyes turned from him to her.

"All right then. How do we express agreement?"

"Ken," the students answered in one voice. There were about ten of them of various ages. All of them were new returnees to Judaism.

"And disagreement?" she asked.

"Lo."

Dawit started noting it all down. When he raised his head, he found the teacher was waiting for him to finish writing so she could continue. From the very first lesson, she was kind to him, having noticed how intent he was on mastering the language. He learned that she had come from the capital, where she'd studied Hebrew at university. The other students weren't as welcoming. It was true that they didn't insult him, but they also didn't show him any kindness. Their wall of suspicion kept him from getting to know them.

The teacher wrote in careful Amharic on the blackboard: "please," "thank you," "thank you very much," "you're welcome." She left space between each word before turning to the class and beginning the lesson.

For the first time, Dawit felt the value of those dull hours at Saba's hotel, when she'd forced him to learn as much Hebrew as possible.

"B'vakasha . . . b'vakasha."

The students chanted after the teacher as she wrote this Hebrew word in the space in front of the word "please." Then she moved on to the rest of the words.

"Toda . . . toda."

"Toda raba . . . toda raba."

"Al lo davar . . . al lo davar."

Dawit was immersed in writing in his book while the teacher waited. When he took a while, she asked him in Hebrew: "Are you done?"

"Slikha."

The teacher was surprised at Dawit's quick response in Hebrew, and so was the rest of the class. Dawit smiled in confusion before explaining that he'd spent some time at home learning new words. He'd just barely memorized the word for "sorry" yesterday, and he was surprised it had sprung to his tongue.

When the lesson ended, and everyone got up to leave, the teacher hung back, waiting for Dawit. She told him that because of his eagerness and perseverance, she would write him a letter of recommendation. That way, he'd get more attention in the ulpan lessons in Israel. He stuttered out his thanks before asking her not to write to the school for immigrants. He wanted to learn the language without any show of favoritism, and no recommendation would actually be more helpful. He was relieved when she agreed—another sticky situation was the last thing he needed with all the gossip about him already making the rounds of the camp.

He moved on to another topic. "Can you give me this pen?"

Without understanding why it was important, the teacher agreed. As he headed out of the school, Dawit ran his fingers over the pen with increasing pleasure.

"How did it go today?"

He found Saba waiting for him, asking about his day with a broad smile. She gave him the choice between getting into the car or walking, and he chose walking. He told her what had happened earlier that day, starting with the language lesson and then moving back to describe the incident with those boys, and, finally, with his awful neighbor. As they walked, he spotted the man in the tattered robe, the one who had smirked and called him a thief. But this time, when the man saw Dawit with Saba, he made a low and polite bow, saying, "Greetings, greetings."

Saba slipped money into his hand, and he humbly kissed her hand before he moved to do the same with Dawit, who avoided him, hardly believing this was the same person. They walked away, and yet Dawit kept glancing back. When the man finished inspecting his gift, he lifted his head, and their eyes met. Now, Dawit spotted the trace of a smile that was just beginning to take shape.

When he told Saba how shocked he'd been at the man's behavior, she gave him a half answer as they walked to a clay bench: "That's how life is here."

Later, he understood Saba's answer more fully: The people here were all like him, seeking salvation with all their might, and they didn't care who fell under the bus. They lowered their heads for the people above them while seizing any chance to humiliate others beneath them. Sometimes survival had more to do with breaking others down than with keeping oneself out of harm's way. None of this was without reason—it was a kind of protection, done in fear of being exposed.

Once, Dawit had finished his religion lesson and slipped out of the camp without the guards noticing. He'd felt suffocated inside its walls day and night. He'd asked Saba to help him sneak out, but she'd refused to violate this most important condition, which had been set when granting him the right to live in the camp. Violating it could mean exposing his whole future to failure. He pretended to be convinced, waiting until she was just about to leave. Then he slipped into the back seat of her car and hid under his white robe until she got to her hotel. There, he crept out, hurrying away. He needed this space away from prying eyes, away from the insults that lay in wait along his path every time he set out. He just wanted to walk without attracting anyone's attention. He wanted to be anonymous again, unlike in the camp, where he was sure that everyone knew his story and where everyone was mad at him.

He walked the city streets, recalling when he'd first arrived. How things had changed! While it was true he wasn't totally at ease, he was no longer homeless, no longer a man who had nowhere to live. Filling his lungs with air, he thought about everything that had happened between that moment of arrival and his fast-approaching departure for Israel. He raised his head up to the sky. He would've liked to embrace the landscape around him, except that, moments later, he had to duck to avoid a stone being thrown at him.

"Get out of here, slave."

A group of shepherds were sitting on a low hill, their cattle grazing not far away. Dawit had barely a moment to understand what was happening when they picked up more stones. He dashed off, his steps leading him back to Saba's hotel. He hesitated a moment before going in, but he had no other choice. When she saw him, he thought she'd be angry, but instead, she laughed.

"I didn't expect you back so fast."

She told him that she'd known he was hiding in the car, and she wasn't going to stand in his way if he wanted it this much. Instead, she'd taken the opportunity to let him see for himself why no one from Beta Israel wanted to leave the camp's walls.

"Did they hurt you badly? I feel guilty, since I let you go out dressed like that. Only people from the camp wear their clothes that way."

This time, instead of worrying about angering *her*, Dawit felt rage swell inside him. "Why do the city people treat people from Beta Israel so harshly?" She said it was a mix—both envy and contempt. On the one hand, people had looked down on Jews here for a long time. On the other, everyone wanted to find even half the food and protection that Beta Israel had. He wanted to ask more, but he realized he was defending the camp even though he'd hardly found shelter and dignity there.

◆ ◆ ◆

"Are things getting better now?" Saba asked, as they sat on the clay bench and watched women straining to cut bare tree trunks with rusty axes. Several months had passed since his arrival in Gondar, and his departure date for Israel was fast approaching. Nothing much had changed—many still treated him cruelly while others ignored him, keeping their distance. But he'd become more immune to it. Sometimes he smiled, ignoring them and moving on. Sometimes he tried to stop whoever was attacking him. He was nearly proficient in Hebrew now, in addition to Arabic, Amharic, and English, which he'd learned while in the military. The religion lessons didn't add much to what he'd already learned from Saba before joining the camp.

Still, despite everything, he felt at home here—even though he dreaded the thought that he might not really leave for Israel. He loved Saba, but he knew her flaws, and he knew she would never have helped him if she hadn't believed he saved her hotel. He felt she saw him as a tool that served a purpose and nothing more, and he was afraid that his credit with her would run out before the date of his departure.

He hated the people here, but he did understand their need to survive. He felt terror, love, fear, hatred, and understanding. He didn't say any of this in answer to Saba's question about whether things were getting better though. Instead, he settled for a half answer: "In part."

The women set their axes aside and made a circle on the ground. One of them began to sing, and the rest followed, their clapping setting the rhythm, picking up the pace. Saba began to tap against the bench in a blissful state as she accompanied their words with a bobbing of her head, before she turned to Dawit, who was watching her with a smile.

"You must have noticed that the people here survive by singing. They sing when they grieve, they sing when they're happy, and they sing when they've got nothing better to do."

Dawit nodded encouragement, and Saba continued: "To them, singing is their mother tongue. They believe they didn't switch to speech until they strayed and mixed with others. So the more they sing, the closer they are to their original selves. Singing takes their souls back to Jerusalem—back to the Promised Land—before their bodies can actually reach it."

◆ ◆ ◆

And here they were in the Promised Land at last. Would they stop singing?

This question rose in Dawit's mind as he found himself among rows of people advancing on an empty hall with booths, where Ben Gurion Airport's passport-control staff were checking the papers of the newly arrived with dull patience. They stamped each of them, allowing the people to pass through a glass door that opened onto a place swirling with people of all different colors.

Dawit's heart pounded wildly as he saw the crowds moving in all directions. The place looked so different! It seemed just right for the life he'd been waiting for, even though he'd never been able to picture it. So this was that other life, the life he'd expected. Now, it had come.

(7)

A man set his bag lightly on the machine and then set off to meet it on the other side. But the soldier across the way stared at the screen in front of him and gestured for the man to go back. As the belt moved in the opposite direction and the bag returned, everyone looked suspiciously at the luggage and its owner. The bag moved again, disappearing into the automated examination box. The man crossed over, waiting on the other side, but the soldier sent the bag back, yet again, from where it had come. The man wanted to ask why, but the soldier was busy talking to a colleague. The man stepped forward a little and got a firm signal to stay where he was. He turned to look for his wife and found she had passed through the inspection and was anxiously waiting for him.

The line behind him had grown longer and sounds of restlessness began to grow, so the soldier ordered the man to stand to one side so they could search his bag manually. He gestured to those behind the man to pass. Again, the man looked to where his wife was standing, how she was seeing all of this. She was a witness to his humiliation in front of all these travelers, as the two soldiers very carefully shook out the contents of his bag in full public view, glaring at him with suspicion.

"Go on."

Dawit, absorbed in what was happening to the Arab in the next line over, was roused by the soldier's voice. Afraid he would meet the same fate, Dawit reluctantly placed his bag on the conveyor belt for the baggage screener. He stood, impatiently awaiting its slow journey, as he studied the features of the security officer, who remained calm. Dawit grabbed his bag and turned to the soldier, awaiting his final decision. He found the man gesturing to another traveler to step forward.

Dawit looked back at the Arab. The man was still in the same position, nervously chewing his nails as he watched his things being scattered, before the signal finally came for him to go and collect them. Meanwhile, the travelers all around him went past, one by one, without any of them being stopped by the machine or the soldier.

Dawit felt sorry for the man. Maybe it was because he knew the taste of humiliation so well. He'd first experienced it in his own country, and he'd gotten used to it in the Endabaguna refugee camp, where he'd arrived jumping for joy, even though he'd been exhausted by his long escape from the Blue Valley to northern Ethiopia.

◆ ◆ ◆

It had been a desperate journey that could have ended in one of two ways: either by reaching his final destination or by being killed by security. Still, "Dawoud" had done it, since life and death had seemed the same to him back in the prison camp in the Blue Valley. But when he'd crossed the border between Eritrea and Ethiopia along with dozens of others, he'd been different from them—he had stopped to look back. He'd wanted to feel the truth of his salvation, the truth that he was leaving this humiliation behind forever. There, beyond those distant mountains that had sapped the group's energy as they climbed up one and wound around another, lay Eritrea. He felt no nostalgia at all. His soul had shed nostalgia at each step he'd taken toward Ethiopia. Now, he was purifying himself by putting distance between him and the Blue Valley, trying to purge the feelings of oppression so he could get back the soul he had before it became so lacerated and scarred.

"Come on, quickly. This way."

At the entrance to the Endabaguna refugee camp, there had been another reason to escape—this time from an Ethiopian soldier who was instructing all newcomers to line up correctly by means of his whip. The whip missed Dawoud, but it struck the woman behind him. The shock of it stopped her from running away. Everyone lined up in a spiral that allowed them to fit in front of the registry office, while the soldier continued enjoying himself by straightening the rows or scattering them if he grew bored with their straight lines. He was sadistically adept at drawing curves with his heavy whip.

The registration desk served as a gateway to the sprawling camp. Behind it were scattered tents of various sizes, most of them so tattered and worn that it was no longer easy to spot the blue logo printed on the front of each one, the mark of the UN High Commissioner for Refugees.

Time passed, and Dawoud's turn didn't come. The crowd in front of him was dense, and the pace of the registry office procedures was slow. Sunlight streamed down from directly overhead. He sat on the ground, absorbed in drawing random circles in the sand and running his hand over the black-and-white woolen bracelet that was tight around his wrist. He closed his eyes, saw the blackness, and opened them to the waiting sun, which stung his pupils. He put his head down between his knees, raised it, put it back again. Nothing had happened. He was still far from the registry office.

"Don't tell them you're a Muslim."

Dawoud resisted the urge to turn toward the source of the low voice. As much as he wanted to listen in on what the two young men were saying behind him, he was afraid that if they noticed him, they might stop talking.

"Immigration organizations won't even look at your file. I've heard it a lot. They'll make excuses without telling you the real reason."

Dawoud knew that Endabaguna was just a reception camp. From there, you had a slight chance of resettlement in some European country, or else you'd be spread out among permanent camps inside Ethiopia. This made him want to join their conversation, to ask more, but their whispers were a sign of its secrecy. They were silent for a while, and Dawoud was worried the conversation would go on outside the range of his hearing.

"So what do we do?"

The other young man's question threw Dawoud a lifeline, and his senses pricked. He took advantage of the opportunity to adjust his position, moving a few inches back and standing still to hear the answer. There was a pause before it came.

"Do like me. I got rid of my identity papers, and I chose a Christian name."

Just before sunset, Dawoud was standing in front of the registry office, shaking out his clothes as he listened to the questions directed at him. He studied the empty box on a piece of paper and the blue pen that was pointing at it. He raised his gaze a little to the veined brown hand and from there to the tightly pressed lips waiting for Dawoud's answer. The employee repeated his question in frustration, while Dawoud again passed a hand over his black-and-white woolen bracelet. Then the employee scrawled the name he'd heard in the box: "David."

◆　◆　◆

"Bo nelekh."

The group from Gondar followed the gestures of a young woman in a black suit who was carrying a sign that read "Beta Israel" in Hebrew and Amharic. The crowd meandered together, enthralled by the gift and liquor shops, before arriving at the towering golden pillars that held up a ceiling studded with crystal balls that lit up the Arrivals Hall at Ben Gurion Airport. The stunned Black mass of humanity seemed to come from some distant era. They caught the attention of passersby, some of whom stopped to watch while others took photos.

Dawit was in the middle of the crowd, tightening the scarf around his head to hide most of his face. He still hadn't shaken off his sense of being exposed, and he still felt sure his facial features stuck out. His features called out to passersby, telling them: *The thief is here, carrying the evidence of his crimes.*

The group walked along a semicircular path that ended at a glass door. As soon as the door automatically slid open, there were shouts and a general hubbub. Dawit didn't know what was going on. Journalists' cameras flashed, and security separated two opposing forces: one of them timidly welcoming the new arrivals and the other bolder, shouting and carrying signs that called on them to take their diseases and go back to where they'd come from.

The group was confused. Some of them wanted to go back inside, but the organizers urged them to keep going.

"Lama bata la'aretz? Lama bata?!"

A white girl's shout pierced Dawit's eardrum as she demanded to know why they had come to her country. He turned to find her glaring at him. She'd picked him out of the crowd. He could no longer hear her shouting; instead, he watched the swollen greenish veins of her neck, pumped full of malice. When he was close to passing her, he looked away and walked faster, leaving her shouts to catch up with him. But as soon as he thought he was in the clear, he turned to see what was happening behind him—and crashed into a bag. Its owner dropped it. He shoved Dawit, cursing, before leaning toward a woman beside him. "These slaves," she grumbled, "they're everywhere."

Dawit didn't respond. Instead, he raised his hands up by his head and apologized as he backed away. He stopped momentarily when he recognized the man's face—this was the same Arab who'd been searched and demeaned by the soldiers.

As Dawit turned and rejoined the group, his gaze fell on a blue signboard inscribed with bold Hebrew, Arabic, and English letters:

"Welcome to Israel."

(8)

"Asnasa . . . asnasa."

David's eyes snapped open. Irritated, he shielded them from the morning sun as he brushed the dirt from his face and hair. He didn't understand why a man was shouting right above his head, telling him to get up, even as he watched the man repeat it to the sleepers beside him.

He and the others had spent the night out in the open because the employee in charge of placing them in tents had left at sunset. David had wandered everywhere, looking for a corner to shelter in, but every time he stumbled into a tent, he found it packed with refugees. Finally, inside a small tent, he found an empty spot that could just barely fit his slight body. But as soon as he stretched out, objections to his presence rose up. In the dim light, he couldn't see anyone's face. He wasn't even sure if he was what they were objecting to. He tried to ignore them, but the protests grew louder. Voices attacked him from every side. Once he realized that, yes, he was the one they were objecting to, he got up. The voices faded, then stopped. Silence fell as he left the tent.

He didn't know what to do. He thought about searching for another tent with a vacancy, but exhaustion had worn him down, and he stopped trying. He chose a nearby tent, mounded a pile of sand beside it, and settled his head on the sand pile. After a while, he noticed others had begun to lie down near him. He made a game of it, counting everyone who joined him in this imaginary tent with its roof made of sky: four, five, seven, ten . . . He fell asleep without finishing the game.

But now, as he looked around, he saw the game could have taken him the whole night.

"Take this. Put it on."

David pulled on a green T-shirt. It was his share of the colorful shirts being thrown out by a person riding atop a pickup around Endabaguna. A few moments later, he spotted a TV camera moving through the camp. Someone was conducting random interviews with refugees who just happened to have gathered before the camera came, following the directions of one of the camp officials. David tugged up his collar. He hid the side of his face and walked away, avoiding the camera's lens.

He went up to the employee responsible for distributing tents to refugees. When the man began to search his records for tent vacancies, David made sure to point out that there was space in the tent where he'd been kicked out. The employee quickly moved down to that number with his index finger, settling on it. He took out a small, presigned card with a seal, wrote down David's name and tent number, then asked him to take it to another employee. David was just about to leave when the employee stopped him, his eyes on the woolen bracelet, woven in intertwined black and white.

David pretended not to understand, so the man was forced to say it out loud: "I don't think you'll need that bracelet here."

He hesitated a moment before taking it off and handing it over. The man hurried to put it on, then promised to help David whenever he needed it. David left with mixed feelings: he mourned the bracelet, but he rejoiced that he'd found a spot. The feeling changed to pure pleasure as he walked alongside another employee toward his appointed tent, holding a blanket and a thin sheet, as well as a piece of bread stuffed with cheese and a juice box—his allotment of breakfast. When he got to the tent, he found fewer people. They turned toward David and the employee as the employee asked about any vacancies. David didn't wait for their answer—he knew the place well enough. He went straight to the narrow corner, as the others stared, and then he spread out his bags and thanked the employee for his help.

It was no longer just a matter of a place to sleep. He wanted *this* tent, *this* corner. He wanted revenge. Euphoria pulsed through his veins and nourished his pride as he boldly met their gazes. This was the first time he'd been able to fight back. Before, he'd always just told himself to lower his head and move on.

As soon as he'd relaxed into this feeling of superiority, however, the employee's voice rang out:

"Watch your stuff—or else you'll be sleeping out on the dirt like a dog."

This was followed by the laughing grunts of other tent dwellers. It dashed David's temporary delight and brought him back to reality.

He sat eating his breakfast in a suppressed rage. A woman carrying a baby came up to him, begging for the juice box. He hesitated for a few seconds, wondering how he would manage to swallow bread this dry. He wanted to ask where her share had gone, although he guessed she was asking for the baby. He gave her what she'd asked for while trying to chew on the bread, but she stayed there, staring at the rest of his bread. He shifted in agitation, turning his back. She moved off, muttering something he didn't hear. He gnawed the bread, and, when he turned, he saw her take one quick sip of the juice, put her mouth to the baby's, and let the juice fall into it. He felt guilty, but this feeling vanished when he saw her empty the rest of the box into her own mouth.

A fat young man walked up, holding his loose pants with both hands, and David hurriedly put the last piece in his mouth. The piece was so large his cheeks bulged.

"Have you come now?"

The young man's question confused him. As he tried to get control of his mouth, he nodded in the affirmative. The young man reached out a hand and shook his. "Yohannes."

Here, it wasn't enough to just nod his head. He gulped down what was left of the bread, which scraped painfully along his throat, and answered, "David."

The young man's face looked briefly startled before he smiled broadly, still holding David's hand.

"Yeah, it's not too big a change. Almost no difference, really. Dawoud, David. That's if we don't count the oldest name, right?"

Nervously, David pulled his hand back. He looked closely at the person standing in front of him, trying to remember if he'd met this man before. He looked younger than him, with childish features that contrasted with a huge, jiggling body. He had light skin but curly hair.

When David got tired of trying to remember, he walked out of the tent, still in shock. He felt a wave of anger when he saw Yohannes hurrying to catch up with him, laughing hysterically. He said, fighting back the laughter, "Well, well, well. So we got to the Blue Valley on the exact same day, right? I saw some of what happened to you there. But in the end, I got here first."

David's mind reeled at being exposed like this, right from the start. He couldn't remember Yohannes at all. Yohannes must have noticed his reaction because his face turned serious.

"Relax. I won't tell. Promise."

David's eyes were still narrowed, so Yohannes went on: "Well, okay, okay. Maybe you'll feel better knowing Yohannes is just a name I'm using to cross through hell."

Slowly, David's expression shifted. A smile rose to his lips. And when he looked at Yohannes's childlike face, they both burst into loud laughter.

Their exuberance attracted the attention of a TV cameraman who was walking near them, just then, with his camera. David noticed too late, his mirth falling away as he tried to hide his face. Yohannes did the same as the cameraman gestured to them, asking them to go on laughing, as if they were acting out a scene.

◆ ◆ ◆

When he'd left the Endabaguna refugee camp, he'd thought he was rid of bothersome cameras. But here, at the entrance to the bus, state TV was waiting for him. A young reporter smiled as she noticed Dawit, whom she marked as a prize catch. She gestured to the cameraman, who shifted the camera on his shoulder to aim it at Dawit.

"How would you describe your joy at finally reaching the Promised Land?"

The reporter asked her question in broken Amharic—it seemed like she had memorized it so she could cover this story.

"Ani khole . . . ani khole."

Dawit tried to avoid her by heading to his seat on the bus while telling her in Hebrew that he was feeling sick. But this only made the reporter even more insistent on interviewing him. She followed him to his seat and asked her question again in Hebrew, and then he realized he had embroiled himself in exactly what he'd wanted to escape.

He told her he was happy, but his confused expression said something different. As he spoke, he avoided the camera—turning his face right and left, then down—and his words came out in unplanned stutters.

When the interview was over, his forehead was slick with sweat, even though it was cold on the bus. He wanted to crack open a window, but he was afraid another camera might appear behind it. When the bus moved off, and he could relax a little, he opened the window and filled his lungs with fresh air before glancing down and noticing that the reporter's earring had fallen off onto his seat. His face brightened as he picked it up and rubbed it with pleasure, forgetting his embarrassment moments before.

The buses drove off one after the other. Next to the driver, there stood a brown-skinned girl with a megaphone in one hand. She spoke Amharic, introducing herself as a Jew from Beta Israel. The bus responded with shouts and applause. The girl laughed shyly before noting that she'd been born in Israel, as if letting them know she was on a different level. She asked them to decide whether she should speak in Amharic or Hebrew, and the overlapping voices were unanimous in asking her to speak Amharic.

"Welcome to Israel. We are headed straight for Tel Aviv, which is a beautiful city, as you'll soon see. You'll be staying there briefly before you'll be sent to cities in different parts of the country. In the meantime, as we make our way to Tel Aviv, I'll be happy to answer any questions you might have. And please, enjoy the journey."

As the young woman wrapped up her speech, she pointed to a large talking screen that hung from the roof of the bus. It was divided into two parts: one part showed a live image of the road, while the other showed a map of the places they would cross. The bus left the area around the airport and headed northwest. Dawit gazed at the tall buildings. On their glass facades, he saw the reflections of buildings on the other side of the street. Cold air struck his face. Cars with yellow license plates streaked past, each plate stamped with bold black numbers and the Israeli flag. There was greenery everywhere. Dawit contemplated his salvation, which he had spent his whole life trying to shape. He compared what he was seeing now to the life he had built in his imagination.

A voice emerged from the screen, telling them to turn right at the exit called "Derekh Kerem." A green signboard hung over the highway's suspension bridge, pointing to the same thing.

"We will soon pass over the Ayalon River."

As soon as their guide spoke, necks turned left and right, although no river appeared. When the driver passed Derekh HaTikva, as the screen noted, he took Highway 1. From there, he merged onto the Ayalon Highway. At that point, it seemed the road was running along a narrow strip of water, and the young woman resumed her explanation:

"This is one of the most famous rivers in Israel. It's close to fifty kilometers long, and it starts in the Judean Mountains."

The river held the passengers' attention for a few minutes before they turned away, preoccupied with other things. Then, the young woman asked them if they knew Hagit Yalu's song "Ha'aliya," which reminded Jews everywhere of the dream of returning to Israel.

Here's the day we're waiting for,
The moment we've been waiting for,
Ha'aliya.
Yesterday has no place here.
Tomorrow has no place here,
Ha'aliya.
Next year, Yerushalayim, is already here,
Ha'aliya.
It's the day we carry inside us,
For all times . . .

Heads swayed and voices grew louder, following the young woman's lead. Little by little, Dawit was drawn into the clamor all around him. First, he watched the state of joy as it flowed from one person to the next, and then he began to follow the rhythm with his fingers, tapping them lightly against the window. Finally, he began to say the words slowly to himself:

Yesterday has no place here.
Tomorrow has no place here,
Ha'aliya.

As the song came to its end, Dawit was fully absorbed in the raucous ecstasy:

Ha'aliya.
Next year, Yerushalayim, is already here.
Ha'aliya.

Unlike the others, he sang to convince himself that he truly *had* reached the threshold of salvation at long last. He was unable to rid himself of the feeling, deep down, that it wasn't quite true.

(9)

The buses passed through a large gate and followed a narrow, winding road that was fringed on both sides with flowers and greenery. They came to a stop in front of a colossal building. Here, the guide on Dawit's bus stood up.

"Here we are at last," she said. "This is the Sheba Medical Center, the largest hospital in Israel. It was established in 1948, the first military hospital to treat the wounded in the War of Independence. We'll carry out some quick checkups here before we continue on our way."

Medical staff stood at the ready, waiting for the new arrivals near the entrance. All of them wore long white coats, the sleeves ending in gloves of the same color, their faces mostly hidden behind green masks. The children were the first to be led off the bus and taken inside, while the others were asked to make a long line. The staff moved aside as someone wearing a white helmet, his face covered except for small holes for the eyes and nose, stepped forward. This person was wearing a blue plastic backpack that ended in a black hose. He gestured with one hand while the other held the hose. The first person in line moved forward until he was facing the white-helmeted man, who asked him to close his eyes and raise his hands high in the air. He then shot him with some kind of liquid before signaling that he could pass.

Dawit watched the proceedings as the line crawled forward, men and women hastening to reach the man in the white helmet, where they lovingly spread out their arms in front of him, making sure they were fully immersed in the sterilizing spray. They even wiped their wet hands on any spots not reached by the liquid, as if this were some new kind of baptism. When Dawit reached the front, he was resigned. He stretched out his arms, relaxed his head, closed his eyes, and felt the pungent liquid engulf his body.

◆ ◆ ◆

When he raised his head, the water dripping off him blurred his vision. His anger grew as he heard Yohannes laughing as he ran away, holding his loose pants in both hands and defending himself: "It was the only way to make you take a quick wash."

David stepped out of the pool, having bathed for the first time since reaching Endabaguna. He hadn't been convinced by Yohannes's idea that they go early. The night before, Yohannes had told him that washing at dawn, before other people arrived, meant you could be sure the water was clean, since the previous day's dirt would have settled at the bottom.

But David found it hard to wake up just to bathe. Still, he gave in to the insistence of his friend, who made sure he was awake. They walked together in the shadowy darkness, guided by Yohannes's lantern. They passed the tents and reached a small hill that David quickly climbed while Yohannes, panting, brought up the rear. In front of them, the last strands of darkness dissolved, revealing a terrifying patch of jungle. David hesitated before he gave in to Yohannes's assurances that the place was safe.

David pulled back the bare branches that blocked his path, feeling his way carefully with his feet. He walked slowly behind Yohannes, who had taken the lead, proud of being in the know about this place, until they reached a rectangular pool that was about twenty feet long. David touched the surface of the still water and found it had stored up all the night's cold.

He turned to his friend. "What do you think about waiting until sunrise?"

But Yohannes insisted on getting done fast. David started to undress and touched the water a second time. He was in nothing but his underpants when he stepped onto the ledge. He stretched out a foot to test the water again, and a strong shiver ran through his body. He wanted to turn and ask his friend to give him a little more time when he was surprised by a shove that sent him flying into the cold pool. He plunged completely underwater, then pushed his head back up, gasping in shock as he felt his skin pucker. He looked around for the runaway Yohannes, meeting his laughter with repeated curses. Still, he was rubbing his head and body, removing the dirt and the stinky sweat that clung to him.

As they headed back, refugees were racing in the opposite direction to bathe before the place got too crowded. Here, Yohannes took the opportunity to remind his friend that he'd been right after all.

Their tent was now half awake as it got closer to breakfast. David sat in his place in the corner while Yohannes picked up his belongings from the other side and carried them over next to his new friend, smiling as he said, "The man who had this spot agreed to swap."

"And who told you I'd be happy?"

Yohannes's smile faltered as he studied David's features. But David couldn't keep a straight face, and he burst out laughing as Yohannes smacked him with a pillow.

The morning passed, and David lounged around in bed. Whenever he tried to fall asleep, Yohannes interrupted him with a new tale.

He told him about half of the people in the tent, about the camp administration, about thieves and smuggling gangs, about beautiful girls, and the ones he described as "girls who were available in times of great adversity." David laughed at this description, and Yohannes sat up excitedly, launching into his explanation.

"Every girl knows how beautiful she is, right? And she acts the part," Yohannes said. "But that doesn't mean we can't make a move."

David turned away, muttering under his breath.

"Just hear me out," Yohannes said. "The beautiful woman is spoiled by everyone crowding around her. She pulls away as soon as you come close, not giving you the time of day. Then there's the girl who is the half beauty. She goes hot and cold. The way to get her is to shake her confidence, and it's already weak. If you want to get close to either of these types, you've got to take risks. The third type is the nonbeauty. Stay away from her as much as possible. But if you can't help it, then give her a compliment, and you'll see the results later when you're in need . . . you know, in times of great adversity."

Yohannes slipped these last words out with a wink, and David laughed so hard he started coughing, his eyes wet with tears. When he'd calmed down a little, Yohannes was ready: "Okay, and listen to this—"

David pressed his hands against his ears to force his friend to stop, before he stretched out again, covering his face with his blanket. Yohannes's enthusiasm cooled, and he stretched out, too, staring up at the ceiling of the tent. A man in the opposite corner cleared his throat. Then, before he left the tent, he tossed out:

"At least tell him about the one who told you all these stories."

David turned briefly toward the man before looking back at Yohannes, waiting for an explanation. But Yohannes ignored him, jumping to another topic. "Tomorrow's the second Tuesday of the month. Are you going to try your luck with the UN office?"

David jerked in surprise before Yohannes clarified: "They're going on a long vacation to escape the summer heat. That's why they moved the appointment up a whole two weeks."

David was filled with terror at the thought that his appointment with salvation was galloping toward him. This wasn't what he wanted. He didn't want the appointment to come late, but he didn't want it to be too early either. There was a sort of psychological readiness that was shaken by any imbalance in time. Sensing his friend's quandary, Yohannes rushed to reassure him: "Nah, don't worry, we'll work together to prep testimony, and you'll get the right to resettle on the very first try. We'll tap into my experience to fill in the gaps. Hey . . . are you listening?"

◆ ◆ ◆

He turned, embarrassed by the man's question. He'd been lost in thought, contemplating his assigned room. The housing officer was making sure he didn't need anything else. They had already gone over the contents of the room: a white bed, a wardrobe of the same color, a TV, an iron, and a small bedside table with a copy of the Holy Book. There was also a painting of Jerusalem at night that hung on the wall by the window, and next to it, there was an instruction card with the day's schedule: breakfast between six and seven o'clock, the Ulpan Hebrew course between eight and ten, then religion classes from eleven to one. Cleaning his room would be left up to him, and the compound's gates would close at ten o'clock.

Dawit read the list before signing the Statement of Commitment. Then he took the key and closed the door behind the staffer. Finally, he was alone with his own tired self, after hours at the Sheba Medical Center, which had drained his energy and his patience. Right after the ritual of forced sterilization, he'd put on plastic shoes and been taken indoors. He'd walked alongside a male nurse carrying a file, who kept his distance. They went down bright, empty corridors that had yellow tape stuck to the floor, a guide for their path through the hospital.

"Elohim!" A female nurse yelped in terror, darting away after almost colliding with Dawit at one of the crossings. She muttered under her breath, and Dawit caught the phrase "filthy slave."

The male nurse turned to her and suggested she wear gloves and a mask, since she'd find many of "them" in the hallways. He cut his gaze over to Dawit to see if he'd understood any of it.

They arrived at the lab. Dawit walked in while the nurse remained outside after giving his blonde colleague all the paperwork he had in hand. He told her that, in the sudden absence of the specialist, it was time for her to prove her worth. Even though she was just a trainee, she'd have to take everything on her own two shoulders.

Dawit sat in the chair opposite the young woman, who busied herself filling out a piece of paper in her hand. From time to time, she peeked over at him and tightened the mask over her face before finally turning to face him. She took his blood pressure, recorded his height and weight, and then moved to taking blood samples. He stretched out an arm and made a tight fist. The girl began to feel around for the location of his bulging vein, and then she pulled on her gloves. When she started to insert the needle, Dawit felt a sneeze forming and growing inside him. He tried to suppress it, but the sneeze insisted. He turned his face to the side and sneezed so forcefully that the woman jolted upright, pushing back in her chair as she readjusted her mask before leaping up from her seat and opening the door.

Sheepishly, he turned to her. Standing stiffly, she ordered him to wash his face and hands. She didn't return to her seat until someone came to wipe the area that had been grazed by the spray of his sneeze. Dawit had to suppress a laugh at her paranoia and how she was treating him like a plague that was looking for a victim to sink his fangs into. Why was she so wound up? He didn't see anything in himself that might cause all this panic.

Part of him wanted to tell her that he'd been subjected to examinations in every place he'd passed through: in the Blue Valley, in Endabaguna, and in Gondar. But her attitude annoyed him, so he tried to enjoy the opportunity to scare her to death.

She stretched out her arm as far as it would go to keep a distance between them, but he suddenly lunged forward. She gasped. He eased back a little until she relaxed, and then he went back to his tricks: once by fooling her into thinking he was about to sneeze again, another time by deliberately coughing, and a third by gagging as if he was about to vomit. Each time, the young woman stood up and took more precautions. When she'd finished taking the samples, she flung her plastic gloves in the trash and called for the male nurse to take Dawit away. Then she left the room, cursing the luck that had sent her to train at this hospital.

Dawit was taken to the radiology department to ensure he was free of all lung diseases, and from there to a large hall without chairs, where he found the others waiting for their results. He chose a corner and sat on the floor. Then, from his pocket, he pulled out the plastic glove that he'd snatched from a container in the moment between the trainee's departure and the male nurse's arrival. He rubbed it between his fingers as he watched the people around him. Most of them had been waiting so long that they'd lain down or fallen asleep. The hall grew more crowded until it was no longer possible to fit everyone unless people stood up.

Finally, salvation came. One person was called to redo their x-rays, while the rest were sent back to the buses, which took them to a residential complex in the suburb of Shkhunat Hatikva, south of the city. Once they got there, they were told that this was their temporary home, and they should be ready to move into a permanent one that would help them quickly integrate into society.

Now Dawit lay on the bed, his arms outstretched, and stared at the ceiling. He closed his eyes, then quickly reopened them. He didn't want any more dreams; he was now living the dream he'd been waiting for. This was *arriving*. This was *salvation*. It was an end to the unjust race. He had taken a place that wasn't his, but in any case, he'd won, and winners could find a thousand excuses for the sins they'd committed along the way. This idea revived him. He got out of bed, pulled on his jacket, and decided to take a victory lap through the streets. When he got to the door, he remembered to glance at the instruction card hanging on the wall.

He grabbed the yellow ID, hoping he'd be able to replace it with a blue one, which would entitle him to resettlement in a country of his choosing from among those on a long list. Would he pick America? Canada? Australia? How about Britain? No, no . . . maybe Sweden or Switzerland. It didn't matter. What mattered was successfully passing the interview with the UNHCR officer, which would take place within the hour.

Yohannes watched David's distraction with impatience before he jumped in, forcing him to listen: "Repeat what we agreed on. I want to make sure you've got the story down cold."

David reassured his friend. He put the ID in his pocket and walked toward the UNHCR office. Yohannes followed, trying to walk beside him, but David's steps were quicker. He was walking without thinking, staring ahead of him but seeing nothing except what was on his mind: the story of salvation that he'd spent the whole night immersed in, repeating it over and over to be sure he was steeped in the story, as though it were his own. He'd heard it for the first time from Yohannes, who had a knack for weaving in the details, and who told it in a more sympathetic way.

"Before the story starts, you've got to *look* the part. Right? You'll wear a huge cross during the interview, and you'll touch it before answering each question. You have to look broken down, so keep your head down. Make your voice tremble. At some point, you'll have to burst into sobs."

Yohannes stopped, pulling his face into a serious look that demanded David's attention. Then he went on: "When you cry, you have to do it honestly, so that the investigator believes it. Remember every bad thing that's happened to you. Think about all the horrors you've ever seen in front of you, and swallow them up so that they show on your face."

If not for Yohannes's stern expression, his eyes popping out and veins throbbing, David might have laughed. As it was, David was silent. Yohannes went on.

"You grew up an orphan, right? Your mother's only child. She spent most of the day working outside the house to feed you. When you got a little older, you had to quit school so you could help her a little, even though it didn't do much. You grew up. Your mama got older, and her health got worse, until she couldn't work anymore. Then the whole burden shifted to you. And when you hit sixteen, on a day you remember well . . ."

Yohannes paused, changing his tone, as though he wanted to separate the story itself from his instructions *about* the story. But he stayed just as serious: "You have to choose a date that seems specific. That's going to make your story more believable. Dates have to be totally memorized. Any mistake and you're done for."

David nodded. He found Yohannes's somber look inspirational. Yohannes went on with his plan: "The Kasha knocked on your door, and then they forced it open. They dragged you to the Blue Valley right in front of your own mother, who tried everything she could, but she couldn't get them to leave her poor son alone. In the Blue Valley, there was nothing but insults and torture until you were a broken man. But the real break came the moment you heard the news of your mother's death."

David focused in on Yohannes, who was now gazing off into the void. David tensed in anticipation of what would come next.

"I suggest that, at this point, you take a moment for the real waterworks. You won't need to finish the story. After that, everything's going to speak for itself. Just pay attention to the number you choose—I mean, the number of years you were in the Blue Valley.

"And now, let's take a walk outside. Keep cool and remember everything I told you."

He heard the guard's voice after he'd taken a few steps outside. The guard reminded Dawit of what time he had to be back, which was in two hours, and said that if Dawit missed the curfew, he'd have to spend the night outdoors. Then the guard asked him to be careful, although Dawit didn't understand why.

He walked without a destination, along the complex's high wall, until the road ended in a detour. A sign in front of him said that this was the neighborhood of Neve Sha'anan, which he'd heard about back in Gondar. Africans gathered here, in an area that looked like their homelands. He felt a chill and pulled his jacket collar tighter around his neck, stuffed his hands in his pockets, and walked down the street in the twilight, feeling a creeping sense of intimacy. A few Black faces walked by him, while others sat on the sidewalk. There were shops and restaurants with Amharic and Arabic signs and familiar music—as soon as he got closer, he recognized Teddy Afro's "Addis Zefen" booming out from a barber shop.

"Hey, handsome. Looking for something?"

The question came from a drunk, half-naked girl who tried to grab him from behind. He pulled away, waving a hand in refusal. The girl gave a vulgar laugh before taking a swig from the beer bottle in her hand. He kept going, looking back to make sure he'd left her behind. He turned down a darker side alley. He thought of heading back to the complex, but curiosity drove him on. He stepped around the beer bottles scattered on the ground, and a musty smell made him stop breathing through his nose. To either side of him, the doors to buildings were open, and strange noises came out of them.

As he drew closer, the noise got louder. A thin curtain came into view, which Dawit slowly pulled aside; inside was a small, crowded bar where the shisha smoke was so thick, he almost couldn't see inside. At the center of the room, there was a large table, and the people around it were clapping and shouting at a girl who was dancing on it in her underwear. Dawit turned, meaning to leave, but he ran into a man with his arm around a girl's waist. He stuttered out an apology and hurried off so he could get back to his room before curfew. But then someone called out and stopped him.

◆ ◆ ◆

He turned to find Yohannes calling out a question as he hurried after him, one hand clutching at his too-loose pants. David stopped impatiently, worried he'd miss his appointment.

"Did you memorize it all?"

"That is the *tenth* time you've asked me the same question."

"There's no other way for me to get you to stop so I can catch up with you—you move too fast."

Yohannes laughed as he said this last part, but then he swallowed his laughter when he saw David's tense expression. When they got to the UNHCR building, David went in while his friend stayed outside, giving him his final commandments.

The lobby was packed. In a corner on the right, there was a door with a small window that opened into the interview room. That's where David deposited his papers before he sat on the floor, waiting his turn. The lengths of the interviews varied. Some ended quickly, and those interviewees would come out with their heads drooping. Others would take longer, without the interviewee showing any external change. David watched the faces of those entering the room, and he studied them as they left. He tried to read their expressions to discover what had happened. Others tried to ask questions, but instructions swiftly rang out: *Those who have finished their interviews must leave.* Next to David, there was a young man talking to his friend:

"I heard that a long, long time ago, there was nothing easier than getting resettled in a third country. You'd make up any old story, and the immigration officer would listen with interest and sympathy, and he'd give you the approval right away. He'd even walk out with you, holding back his tears and promising he'd pray for you. But by now there are so many people that all the stories have been taken, and we have to do the impossible to convince them of our right to resettle."

Then, finally, he heard his name.

As he dragged himself into a standing position, the eyes of everyone followed his movements. The roles had flipped—now he was the focus of people's attention, and they were studying *his* features, comparing them to whatever his features would look like when he walked back out.

He went in and closed the door behind him. It was a small room, painted all in white. At the center was a brown desk, and behind it sat a European man with light-blond hair and thick glasses. He seemed to be in his fifties, but fit. Next to him were two young Ethiopians, one who was translating and another to document the interviews in a large notebook.

David sat down opposite the European, letting his gaze fall to the floor. The employee doing documentation asked for his personal information, which David answered without lifting his gaze. Then it was the European's turn. He spent a while inspecting David's face before tossing out a question in a voice so hoarse it made David shudder. "What makes you think you deserve to be resettled in a third country?"

◆　◆　◆

The man's question sounded odd. Dawit looked into his eyes, seeking clarification, and the man repeated his question more aggressively and with a heavy tongue: "What are you doing here?"

Dawit hadn't even formed an answer when the man tried to punch him. But he missed, lost his balance, and fell to the ground. Dawit ran for the residence, trailed by the man's curses. The road seemed to have gotten darker.

When he arrived at the complex, he was panting. The guard opened the gate with a broad smile.

"Ah, well, it's nothing new. Seems like they gave you a good welcome."

(10)

"Deep down, I knew they were going to come. I couldn't escape conscription forever, since nothing in Asmara stays hidden. I was bound to be ratted out by enemies, friends, or even people who had nothing to do with me. Everyone wanted to survive by pushing others into the trap. Still, I wanted my mother to feel at ease, so I hid my fears. I tried to keep it together for her sake, and she did the same for me, trying to hide her rising panic that they would come. We were both playing, while our vulnerability ate away at our souls.

"When they knocked on our door, I was sure this was the moment of terror that we'd hoped would never come. I hugged my mother, or actually I clung to her, as the knocking at the door grew fiercer. I stuck close to her trembling chest, her breaths rising and falling, her heartbeat sounding in my head as her panic rose.

"'You won't take him. You won't.'

"As soon as they began to break down the door, my mother shouted and made a run for the kitchen. She grabbed a long knife and told me to get behind her. Even though I was scared, some part of me was filled with pride. My mother had always seemed helpless to me, but now here she was, standing up for me. So when they broke down the door and grabbed me, and one of them slapped me, it didn't even hurt. I was filled with a strange calm that radiated from my mother. I saw her being slapped, but without giving in, growing even firmer in her resistance.

"I wished I could make her like me: oblivious to pain, to all those painful feelings."

David fell silent for a moment, keeping his head down, while the European waited impatiently for the story to continue. The European fiddled with his pen and resettled his glasses, which had slid down his nose. He gave the translator a bored look, and then made a shocking suggestion: "How about we go straight to the Blue Valley, and you start with the torture there."

For the first time, David lifted his head, shock written all over his face. All his efforts to pretend to be in mourning now appeared pointless; the European seemed to know the story by heart, even before he said anything. The man hadn't just ignored what he heard—he'd jumped with deliberate indifference to what came next. David cleared his throat as he tried to get back into the rhythm of his sadness and to take up the thread of his story once again:

"In the Blue Valley, torture was our daily bread. The goal wasn't that we become strong soldiers but that we be submissive slaves. It was an eternal slavery, inextricably—"

"And when did your mother die?"

David covered his face with his hands, plunged into a swirl of embarrassment and rage. This confirmed it: he was telling a story the European had heard thousands of times. He'd fallen into this stupid situation, where he was the butt of a joke. How had he missed it? How had he failed to ask Yohannes if the story he'd donated was new or if many tongues had used it before it had reached him? How had he put such an important task into someone else's hands? He bit his lip with bitter regret. He thought about getting up and walking out of the meeting, since his fate was already clear. But then a new idea took hold of him, filling him with energy. *He would tell the truth.* He would tell his own story, and the European would hear something he'd never heard before. He would tell his own great secret for the sake of his salvation.

Again, he lifted his head. The European's lips still held the traces of a smirk, but this quickly slid off when he saw David staring into his eyes so firmly it confused him. The European set the pen aside and resettled his thick glasses, then clasped his hands and placed them under his chin, looking keenly at David.

David said: "I'm Free Gadli."

The translator faltered, then dropped into silence and turned to the session's secretary, who hadn't written a single letter but was instead staring at David in astonishment. The European was confused as he saw the young men's expressions but couldn't understand what was going on. He angrily ordered his translator to explain. The translator looked at David, as if giving him one last chance to take it back. Then he cleared his throat and translated in a low voice: "He says he's one of the 'fruits of the struggle.'"

The European understood nothing from this literal translation, so the translator had to explain the meaning. "In Eritrea, that's what children are called if they're born of a relationship between soldiers on the battlefield that goes against religious law."

The European knit his brow and said with great interest: "This is new." Then he urged David to tell his story.

It was only at this moment that David felt the enormity of his decision. It wasn't easy for him to pull from his chest a story he'd grown used to hiding in the dark. But on the other hand, he wanted to survive, no matter what. He hesitated, before he noticed that the European was growing restless again. So he made up his mind and began to speak, hoping that his secret would never, under any circumstances, become public.

"I was seventeen at the time, even though I looked a lot younger. I was crammed with a bunch of others into the back of a truck that was part of a long column of vehicles going from Massawa to Asmara. I managed to climb up on one side of the truck bed and sit on the edge. Dozens of trucks, tanks, and smaller cars were following each other on the winding Qalb Tigray road up to the capital. In front of us, there was a tank spewing thick black smoke right into our faces, with exhausted soldiers sitting on top of it, waving their rifles and crutches to the people lined along the sides of the road. The soldiers didn't let a single truck pass without leaping onto it, so that it would bring them to their final destination, where people were celebrating the liberation of Eritrea. If a soldier couldn't find a truck or walk there on his own two feet, then the people from the villages scattered along the road would stop him, embrace him, and carry him on their shoulders. They would dance with him, for him.

"I was thrilled as I watched the celebrations. I wished I could get down so that the people would celebrate me, too, but our instructions were strict—*we* had to stay in the truck until we got there. I was filled with pride in our victory. It's true that I didn't do any of the fighting because they used to put me in the back, far away, where I'd carry water and help the nurses. I'd been too far back to be touched by victory, too far to be touched by defeat. Still, I'm the son of this revolution, and if liberation had come just a little later, I would've been one of its heroes carried on people's shoulders.

"When we got to the edge of Asmara, everything stopped, and crowds filled the streets. I could see it all from where I was sitting. Women came, and even invalids came in their carts, tossing corn and leaves at the fighters. The whole city was trilling, dancing, and weeping. Everyone was hugging the person next to them in a kind of hysterical joy. I saw a person run full speed in one direction, then turn around and race in the opposite direction. I saw another jumping up and down in place and a third pounding his chest and wailing. I saw a disabled man standing on one leg and waving his prosthetic leg up over his head. The people of Asmara couldn't find a way to express all their happiness. The victory was so huge and overwhelming, and it had come after so many setbacks—their spirits had been pierced with a despair that almost pushed them to surrender.

"When the trucks couldn't go any farther, the orders came, telling us to get off.

"Right away, I leaped off and dove into the crowd. I was proud of my uniform, which had been hemmed up to fit me, and I wanted everyone to see me in it. A woman seized hold of me and hugged me, shouting, 'Ohh, you're just a baby.' That irked me, so I slipped away from her and went toward the groups carrying soldiers on their shoulders. It was hard to get through the crowds, but finally a man noticed me and lifted me up, and I was surrounded by a circle of women. I was elated as I pulled the corn they were tossing on me out of my hair, and I started waving back at them. I was like a great leader returning with badges on his chest after he'd brought a major victory to his country. I didn't want the moment to end. I was afraid the man who was carrying me would get tired or bored, and then I'd go back to being a young man who was too short to see what was happening around him. But I felt at peace as he carried me around like a wild ox. I'd barely gotten a look at one side of the street before I found myself being carried to the other. But it wasn't confusing so much as joyful, as I looked at the faces staring up at their hero—until I saw her, and I wanted everything to stop instantly.

"She was staring at me, but if I looked back at her, she'd lower her gaze. She'd look away, raising the edge of the shawl around her neck to cover her lips, but then she'd drop it when she turned back to me. The man took me on another circuit, and I twisted to see if she was still with me. He took me to the opposite side of the street, and my neck almost twisted off as I tried not to lose the line of sight that connected us. Then he brought me back, right in front of her, and she smiled so shyly I almost lost my mind. I asked the man to put me down, but he ignored me and kept going. I begged him as I cursed his unstoppable energy. Finally, he spotted another soldier, dropped me, picked him up, and went back to his rampaging dance circle.

"When I looked around, she was gone.

"My head swam. Now that I was standing firmly on my feet, I felt dizzy. I spotted her stepping into another circle as she glanced behind her, holding the edge of her shawl close to her lips. Our eyes met, and the smile she'd had before returned to her lips."

David paused for a moment to check the effect his speech was having on the European. He found the man smiling stupidly and waiting for more. The session's secretary asked whether all this was worth writing down, and the European scolded him, telling him to just write without sticking his nose into what he was hearing.

David felt even more encouraged. For the first time since he'd arrived in Endabaguna, it seemed that destiny was being kind to him.

"When she saw me coming closer, she moved faster, sliding through the mass of body against body, until she emerged from the packed circles onto a side street off Komochtato.

"There, she slowed down, as if giving me a sign to follow her. She stopped completely at a Neapolitan pizzeria, which the owner had apparently shut down before going out to join the crowds.

"The crowd kept me a little ways back from her, and I struggled to get through the bodies and turn into the side street behind her. Then I saw her in front of me. But it was a shock, since someone else was holding both her hands, gazing into her eyes with a hungry desire. I was so overwhelmed by confusion I didn't know what to do. I thought maybe I should go back to Komochtato Street. But at the same time, I thought maybe I should walk past them, as if I were just casually passing by. Indecision paralyzed my legs, and I kept looking at them with a grief I couldn't hide. The young man turned to me, stunned by my gaze, and she turned to see where he was looking. Her eyes met mine. I smiled, my forehead dripping with sweat, before I turned and went back with the same speed I'd used to come that way, cursing the stupidity that had thrown me into such an embarrassing situation. She hadn't been looking at me. She hadn't been giving me a sign. And, idiotically, I'd bumbled into the meeting between her and her lover. I imagined them laughing as they thought of my shocked expression, before forgetting me forever.

"I found Komochtato in a state of wild dancing, but with my broken spirit, I couldn't feel anything. I pushed my way into a corner and leaned back, sullenly watching the beaming faces.

"I don't know why I remembered the first time I'd ever been attracted to a girl, which I used to find so intimidating. I was in the military, undergoing training. I was afraid of any kind of relationship, afraid of even trying, until people started to say I wasn't fit for love. Until *she* came.

"She was a soldier, older than me, and whenever we passed each other, she'd give me this mysterious smile without saying anything. At first, I thought it was just a casual greeting and that she repeated it only by accident. But, over time, I noticed the girl seemed obsessed with me, and when I turned to find her glancing at me, I began to deliberately put myself in her field of vision. Then she'd stop and watch my movements. I was taken with her obsession with me, until I became the one who stalked her, provoking her mysterious smile and building her trust in me. I put a lot of time and effort into being daring and trying to get close to her. Once, I succeeded, but I couldn't say anything, silenced by a deep fear that leaped up from the bottom of my soul. I cursed myself for my hesitation, since she seemed to be waiting for my next move.

"The next time, I gathered my courage and went for it. She was waiting for me with that smile, which had given up its mystery and become more obvious. She invited me to be braver, and so I was.

"'Can I talk to you for a minute?'

"I don't know how the words came out, but I finally said them. The girl's smile widened, and her voice sounded eager when she said I could meet her at nightfall behind the hill. That whole day, I was anxious, imagining what we'd say to each other. How would I be able to chat with her when saying just a few words tormented me? I thought about skipping our date, but I knew this was not just my first chance—it might be my only chance.

"When the time came, I headed toward the place we were supposed to meet, more anxious than before. My heart was pounding, and my feet hurt, even before I'd started out. I stood for a while in front of the hill, filled my lungs with air, and made a half turn to find her right in front of me. She was looking in another direction, so it was a moment before she realized, confused, that I was coming. She seemed to be like me, then—tense. She boldly reached out her hands, and I walked toward her with the same boldness. I liked the synergy between us, how we were stronger together. She grabbed my hand and my body shuddered, even though I made sure to hide it.

"'Do you love me?'

"Her question startled me. It seemed like a step too far. Still, I was amazed at her audacity. I liked being driven by this sort of madness. She smiled, and I answered her confidently: 'Yes. I love you.'

"As soon as I answered, hoots of laughter came from every side, and flashlights shone on us.

"'I won, I won!'

"The girl jumped up and down, her friends surrounding us. They were split in two groups: those who congratulated her for winning the bet and those who laughed at me. It took me a minute to realize what was going on and slink away, broken. My steps were slow, probably because I was waiting for the girl to call out a quick apology, but in her joy at winning, she forgot. I have never forgotten.

"So. Back to Komochtato.

"Not much time passed before I caught sight of the shawl-girl again. This time she was alone, walking around and looking for something. For a moment, I considered appearing in front of her in an apparently spontaneous way. At first, I was relieved that her boyfriend wasn't there, but then I quickly fell into a state of rage when I remembered how shattered I'd been in front of the two of them.

"She noticed me, and I quickly turned my face away, then peeked to see her walking up. She stood beside me, waiting for me to notice her. I glanced at her, casually, and met her broad smile with a lukewarm one.

"'Where were you fighting?'

"'In the field.'

"As I answered, I deliberately distracted myself by watching the crowds all around me. She wanted to ask something else, but I walked away before she could finish her question. I took a few steps, then looked back to find her face twisted up with irritation before she, too, walked away. I fought a twinge of guilt and immersed myself in the noise of Komochtato."

The European knit his brows, then asked with irritation, "But why did you do that?"

David hid a smile, proud of the impression this story had made on the man. He imagined himself walking out of the office with a blue card in hand. Only time separated him from this moment. He would brandish that card at the anxious people waiting outside, and it would prove to all of them that he had a different story, that he might have been the last to reach the camp, but he was the first to achieve his goal.

"I'll explain everything."

With the same pride, the words poured out of David's mouth. He knew exactly where to strike next.

(11)

Dawit was still eager to explore the city, despite his outing the evening before.

This time, he left the residence during the day as soon as he'd finished with class. He wanted to see Neve Sha'anan in the daylight. He walked with confidence, keeping a neutral expression as he looked around. There was constant motion in all directions, as well as people of all nationalities, although Black was the dominant skin tone. He spotted a police vehicle blocking the entrance to the neighborhood, but the Africans walked past it without taking any notice.

He passed a group sitting in front of an Ethiopian café. One of them called after him and alerted the others. Then someone said, in Amharic, "Welcome, new guy."

Dawit gave a brief wave, returning the greeting. After that, he hurried through the crowd until he'd gotten past them. Another man rushed up and spoke in the same clear Amharic: "You're lucky, slave."

He ignored the slur and kept going, but without failing to notice that this particular insult haunted him wherever he went. He turned right and found a bric-a-brac market, where he stopped in front of a watch cart. The seller walked up, showing off his wares.

"This one just arrived. Costs two thousand shekels, but it's yours for only a thousand."

Dawit flipped over the seemingly new watch, with its glossy black metal rim and silvery face, before putting it back. The man made a new offer: "Five hundred. That's my last price."

Surprised by the huge range, Dawit decided to test him. "What do you say to two hundred?"

"Take it."

Dawit hesitated for a moment, turning the watch over again, afraid of being tricked. He wanted to offer an even lower price, but he was afraid of angering the seller. So he paid the man and went off, proud of his left wrist.

The street ended in a large, untended park, where scattered groups of Africans mingled. Most of them were speaking in Arabic, with a few foreign languages. He walked among them, feeling encouraged, since most people didn't seem to be staring at him, despite a few curious looks. The Sudanese dialect grew clearer, and he sat down near a group that was talking loudly, joking, occasionally bursting into fits of hysterical giggles.

Next to them, another group was lying on the grass, silently staring at the sky. He noticed a group of Asians gathered around their bags, and others who were hanging clothes on a nearby tree trunk.

It was time for afternoon prayers, so some were headed for the mosque, which overlooked the park.

A small truck pulled up, and the Africans inside started handing out water to everyone. Dawit watched as people grabbed the bottles that flew at them. He waited for one to be tossed at him. After he'd waited a long time, he pointed at the nearest man in the truck, but nothing happened. He walked toward the man, stretching out his hand. The man almost gave him one but then suddenly stopped, examining Dawit before passing the bottle to another man beside him. Dawit stepped back, having lost all desire for water.

A girl walked past, handing out leaflets, and she was met with a cold shoulder. A young man standing nearby dropped her paper after glancing at it, and Dawit picked it up. It was a leaflet about AIDS prevention, printed in Arabic and Amharic; he folded it and put it in his pocket. Then he heard a voice say: "There's nothing free here except advice."

He turned, looking for the source of the voice, which went on without waiting for his response: "Except for what *you* get, of course." Then the speaker gave a nasty laugh.

Dawit was clearly puzzled by that last comment, and his bafflement seemed to throw the young man into doubt.

"Aren't you Falasha?" the man asked. "Sorry, but you're wearing their clothes."

Dawit looked down at what he was wearing, trying to see what made him so obvious. He was in white track pants and a blue shirt emblazoned with a six-pointed star. Under that, in neat letters, it read: BETA ISRAEL. So *that's* why he'd been stalked by glances in the garden and insults in the market. Was that why he hadn't been offered a bottle of water?

The man was still waiting for a response, so Dawit let go of his misgivings and answered in Arabic. This gave the other guy—who had been speaking in broken Amharic—a jolt of surprise.

"Yeah. And you? You're from Sudan?"

The man fell silent for a moment before he brushed off his confusion. "I'm Yaqub. From Nyala."

Yaqub rushed right past the getting-to-know-you part and jumped straight into questions, clearly driven by the curiosity that creased his expression.

"So tell me, man, how do they treat you? Is it true that these dogs give you a whole two thousand shekels a day, while they let us starve? And that you have jobs waiting for you before you even get here? How do they make sure you're Jews like them? And you're going to join the army, right? I heard your salaries skyrocket when you're in there—like, the more you kill, the more you make. Tell me . . . come on, come on."

Pummeled by Yaqub's questions, Dawit didn't know where to start. He wasn't sure if he could answer without revealing too much. Plus, it seemed less like Yaqub genuinely wanted to know and more like he was just full of rage. Finally, Dawit picked a vague answer: "If only things were so sweet."

Yaqub paused, trying to make something of Dawit's answer, before he attacked again: "Yeah, yeah. Is it true that most of you buy a Jewish ID in Ethiopia? How does that even fool these fuckers? Come on, tell me, how much did you pay to become a Jew?"

Dawit was horrified as the young man shifted from rumors to dark secrets. He realized now that he didn't want to play this dangerous game. This time, he didn't have a vague answer. He chose to cover up his anxiety by returning Yaqub's attack.

"You tell me, when and how did *you* get here? Are you going to stay here, or will you go back?"

Yaqub adjusted his position as he considered his answer. But then a brown-skinned girl appeared, wearing a short skirt that revealed her thick, dimpled thighs. She called for the young man to come.

Yaqub winked at his new acquaintance, promising to answer soon, and then sprang up to join the girl. Dawit was relieved to have gotten himself out of this predicament. He didn't care so much about the answer to his question—just about escaping Yaqub's barrage of questions.

He, too, got up and walked quickly back to the residence before another one of the curious onlookers could latch on to him, keeping him in Neve Sha'anan.

◆ ◆ ◆

The next day, he was scheduled to meet with a counselor.

The bus took them down Retsif Herbert Samuel Street to the Matzpen Mental Health Center, located right next to the Corniche. Strangely, he didn't really care where they were taking him.

He sat at the front of the bus and put his name down at the top of the list, feeling tranquil and at ease. He didn't know if he felt like this because he'd finally reached his destination or because they made the visit seem routine and unimportant, a thing ordinary people would do in the course of an ordinary life.

He walked into a small room. The lighting was soft, and there were two comfortable chairs in the center. He sat in one of them. In the opposite chair was a blonde woman in her forties, her thick hair held back in a big black clip.

She had one leg crossed over the other as she browsed his file, giving him a smile every now and again, until she turned her attention on him.

"Okay, Dawit. First off, you should know that this is a completely routine procedure. Also, it's normal for you to need help. Anything you say will be useful, no matter how insignificant it might seem. And anything you say in here won't go beyond the walls of this room."

He nodded, rubbing his hands together. He didn't know why he'd started to feel a strange tension, as if this was the interrogation he'd gone through in the Endabaguna refugee camp all over again. The woman seemed sympathetic, but he'd learned not to trust anyone, especially people who seemed to be treating him with too much kindness.

"Tell me about yourself."

Dawit didn't like this question. He felt it gnawing at his disguise, peeling back layer after layer to reach where he was hiding. Even if he didn't answer . . . well, what the breast hid, the face revealed.

"Where do I start?"

As soon as Dawit tossed out this question, he recognized its futility. But it bought him time to search for a story that would keep him safe. Usually, he felt okay about weaving tales, the way he had back in the army while he was working with the army's theater troupe. He'd spent time watching the performances, and he'd paid special attention to how actors spoke, telling story after story without the help of the printed page. He was amazed by their ability to emerge from one story and slip right into another. He would memorize everything he heard, and then he'd take pleasure in reenacting all the parts when he was alone. He was overjoyed when they gave him a small role—he spoke a single word in the middle of the market ("Cloth, cloth"). After that, his job had been limited to fetching water and carrying and arranging the chairs.

But that night, he'd slept as well as he ever had, and he dreamed that his roles would grow and grow until he became the most important actor in the whole military troupe.

"Wherever you like. But maybe if you talk about your childhood, that would be a good place to start."

Here, the counselor pulled him out of his comfort zone. At the word "start," he froze. He realized he was being lured into something that would not end quickly. He cleared his throat, feeling pressed into a new lie.

But at the same time, he felt a thrill, because the counselor's pen cap had tumbled under his feet, and she didn't make a move to pick it up.

"I was born in Makaly, where I spent my first years. Our mud-brick house was at the middle of a square that was linked to the city's outdoor market. We had a small yard that stopped at our door, and it was open onto the neighbors' yard, which was open to another yard, and so on, all the way until you got to the start of the market.

"I spent my days going from house to house. No door stopped me, and I was friends with everyone I found along my way. When things were good, the lucky owner of a soccer ball was generous and let me join their group. Then I'd spend the whole day playing soccer.

"Later, my father bought me a bike. Then *I* became the lucky one, and I could give anyone I liked a quick spin around the neighborhood. In the evenings, I'd come home covered in dirt, and my mother would place me under the tall faucet, naked, while the neighbors laughed and chatted all around me. I liked the evenings best, when I would sit and listen to the women's conversations. My mother always let me be, except when she was talking about 'adult things,' as she called them, and then she'd make me go inside. I would pretend to obey her, but really I'd stand by the door and listen to one of the trashy neighbors, who described in detail how her husband rode her like a bull while she moaned underneath him. My mother tried not to leave me alone with this neighbor, who kept repeating the same story, again and again, with only a few changes. The other women would laugh while my mother just smiled, anxious about anyone who might overhear. Once, this neighbor raised a topic that my mother had been trying to avoid. But when the other neighbors insisted, she finally gave in.

"The trashy neighbor said: 'The first thing I see when my husband steps in the house is his cock. It almost seems like it's suffocating in there, like it's trying to escape its cloth shackles with every step. I hurry to the man to take whatever he's carrying, and, as I do, I deliberately rub up against what's grown into a third leg. And what about your husbands?'

"The women covered their faces with fake shyness, before each one started to talk about her husband's length. By the time it came to my mother's turn, her shyness had fallen away a little. She was silent, her head lowered, a smile creeping over her face as the women erupted with cries of encouragement.

"'It's long enough.'

"Then she lowered her head a little more before she was totally caught up in the mood of the discussion: 'It's enough and more.'

"I felt proud, because my father wasn't less than the others. I wanted to come out of my hiding spot and tell them a story about something I'd seen. I wanted to tell my mother, most of all, how I'd passed by our trashy neighbor's house one night to hear her cursing her husband as she asked him to bring a mirror to put under his potbelly to look for his organ, which was hidden like a trembling thief. That night, I'd left the woman cursing her fate, wishing she was as lucky as her friends in the neighborhood."

Dawit looked up into the counselor's eyes, expecting to see her flustered, but he was surprised to see her taking notes with a calm smile that transferred the flustered expression onto his face.

By the time he left the clinic, he was exhausted by the stories he'd had to tell. Some of them he'd made up and others he'd heard in places he could no longer remember. This was how he dealt with things— turning everything around him into an exciting story. He could even come back to them dozens of times. He rearranged events, added to them, shucked off their husks and appendages, moving in toward the body. The story would start out strong, then slow down before rising up again and taking his listeners' breaths away.

In bed at night, he was proud of his ability to invent elaborate lies. He was even happier to be stroking the counselor's pen cap he'd snatched up before leaving the clinic. He would add it to his collection, along with the napkin from the waitress in Ethiopia, the pen from his teacher in Beta Israel, the glove from the nurse in Sheba Medical Center, and many, many more . . .

But then an incomprehensible feeling of unease returned, seizing hold of him. The counselor had been happy just to listen, and she hadn't told him the results of their meeting. He closed his eyes, hoping he hadn't incriminated himself, spoiling the salvation he'd worked so hard for.

(12)

"So I tried to forget about the girl by distracting myself with the celebrations. But it didn't work.

"I felt a huge desire to go look for her, talk to her, or at the very least, get close to her. My eyes darted all around, but she wasn't there. I walked in the direction I'd seen her go, and then I was running through the crowds, crashing into sweaty bodies, my shoulders rubbing against large breasts. But none of it stopped me. There was no sign of the girl.

"Time passed, and my urge to see her grew.

"I felt it was futile to look for her, especially since I was too short to see over the tops of the too-tall bodies around me. I found my way to a high bench and climbed onto it. Now the whole area was laid out in front of me, and it was such a delicious feeling that I envied the tall people. Now, I could look around more confidently. Not far off, a young man had wrapped an arm around his sweetheart. An old woman was kissing what was left of her son's amputated arm. A few meters from that, one of the fighters was weeping in front of Cinema Roma and stopping people, who looked at him in confusion.

"And on the other side of the main road, the girl stood, playing with a homeless child.

"I leaped off the bench and pushed my way toward her through the throngs of people. She didn't notice me until I was standing right in front of her. She seemed a little confused, but even once she recognized me, she went on acting like she was busy with the boy, even though she was obviously pretending. I took out ten cents and put them in the boy's hand, and he left the girl to move toward me. I patted him on the head, looking at her, but she ignored me. I whispered in his ear, and he darted off. I moved toward her, and she took two steps back. Confidently, I bridged the distance. 'You didn't tell me your name.'

"She smiled faintly and went on staring into the distance. I seized hold of her hand, and her features tightened as she snatched her hand back and turned away. My confidence was shaken. I was about to walk away, but a fear of losing her completely fixed me in place. I played my last card: 'I'm sorry. That was rude, and rudeness never suits a beautiful woman.' From the side, I spotted a half smile, which she was struggling to hide, and felt encouraged. 'Still, just the same, it doesn't suit a beautiful woman to be cruel.' Here, the blockade broke, and I heard what sounded like a chuckle. But she still didn't turn fully toward me.

"I inched closer. She still had her back to me, her right hand holding the edge of her shawl up to her mouth. I moved around until I stood right in front of her. She let the shawl drop, revealing her whole face. I was mesmerized by her features: her short coal-black hair, her sumptuous dark skin, and her round glasses, which gave her a look that was both innocent and seductive. She had jutting cheekbones, a slightly plumper lower lip, and the trace of a small wound at the tip of her upper lip. She also had a large mole on her throat, right where it met her chest. She noticed me devouring the details of her face, so I adjusted my gaze, looking up into her eyes, which I could do as much as I pleased without embarrassment.

"It seemed like she was waiting for me to make a move, but I was confused about where to start. I wanted to step past any sort of beginning and tell her how beautiful she was. It wouldn't be right to just have an ordinary conversation with her, since this sort of thing didn't happen every day. I was unable to resist moving my gaze over her face again, and she lowered her eyes and raised them to find me in the same position.

"I didn't know exactly what was going on, and she probably didn't either. I didn't know why we seemed to be picking up something we'd started a long time ago. There was a familiarity to our meeting, as if this were the tenth time we'd met and not the first. And it wasn't just about the two of us—there was something else motivating us to be here, pushing us to face our beautiful destiny. A supreme energy was willing us to do it, and we obeyed without argument. I don't know why I felt a spiritual reverence in front of this face, or why I felt her soul was also leaning forward, kneeling, prostrating, holding the position.

"'Aisha.'

"She mumbled it, finally answering my question. At the end of the word, shyness swallowed her voice. Still, I felt the whole of her name. I was able to taste it, smell it, touch it. It was as if she were giving me one last chance to step forward. After such a long wait, she had finally answered.

"And now she'd led me to another dilemma: What should *I* tell her? Did I give her the name I'd once used? *Adal?* She would know what it meant for a person to be named after a mountain, or a valley, or a battle. I wouldn't be surprised if she felt disgusted with me and left without even trying to hide her disappointment. Maybe she would be more sympathetic and find some more merciful way to pull away. But at the end of the day, the result would be the same: she'd be gone.

"'Dawoud. My name is Dawoud.'

"The words came out slowly, as if I had to work to pronounce them. It was as if, like her, I was hearing this name for the first time.

"She smiled as she whispered, 'That's a beautiful name,' and it lifted away the shame of my lie and shot me full of courage. I stretched out a hand. She reached out hers, and our palms pressed powerfully together. I felt my hand clutch hers, begging her to be there forever. For some reason I couldn't understand, her tender brown hand made me sad.

"'Your palms are rough.'

"She said it with a shy laugh, and I pulled my palm back in embarrassment, since my hand had known nothing but wilderness and hard work, and it hadn't been ready for a great day like this. If I'd known what a beautiful fate was waiting for me, I would have hidden my palm from the world until this very moment. Seeing how her words had struck me, she clasped my palm in hers, trying to erase their impact.

"'But it's *this* palm that's defending us. Isn't that so, Dawoud?'

"I was filled with pride. I loved my new name, which seemed to have been mine since birth, from the moment my parents fought about it, each wanting me to have a name of their own choosing. Perhaps, to settle the dispute, they'd ended up drawing lots, and that had led them to the name Dawoud. What a name it was, especially when Aisha spoke it, filling it with so much music! No doubt, this was the name for me. I slipped further into my imagination until it occurred to me to wonder: What would have happened if a different name had been chosen for me? How much would I have lost if I'd missed out on the beautiful way she pronounced 'Dawoud'? But I decided that any name would have been delectable as soon as Aisha said it, even if it was Adal."

"So then you're not David. Aisha wasn't the only one you lied to."

The session's secretary yanked David out of his story and back to reality. This one sentence shook off the sweetness of Komochtato Street and threw him brutally back into the mobile office in Endabaguna, where he was facing an investigation that would determine his fate. David stuttered—he who was Dawoud in Asmara, and before that Adal at the front. But a sign from the European told him to continue with his story. It was clear that the decision maker had been absorbed by the story, and he would not brook any interference, even if there was a lie in the man's basic information. David ignored the secretary's angry glances and continued.

"We sat out on the patio of a restaurant, near the front door. From that spot, we could see all the loud celebrations out on Horreya Street. But we were also far enough to feel alone in all of Asmara. Music and chanting were the backdrop for our private meeting. It was as if the whole city had come out just to crown this event, to give it everything it deserved. Aisha shifted her gaze between me and Komochtato, while I was lost, gazing at her face, content in her presence.

"There was a silent agreement between us: we wouldn't ask what was happening in that moment, what was fizzing through our blood-streams. We were just living it, performing the roles entrusted to us as sacred missions.

"'Tell me about you . . .' She was silent for a moment before she clarified. 'About your fighting at the front, I mean.'

"Her clarification saved me, because how could I tell her I had no life outside the front? I'd had no childhood in any village or city. The first time I'd opened my eyes, it was on a battlefield. I had moved from one babysitter to another, and they were all my mother. The fighters took turns tying me to their backs. With them, I would go up hills, down across the plains, and stretch out in the trenches. The first toy I ever played with was an empty Kalashnikov—or maybe it was loaded, who knows! The first word I ever spoke was a bad attempt to imitate the sound of someone ordering an artilleryman to fire. Before that, I had been happy imitating the sounds of shelling, with perfect success.

"Aisha's clarification saved me, because I wouldn't have been able to tell her that I'd been helping the women soldiers drag the wounded away from the front. I had grabbed the half-amputated hands, walked up to the broken faces. Once, my clothes got so soaked in blood that a woman soldier surprised me, grabbing me in a panicked hug before I gave a mischievous laugh. She scolded me, telling me to help her carry one of the newly wounded.

"It wasn't like that the first time I handled a broken body—I wasn't nearly so calm. The first man wasn't one of the wounded, or rather he didn't stay that way. That first time, I'd helped drag a young man with a staved-in head. Sometimes he moaned, and other times he cried out loudly, asking the women soldiers if he was going to die.

"I had looked at him in horror. As soon as he turned to me, I looked away. I avoided his repeated question, 'Am I going to die?' because I wasn't prepared to lie but I also couldn't tell him the truth.

"A woman soldier stood steadfast by his head, trying to stop the bleeding as we waited for the doctor. She glanced at me and ordered me to bring her more bandages. I didn't move. It looked like I hadn't really heard her. She repeated her order, louder, but I still didn't move. I was paralyzed by the sight of blood coming out of the young man's head, his intermittent weeping, and his hope that they would do something so he'd survive. He didn't make it.

"For days, I shivered with fever, and my stomach emptied out any food I put in it. I had hallucinations and nightmares, and they were all full of blood and cracked heads.

"I couldn't tell Aisha about that kind of weakness. I also couldn't tell her about how, after, these things became normal. How I could see Death hovering over the head of a wounded man even before the doctor came, and how I accepted it in the lukewarm way you accept any kind of habit. In time, I was able to see Death in the eyes of the people around me, even before the battle would start. There is a state that bodies enter when Death is approaching, even if they're still in the peak of health. I can't explain it, but for some reason, I can see it.

"Anyhow, Aisha's clarification saved me from all that, even though it dropped me right into another dilemma. So I started to spin lies from nothing. I said:

"'A bunch of times, I tried to persuade my parents to let me join the revolution. But they totally refused, claiming I was too young. So I had to run away to join the front. There, I learned how to use weapons, until I got so good they made an exception, and I was allowed to join the battles, unlike the other kids my age, whose main job was helping the women drag the wounded and the dead into the ranks at the back. You could tell that the other kids burned with envy at my combat performance and at the constant praise I got from my superiors. Some of them even made a public protest, which got them punished. Although the punishment only made them even more determined to get their revenge.'

"After that, I was silent for a moment, afraid I'd drifted too far into exaggeration. But I found Aisha looking at me with pride, as if she were gazing at a hero who had successfully returned from his mission without a scratch and not at a young guy she'd just met. That pride passed on to me, and I raised the ceiling of my imagination.

"'I don't know if I should tell you, but as I did my duty, I was forced to . . .'

"Eager interest appeared on Aisha's face, and she seemed to be urging me on.

"'I was forced to kill.'

"The girl drew in a breath and placed a hand on her mouth, so I seized the moment: 'It was just that . . . I mean, I was defending a soldier who nearly took a bullet in the back. But I charged at the attacker and shot him, which killed him straightaway.'

"Aisha's smile grew, and a spark of gratitude settled in her eyes. I became even fonder of my imagination's ability to take flight. In that instant, it occurred to me that I could test my own worries, so I added, hesitantly: 'The soldier whose life I saved was one of the "fruits of the struggle." You might have heard about how highly trained they are. Saving him made me a strong candidate for the same privileges.'

"At this, Aisha's smile shrank. Her features shriveled with disgust for just a moment before the smile returned to her lips, although now it was a little more half hearted."

The European gave a loud laugh, which was followed by a stuttering cough. He gestured with a hand and said, "Go on, go on."

David felt that the deeper he dug into his story, the closer he was getting to his goal. Maybe after he was accepted into the resettlement program, *his* story would be turned into one that other refugees adopted as a means of survival, and others would spend their time trying to learn it by heart. He would go back and tell Yohannes about how he'd abandoned that old story and sailed along on a new one, which had taken him to his safe harbor. He reached out a hand with a boldness he didn't really feel and took a sip of water from a bottle in front of the European. He deliberately didn't turn to the session secretary. Instead, he cleared his throat a little, until he was ready to go on with his tale.

(13)

The room phone rang. The building's guard told Dawit that his friend was waiting for him at the gate. Dawit was surprised, and he kept guessing who it might be until he found Yaqub in front of him, his lips parted in a broad smile.

"I thought you might want to get out a little."

Dawit flushed as he tried to think of an excuse that would mean he didn't have to go out with this irritating guest. He remembered the man's curiosity from the day before, which had so completely trapped him.

"Come on, man."

Yaqub's insistence cut off all paths of escape. Dawit gave an unenthusiastic nod, not that it changed anything.

"Today, let's talk all about you. I want to know everything about you, my *friend*." Dawit leaned hard on the last word. This was his only trick to evade interrogation, and he felt pleased by Yaqub's instant approval.

This new friend took him to the heart of the Neve Sha'anan market. Everyone seemed to know Yaqub, and they all passed on news and greetings. They walked past the guy who'd sold Dawit the watch, and Yaqub said hello before turning back to his new friend, telling him that the best stolen goods in all of Tel Aviv found their way to this vendor. Dawit couldn't hold back his laughter. Now everything was totally clear. He wished he could find something in the market that really interested him—the watch with its shiny black metal rim had stayed in his drawer, since he wasn't used to wearing a wristwatch.

Then Yaqub disappeared for a few moments, slipping into a beauty salon and coming back out with a mysterious look on his face.

"Man, you've got heaven's luck. This piece is Afghani."

Dawit looked into the other man's hand, where he found a joint of black hash. He looked around anxiously before his friend gave a burst of reassuring laughter. Dawit remembered when he'd been close to smoking hash for the very first time. He'd heard so much about it that he'd started to crave this unknown flavor. He had managed to get hold of one single joint that he'd hidden for a long time, waiting until he found the right opportunity. But then he'd panicked at seeing a police car drive up Komochtato Street in Asmara, and it had fallen from his hand, straight into a sewage-filled ditch.

But here was luck, throwing his wish right back at him.

They turned into an alley, and Dawit watched his friend light the end of the joint with a gentle flame before mixing it with tobacco that he'd emptied out of a worn cigarette. Then he rewrapped it with remarkable deftness and offered it to Dawit.

Dawit drew in a deep breath, which burned his throat and chest with sudden fire, before he coughed out forcefully.

"Slow down, man, take a breath. Don't mess with the rocket, or it'll mess you up."

Dawit tried the joint again, although this time more slowly, feeling the smoke creep into his lungs before it rose into his head and settled there, making him feel numb. He blew it out again, and his sense of ease grew.

"Give it here, man. Haven't you ever heard of socialism?" Yaqub chuckled before taking the joint, while Dawit let a thread of numbness run through his body with a delicious slowness.

"You know, I was one of the first guys to come to Israel. If it hadn't been for my bad luck, I would've gotten residency by now."

Dawit tried to focus his attention on his conversation partner, but something convinced him not to leave the joint's zone of influence. He wanted to breathe in the smoke that was coming out of Yaqub's lungs.

"When me and two friends left Darfur, we went to Cairo. We meant to get refugee status and fly to Europe. But there was this long wait with a huge number of asylum seekers. They were from all these different African countries, except all of them claimed they were from Darfur. It was weird, or shady I guess, how they all had this deep knowledge about the geography of *my* country.

"Anyhow, after we spent the last pounds we had, a bunch of us got together in Mustafa Mahmoud Square to pressure both the Egyptian government and the UNHCR. Almost four thousand of us waited out there. It got to be our third month of pointless waiting, and we were being battered by the cold and the rain, with nothing but plastic bags to wear on our heads. And then, on New Year's Eve in 2005, just before midnight, we were surrounded. It was security, and there were about two thousand of them. At first, we thought they just wanted to scare us, and that's what people said, passing the news through the group.

"But on a Friday morning that I still remember crystal clear, the protestors resisted. After that, security started firing water cannons at us and slamming us with batons. Man, it was total chaos, and we didn't know where to turn. Families were separated, and the people who were running away trampled other people who fell. When things finally calmed down, we found out how bad it was: twenty-five souls were lost that morning. One of them was my best friend.

"The faces of the dead are still there, still haunting me, no matter how hard I try to forget. I don't even know how I survived it. It was the kind of death carnival that nobody's supposed to escape."

Yaqub's voice shook as he handed over the joint, which was now just the length of a fingernail. When Dawit took it, he sucked in a drag so deep that the flame reached his fingertips, but he didn't care.

"We were in a real mess. The UNHCR threw us scraps to soak up our anger. I don't know how the idea of immigrating to Israel started, but I just heard some of the guys whispering that a few people had already left, and they were welcome. In the beginning, I hesitated. But the shit conditions forced our hand, until—"

"Hey, listen. Do you have another joint?"

Yaqub was silent for a second, shocked by Dawit's hunger for a fix, so strong that he wasn't even listening. He took out a small piece and started to pass it over the flame.

"I meant to save this for tonight, but it's okay, man. It's yours."

Dawit's eyes glittered as he took the new joint and asked, with fake interest, for his friend to go on with the story. Yaqub hesitated for a moment, but then he made up his mind when Dawit insisted.

"Yeah. We crossed into the Sinai. Seven of us. I'm not going to pretend like I wasn't scared shitless at the idea of falling into the hands of Israeli security. But the shocking thing was that we were shot at from the *Egyptian* side. This guy I didn't know was injured, but the rest of us made it. We got to the high fence that separated us from Israel, and we worked together to get over it. Then we found a sign welcoming us.

"I remember it perfectly—how I stood in front of that sign, like it was the boundary between the shit life I was leaving behind and the comfortable one that was waiting for me. But no, man, that's not what happened. A group of Israeli border guards met us, and they took us to Ktzi'ot Prison in the Negev. They told us we'd be going through some routine procedures that would just take a few hours. Yeah. Most of us were there for months."

Dawit's eyes drooped as he continued to take greedy drags, afraid his friend would notice and remind him about socialism. But Yaqub was so deep in his story that his speech slowed down.

"I left Ktzi'ot after six months with a bus ticket to Tel Aviv and a card saying I was on temporary release with no right to work. I knew my new status made me an illegal, not a refugee. But by the time I realized that the door was totally shut, and they weren't ever going to accept my documents, it was too late. Not everybody was like that. Some guys came out with a refugee card, and today they're like half citizens. They don't have to work long hours in the vineyards for a handful of shekels, like I do, and they don't have to sleep out in the open because they're still out a few minutes past six, when the public shelters close. Maybe you're curious about why some people are rejected and some are accepted . . . well, trust me, man, nobody knows."

In truth, Dawit wasn't interested in the question. He dropped the butt of the joint and crushed it beneath his foot in apparent ecstasy, redness spreading through his eyes. When he turned to Yaqub, he found his friend gazing absentmindedly at the joint's remains.

(14)

"The next day was the first of our Independence.

"Even though none of the streets or buildings had changed, Asmara looked totally different. The change was in the souls of its people. Even though they'd stayed up late the night before, they were back in the streets at the break of dawn, as if they had to make sure the city really was liberated, and they could keep everything in this new form. Everyone seemed to be a police officer, guarding their property.

"Like them, I went out to Komochtato early, although my reasons were different.

"*Let's meet tomorrow.*

"I carried Aisha's promise, which she'd made before leaving, like an amulet that helped me face the world. She hadn't told me exactly when she would come, but to avoid missing her, I hurried to the old Komochtato, which was now called Horreya Street, in the early hours of the morning. It helped that I hadn't been able to sleep for the last two hours of the night.

"People like me, Free Gadli, had been instructed to sleep at the residential quarters of the Revolution School. I wouldn't have been embarrassed about this if it wasn't for Aisha, who had come into my world and changed everything. I didn't want her to get close enough to see who I truly was. Everyone knew that the Revolution School was for the members of Free Gadli. So when I left her, I made sure to go a completely different way, taking a side road toward the Central Post Office building and from there to the fish market. I made a full circle around Komochtato until I came out on the other side. The whole time, I kept checking behind me.

"I walked around for a while until I got to Mikael's Bakery, which was right in front of the school. But again, I decided to wait and check out the faces of everyone passing by. I don't know why I thought Aisha might follow me in disguise and catch me red handed in a lie. But I kept my excuses stacked on the tip of my tongue, so that I could spit them out as soon as she showed up. When I finally went inside and shut the school door behind me, my nerves calmed. But then my anxiety returned. I tossed and turned in bed.

"People always envied us, the 'fruits of the struggle,' since everyone could see how we were being prepped for the future of the country. They knew we were getting ready to be the backbone of the homeland. We were given a university education, plus we had to master more than one language and learn how to handle light weapons. We were orphans, without tribal or religious ties, so the revolution was our only goal, our mother and our father. For me, the whole thing was kind of confusing.

"I mean, on the one hand, I was happy for the help from our leadership and the envy that welled up in the other kids' eyes. But that never really helped me get rid of my feeling of loss, of being without a father or mother, without brothers, without a wall to lean on, without history, without memory. I grew irritated whenever I caught sight of other people's mocking looks—those were the people who didn't dare say out loud how they felt about me. Basically, the care they took in raising 'us' wasn't enough to make us forget that we were a product of a moment's pleasure at the front lines, and that the pleasure seekers hadn't made any effort to turn around and check on that moment's result. We weren't supposed to be attached to anything except the revolution, which was why women soldiers took turns breastfeeding us, so that they wouldn't take the revolution's place as our mothers.

"My affections were scattered across many women. My mouth would scarcely get used to one breast before it was replaced by another, and I'd have to start the journey of getting to know someone all over again. I would barely get used to a fighter's smell while I was tied to her back, and then I'd be changed to another. Once I'd grown up a little, I started to wonder whether my real mother had slipped away from the revolution and come to look after me as a nurse or a babysitter. Which of these smells, exactly, belonged to her? Had she intentionally left me something of hers? Had she tried to leave me a sign, except she'd been stopped by fear of punishment? Had she even wondered about me? Was she one of those women whose faith in the revolution led them to bear children just to pump up the number of fighters? Had I come into the world without even that momentary pleasure?

"These kinds of questions pulled me out of the moment. But, in the end, I came back and looked around, realizing I was better off than lots of people who had family but lacked everything else.

"But now—what could I do when I was with Aisha?

"How could I hide all that history and walk up to her a new person? I felt her seductive features lining up with the edge of my ache, tipping the scales to remind me of my loss—no community, no family, no one to call my own. I couldn't shake the disgust I had seen on her face when she heard the phrase 'fruits of the struggle.' She would drop me if she knew I was one of them. Everything people said about us would stand as a barrier between Aisha and me, and she would never be able to get past the details that people whispered in secret: the daytime rifles shot into the air, which led to nighttime assignations between male and female soldiers. Eager to have children to complete their patriotic duty, they would devote themselves to personal pleasure with no sense of shame. And then there were our names: mountains, battles, valleys, and villages. There was always a dilemma when two of us had the same name, since there was no family or father's name to distinguish us. The others resorted to gimmicks, like Big Adal and Little Adal. Or else they'd add one of our most visible qualities, like Adal the Cripple or Adal the Swift or Adal the Squint Eyed, or other stupid things like that.

"'You got here first!'

"Aisha, with her cheerful tone, put an end to my thoughts. I studied her morning face, which looked delicious. Her eyes still held a little of yesterday's fatigue, which filled them with a charming drowsiness. My gaze flicked toward her tight-fitting white shirt, her breasts straining so hard they almost leaped out at me. I wanted my gaze to fall even farther, to settle on her legs, which were exposed beneath blue shorts.

"'I couldn't wait to see you.'

"I don't know why I blurted this out. If she noticed how much I needed her, I might lose her. I wanted to stop my soul from moving toward her with such fierce intensity so that I wouldn't destroy myself completely if the worst happened. I don't know. I was very careful—I didn't want to come back from my outing with her disappointed, when I still didn't know just where this would take me."

David stopped when the European lifted his pen. He brought it to his mouth, as if he were hesitating between speaking and staying silent. In the pause, the European didn't come to a decision. He just kept chewing on his pen, silent, as if he were about to say something.

The interpreter and the session secretary both turned toward the European. He seemed to feel the weight of their anticipation and finally said: "Let me guess. Ultimately, it all came to an end. Because if that wasn't true, we wouldn't be seeing you here. Am I right?"

David had barely started to answer when the European changed his mind, begging David to ignore the question and finish the story as he liked. David smiled, turning to the session secretary with a confident look until the secretary lowered his gaze in surrender, giving in to how this story had seized the European's imagination.

"It's definitely not done yet."

The European seemed comfortable with David's assertive answer. Then he urged him, again, to go on.

"'Come with me.'

"Aisha pulled me by the hand. I went with her, renewing my promises to her soft hand, feeling embarrassed by the scratchy touch of my own. She led me through the side streets to Travolo Street, until we reached the La Madia restaurant. Inside, there was a glamorous woman in her forties.

"'Mama, this is Dawoud.'

"As I reached out my hand, I saw where Aisha had gotten her sleepy eyes. This was how my girl would look when she was older. She would add a few years to her features but without losing any of their charm.

"I reached out my hand, and the mother reached out her pale white one. I took it and caught a glimpse of green veins before I released her hand, having felt it was strangely restless.

"'Mama, Dawoud is one of our fierce fighters.'

"The mother shot me a suspicious look, and I lowered my head, busying myself with the elegant tablecloth that covered the glass table. Aisha sat across from me, her hands under her chin, giving me a confusing smile. Her gaze seemed to slowly creep over my face. I was ashamed by my features, which I knew well. I wished I were handsome, or even just average, so that she'd have something to look at.

"I broke free of her gaze and turned to the pictures hanging on the walls. There were old photos of Asmara next to others of Rome. There was a black-and-white photo of a young man standing next to a race car, flanked by two girls in short pencil skirts.

"'That's my grandfather. People say I look a lot like him. What do you think?'

"As she turned toward the picture, I took the opportunity to steal a quick glance at her bare thigh, as her shorts pulled up even farther. When she turned back, I had my answer ready: 'There's no one like you.'

"I gave a numb smile, and she went back to devouring my features, and I went back to looking around the room. From a distance, her mother stole glances at me. An employee came in carrying two plates, and he set them down between us.

"'You're about to taste the best omelet in all Asmara. Nobody can beat my mom's restaurant in that.'

"Aisha grabbed a knife and fork and began to eat breakfast with a gentility I'd never seen before. She cut the eggs and mushrooms into tiny pieces, and then she slipped them into her half-open mouth before picking up a small piece of bread. Her chewing was calm and even. Awkwardly, I tried to copy her. I'd never had a barrier between my hands and food before. I couldn't remember having a plate that took me any time to wipe clean, but here I was, facing a difficult test. The pieces of food slipped away from the fork, and the more I tried to bring the food close to my mouth, the more it fell onto my lap. Aisha reached out, handing me the pink cloth that sat in front of me. I wiped off what had fallen on me before I put it back on the table, and then I noticed that she'd put *her* cloth on her lap. I took mine and did the same.

"'Eat your breakfast however you like.'

"I shifted, embarrassed at how she'd pointed out my ignorance, but I was determined to keep up with her. And when I couldn't, I pretended to be full, even though the damn hunger was chewing away at me.

"As we walked toward the door, I thanked her mother for the delicious meal. She gave me a frosty smile before calling to her daughter. I stayed near the door, watching them whisper to each other. When we left, Aisha's face was a little clouded over."

David went silent as he lowered his gaze to the ground and nervously rubbed his hands together.

"Damn mothers. Don't tell me she set your girl against you?"

The European's curiosity had now turned into clear indignation. David ignored the question and went on with his story.

"Two weeks passed, and I met Aisha every day. I made excuses to avoid going back to the restaurant. Sometimes, I'd say I had my breakfast early. Other times, I'd say I didn't feel hungry. Or else a third way was to invite her to a *new* restaurant. I was anxious about seeing her mother again, whose features were both gentle and tough. And whenever I had trouble finding a new excuse, I found Aisha wouldn't mention the restaurant. Sometimes, I thought her repeated invitations weren't actually serious but instead were a way to dispel any doubts I had about her mother's feelings toward me, since we both knew she had a say in our relationship.

"And so there we were, sitting on the steps of St. Joseph's Cathedral, watching the people passing by. Aisha pressed up against me like she never had before. I could feel her thigh rubbing back and forth against mine. She put a hand on my shoulder, and she drew me even closer.

"'Do you know that I love your strong shoulders?'

"A faint tremor passed through my body, and I dared to wrap my arm around her. She leaned her head against me and put a hand on my back, which totally destroyed my cool.

"'And your back too . . . I love it.'

"Was this real? Was there anything about my body that could attract a gorgeous girl like her? No one had ever stopped to comment on my looks, except sarcastically. For a moment, I thought maybe she was bullshitting me. But her sleepy eyes were totally sincere.

"What should I say? How long would it take to tell her all the things I loved about her? That I desired about her?

"Her soft hand, which was now stroking my back with its fine nails, was everything I'd ever wanted. I wanted her to stroke every inch of my body, to be remade by her.

"But as much as I wanted it, I was terrified she might find out my identity, that I was a 'fruit of the struggle.' That phrase haunted me, and it was going to grind down our intimacy until there was nothing left. Until that point, I'd succeeded in hiding my great secret. I avoided Aisha's curious questions about where I lived. I took her home first, and then I'd go a roundabout way back to the Revolution School, and I wouldn't set foot inside until I was absolutely sure the road was clear.

I avoided my fellow recruits on the street, and I would go back and apologize to them every night.

"But all of that wasn't enough anymore since the Revolution School would soon begin in earnest. Once it did, I'd be in training twenty-four seven, with no chance to meet Aisha for long stretches, even months at a time, and with no convincing reason for my absence.

"Tremors fluttered through my back and flowed through my whole body, and Aisha could feel it. Her gaze turned insistent, and she projected that insistence through her hand on my back.

"She was still speaking to me with love.

"She told me about her childhood: about her Italian maternal grandfather, who had brought race-car driving to Eritrea; about her father, who had left when she was still little, even before she had any happy memories of him; and about her good-hearted mother, who had taken charge of raising her and who'd closed the door on a long line of suitors.

"I couldn't give her my full attention. I was obsessed with making sure it all continued, that she kept getting close to me with her hand, her shorts, her hip rubbing against my thigh, her tight shirt. We were complicit in staying close without asking why.

"She noticed my distraction and said my name. I turned and she surprised me, for the first time, with a long kiss. Then she ran off.

"I spent the rest of the day in silence, not wanting anything to mix with the trace of her saliva, which she had left on the edges of my lips."

(15)

At the sound of police vans rolling up to the entrance of Neve Sha'anan, passersby anxiously turned around. Dawit felt a pang of fear, and he searched for reassurance in the faces of Yaqub and his friends.

Finally, with Yaqub's help, he'd been accepted into this neighborhood. Maybe his friendships weren't deep, but they were a lifesaver in this place, where a person could drown in the abuse of power. There was a group he hung out with, and they would ask after him if he wasn't there. He'd been suspicious of whether they really cared about him until he found them welcoming him even if his friend Yaqub wasn't around. They asked him to hide the fact that he was one of the Falasha, though. They asked him not to wear their clothes and not to go into his residence if anyone was looking. As for the rest of it, well—he should leave it to them.

"Did anyone hear the warnings?"

The group shook their heads. It was strange for the police to enter the neighborhood without a few of the residents calling out warnings. Dawit could read anxiety in some of their eyes.

As the armored police vehicles advanced, street vendors gathered up their wares, and some of the shops closed their doors. A young man with Arab features walked in their direction carrying a sign that read "Not an Arab." An officer checked his papers and let him walk on.

"Remember that dog's face and make sure to keep him out of here."

Dawit asked Yaqub what that was about, and Yaqub said that some Middle Eastern Jews came into the neighborhood to buy hash, taking advantage of their shared features.

"What, Jews aren't allowed into Neve Sha'anan?"

The group laughed at Dawit's question before one of them volunteered that Jews had fled the neighborhood after the influx of African refugees, when people started to call the place the African Republic of Tel Aviv.

"Remain calm, Sudanese. You, Sudanese, stay calm."

Yaqub explained this to Dawit before he could ask. "For them, every Black is Sudanese."

Dawit understood that something big must have happened in the neighborhood, since the police weren't interested in undocumented migrants, or the drug trade, or sex work. His friends speculated that they were looking for a murderer or some other high-profile offender. The police vehicles drove past them, the soldiers looking at them carefully before they went deeper into the neighborhood.

"Seems like they know exactly who they're looking for."

After Dawit spoke, he was startled to find the group staring at him in amazement.

"Oho! Looks like someone's become an expert in the business of Neve Sha'anan."

Dawit felt flattered that Yaqub had noticed. It wasn't long before the soldiers returned. They put a handcuffed young African man into one of their vehicles, then left the neighborhood completely.

"Anyway, warnings don't do any good. The police know that, and they let us be fooled into a sense of security. When they're after a big fish, everyone puts themselves first and keeps their mouth shut."

The group fell silent, acknowledging what the man had said. As for Yaqub, he stepped toward Dawit and whispered near his ear: "How about we forget about all of today's stress?"

The two of them left the group amid mocking murmurs, since the others knew exactly where they were headed. The pair walked through twisting alleys until they stopped in front of a house with a red light. Yaqub turned toward Dawit, his eyes mischievously promising a different sort of night.

When they knocked on the door, the response was slow.

"Don't worry. It's just security precautions."

Dawit snorted at his friend's remark and then went silent at the sound of a key turning in the lock. A brown-skinned girl appeared, chewing gum and pushing a hand through her badly dyed blonde hair. Yaqub kissed her and stepped inside, and she kept staring at Dawit until she got so close that he could feel her breath. He gave her a flustered smile and moved past her. She slapped him on the ass, giving a lewd laugh when he jumped as though bitten.

Inside, they were greeted gleefully by an older woman who jiggled her buttocks as she adjusted her huge bra. She asked Yaqub about the new guy.

"This here is my friend. I really like him, so he better leave this place fully satisfied. Or if he never leaves here at all, even better."

Yaqub tossed off this sentence, following it with a laugh as he stepped into one of the rooms, trailed by a girl of average looks. Dawit stood there, baffled, until the old woman pushed him into a nearby room and shut the door on him. The minutes passed slowly, charged with tension. He considered leaving, but his desire to see this thing through was stronger.

The old woman came back and stood beside the open door as a flurry of girls passed by, offering themselves to Dawit. He was disgusted by the first one, whose face was covered in splotches. He didn't like the big mouth on the second. As for the third, he didn't like the warts that covered what he could see of her body, and he didn't like the stupid look on the fourth. He ignored the fifth, who seemed to be proud but incapable.

He finally found one who looked kind of agreeable. He pointed her out to the old woman, who dismissed everyone except that girl.

When the door had closed behind them, he noticed her confusion. She was tall and white, with ordinary features and sagging breasts. He waited for her to take the initiative, but she stayed where she was. He walked up to her, and he felt her grow even more confused. He stroked her hair, trying to relieve her stress, and she finally said, "I'm new here. Please don't hurt me."

Dawit didn't understand, so she pointed at what was between his thighs. He laughed, proudly, but then he went back to reassuring her. "Don't be scared. I won't hurt you."

She undressed slowly, and he also started to take off his clothes as she glanced down at his belly. Then he remembered something, and he asked if there was anyone in the place who wore round glasses.

She was surprised by his question. After a short silence, she said that there wasn't. Once he was totally undressed, she let out a shameless laugh and said she was sure *he* wouldn't hurt her. Dawit was seized by so much rage that he wanted to slap her—that way, at least, she'd understand he could hurt her.

When he finished, he found Yaqub waiting for him. The girl walked by, whispering in his ear, *Come back any time, little one.* Laughing, she emphasized the last two words.

(16)

"Then the moment I'd been fearing arrived: the start of the Revolution School and my training.

"That night, I told Aisha I'd be gone for a week, visiting my relatives in Massawa. It seemed to take her by surprise, and her expression turned sad. This was the first time that something came between us. Then suddenly her eyes flashed with an idea that she shared with glee. She asked to come with me, and started telling me how she was going to convince her mother. She was sure she could do it. She told me how excited she was to visit Massawa with me, how she wanted to swim in its clear blue seas. I flatly refused, and a cloud of sadness settled back over her features. I had no idea what I would do after this lie had passed and I was faced with the same situation again and had to disappear again. But all I could think about now was that it would buy me a little more time to find a way out.

"She walked off and left me feeling disoriented. I thought maybe I should run after her, tell her I'd changed my mind—that without her, Asmara was bleak, that it made me feel a heavy pressure in my chest. But I couldn't. I let her go and turned to face what was waiting for me.

"From dawn the next day, I threw myself into my new assignments at the Revolution School: morning lessons, political rehabilitation, difficult exercises. Even though all these things kept me busy until the night, Aisha didn't leave my mind for a single moment. Still, I would have liked the day to stretch out so that time didn't pass, and I would never have to crash into the wall of lies I'd told her.

"Once the week had passed, I asked for leave. I was entitled to just one day a month until I'd finished my third month, when I would finally get a regular weekend. This would create a new dilemma, but my heartache for Aisha blinded me to all my worries about what would come next.

"I knocked on her door, hoping I wouldn't come face to face with her mother. I waited, but there was no answer. I got ready to knock again, and then the door opened. It was Aisha, wearing long cotton trousers, which were partially covered up by a shirt of the same pinkish color. Her glasses were stuck into her tousled hair, her face was pale, and her eyes were dull and swollen.

"When she realized it was me, she pulled her glasses down over her eyes, which widened in shock before she cried out my name, sobbing and hugging me.

"'You won't leave me, will you?'

"I hugged her fiercely, my face pressed into her neck. Nothing I did calmed her. Words didn't help, so I settled for this scorching proximity.

"Once she'd calmed down a little, she invited me in. I hesitated a moment, and she gave me the smile I knew so well.

"'Don't worry. My mother's not here.'

"The house was elegant without being overstated. There was a spacious living room, mostly done in white. In it, two brown sofas stood opposite each other, alongside a third smaller sofa. I sat on the smaller one, and Aisha disappeared for a few minutes. In front of me, there was what seemed to be a family portrait: a handsome, young, brown-skinned man hugging a young girl, and beside the man, his charming wife. I liked the father. He radiated confidence, and his smile was clear. He wrapped both arms around Aisha as though he would never let her go.

"Aisha came in carrying a woven coffee mat and water jug, followed by a member of the kitchen staff who carried the portable stove and clay pot. Aisha sat down in front of me and asked the other woman to leave her to finish up. I watched Aisha fondly as she roasted the coffee while shooting me loving looks. Her face had regained its color. She had brushed her hair and put on a long skirt, and she looked very attractive. I was annoyed by the distance between us. I wished that she would come closer, that she would bridge this gap. Aisha could read my wishes, and she fulfilled them.

"'Come.'

"I sat down next to her, and she pulled my hand against her. Now, my fear returned. Just being this close to her made me feel the enormity of all that time I'd spent without her, all those days I had lived without her gorgeous, drowsy eyes.

"I finished my third cup, and we went out. She held my hand as she walked me toward the steps of St. Joseph's Cathedral, the place where we first kissed. She knew when I was speaking the truth and when I was showering her with lies. She greeted my tales about my relatives in Massawa with a smile, without worrying too much about the holes in my story. It seemed to me like a beautiful complicity—I would lie, and she would enjoy letting the lies pass by unchecked. Then it was her turn to tell me about her week. She seemed to want it to look full, but she failed. Words crowded her mouth without coming out, until she chose to just be herself: 'The days were empty.'

"I didn't know if I should be flattered, or if I should mourn the sadness that she'd felt without me. But we were on the same path—we were fulfilled when we were together, and we lost hold of life's meaning when we were apart.

"The street was crowded with people. An attractive woman passed right in front of me, and I found myself following her with my gaze before I noticed Aisha's angry glare. I wrapped my arms around Aisha and put my face into her hair. I *loved* the smell and taste of her hair, and so I dove into it, not pulling away until her face had shed its anger.

"All the way home, I was busy thinking about how to explain I would be gone the next day. It seemed like it was going to be nearly impossible, since I could clearly read the fear in her eyes. For the first time, I wasn't alone with my fear. Yes—for the first time, a woman shared my fear of loss.

"This was the fear that had haunted me the whole time I had been growing up on the front lines. If I liked a girl, I would ask myself a thousand times whether she'd accept me or whether she would meet my advances with contempt. And so I never put myself out there, never saying that I liked anyone, even if that meant I missed one opportunity after another. And if a girl took the initiative, then the questions still wouldn't leave my mind: Is she going to leave me? And if so, when?

"I was constantly afraid that the girl would leave me first, which was why I usually ran away from my fear of abandonment, finding my escape in abandonment itself. I would leave the relationship as soon as I felt the slightest chill when looking at her from a distance.

"To leave first—well, it gave me some comfort. I could feel like I'd been in the wrong place and like *I'd* been the one who made the decision to leave. As for the opposite, it definitely meant I was less than desirable.

"But Aisha was different. She was two steps ahead of me in her fear of abandonment, which was why I found myself completely overwhelmed by my feelings for her. Then we were in front of her door. I was all set to invent a new lie, but she jumped in eagerly: 'Tomorrow, I'll bring you a little surprise.'

"I swallowed my lie and nodded in agreement. I kissed her forehead, but she pulled me down to her hungry lips, and she didn't let me go until she'd bitten down hard, puncturing my lip. 'That's so you can remember how painful it is when you're not around.'

"Back in my bed, I happily ran my tongue over the wound. I pressed down on it, and the pain made me euphoric. By the time I closed my eyes, I had made up my mind."

(17)

At the end of his third month in Tel Aviv, Dawit received a letter telling him to prepare to move to his permanent residence in Jerusalem.

He was just starting to get used to Tel Aviv—to his wild nights with Yaqub and to Neve Sha'anan, the piece of Africa in the heart of Israel. The announcement that he was leaving left him a little downhearted. He wanted to stay in Tel Aviv, in his new circle of safety, in the place where he was able to plunge into the depths instead of paddling around at the surface like he had all his life. Here, he had finally stopped paying attention to the others who'd come on the same flight from Gondar. They could still hurt him, sure. But at the same time, he wasn't afraid of them anymore. He had beaten them—he was the first to reach the soil of Tel Aviv, to mix with it.

This feeling put him so much at ease that he even dared tell Yaqub his forbidden story. He told Yaqub how he'd left Eritrea with one name and entered Ethiopia with another before heading out with a third name on the journey to Israel from the Gondar refugee camp. He hesitated, unsure whether to tell his friend that before all this he'd had a *fourth* name, which had nothing to do with all the others. Yaqub could hardly believe his ears. At some points in the story, his eyes bulged out, and at others he would cry out and clutch his head, while some of the details made him laugh.

Dawit considered telling his friend the story of Aisha, but then he stopped. *That* story, he realized, was hidden in the deepest part of him. He could peel away layer after layer, but he would only reach those depths by destroying himself. Still, he wasn't sure whether he was hiding the story from others or whether he was hiding it from himself.

"Man, show me how to join you. Should I say we're brothers? Should I go to Gondar and ask Saba for help? What do you think?"

Dawit now saw the mess he'd gotten himself into, as he could see his story ricocheting back and creating unforeseen complications. He tried to be vague about it, but his friend intensified his siege and Dawit found no escape except to give his friend the hope he wanted.

"Maybe if you move to Gondar, sure, you'll find the right opportunity. Just tell Saba that you're with me."

Yaqub's face filled with joy at what seemed to be the salvation he'd been waiting for. Dawit wasn't sure how he felt—whether he was happy to be out of his predicament or whether he despaired at having given his friend false hope. But what sealed it, in the end, was that he knew Yaqub's personality. His friend wouldn't really do anything more than seek out short-term pleasures. Let him have them, then. The problem would end right here.

Dawit knew his friend avoided the things he wanted as soon as difficulties cropped up. There was the time he had avoided taking a job, since it would have meant staying away from his woman in Neve Sha'anan for long stretches of time. Also, Yaqub always completely immersed himself *in* the moment, as if running away from some mysterious thing.

He still didn't know how to tell Yaqub that he was leaving for Jerusalem, and he didn't know how sad it might make him.

The next time they met, Yaqub was just coming back from his girlfriend's, euphoric and boasting of a virility that he could not stop showing off. "When I came, she was laughing, and when I left, she was moaning. She couldn't even stand up to go to the door and say goodbye. I gave her a last quick glance, an air kiss, and left."

As usual, the only way Dawit could respond was to show an exaggerated envy and amazement at his friend's extraordinary abilities, which ordinary folk surely could not attain. But this time, he fulfilled his role perfunctorily and quickly moved.

"The order for my transfer to Jerusalem came through. I'll be there by the end of the week."

No sooner had he finished speaking than he noticed, in his friend's eyes, a shock that quickly faded into sorrow. The talk about his girlfriend and his exceptional virility disappeared, replaced by silence. There was a long moment when Yaqub just hung his head.

For the next few days, they walked for hours down the streets of Neve Sha'anan with no particular destination. Dawit repeatedly tried to break through Yaqub's trancelike state, but to no avail. He wanted to cheer up his friend, so he said that he would keep on visiting him— reminding him that it wasn't far from Jerusalem to Tel Aviv—and telling him how attached he was to Neve Sha'anan and how no other place could take him away from it. But all of these calming niceties evaporated in front of Yaqub's rigid face, before Yaqub finally said: "Yeah. You'll go to Jerusalem and find a permanent job. While I'll stay here to entertain people like you until their lives begin."

Dawit tried not to show his shock. He changed his expression to a confused smile, and he gathered up a few words he didn't really mean. "Who knows. Maybe I won't like it there, and then I'll be back here in no time."

At that moment, just as he was tossing out these words of consolation, Dawit realized that Tel Aviv had been yet another superficial surface that he'd stood on rather than diving in and becoming a part of it. Was he being too hard on the place? But what are places if not their people?

On the bus with twenty-two others, he sat by the window, as if repeating the first stage of his journey from Gondar to Israel. It was morning, and he took one last look at the nearly empty streets of Neve Sha'anan. This was where he'd met Yaqub for the first time. On that bench, his relationship with the neighborhood and its people had grown stronger. In that alley, he had faced his fear and smoked hash. This wasn't nostalgia. It was more like he was plucking out his feelings, returning each piece to the place where it had come from. He wanted to leave the neighborhood just the way he'd been when he first arrived: anxious and neutral, and not having told his terrible secret to anyone.

The bus left Tel Aviv and headed east. Highway 1 looked like a large cleft between tall mountains that were topped by dense greenery. The guide pointed to a nearby depression: "This is Ayalon Valley. It will bring us to the Gate of the Valley, or Sha'ar HaGai. In a little while, we'll pass through the Town of Forests, Kiryat Ye'arim, which is mentioned in the Torah eighteen times."

As she returned to her seat, the young guide folded up the piece of paper she'd been reading from. There, she entered into a whispered conversation with the driver.

Dawit went back to looking out at the road around him, the pressure in his ears increasing as the bus got closer to Jerusalem. From where she sat, the guide pointed out the housing complex on the right, reminding them that the place was called Kiryat Ye'arim. Several houses were perched on a green plateau, all of them with sloping orange-brick roofs, surrounded by an impregnable wall topped by barbed wire.

One of the passengers asked about the tunnels running through the mountains beside the road, and the guide looked confused before the driver spoke to her. Then she got up to face the passengers with a confident smile.

"These are the routes for the Tel Aviv–Jerusalem train, which will shorten the time it takes to get between the two cities to just half an hour."

She had barely sat down when the driver veered onto a side road, telling her that they were about to arrive. His voice was audible throughout the bus because he was close to the microphone the young woman was holding. She was confused again and asked him, "In Jerusalem?"

The driver couldn't hold back his laugh as he corrected her. "In Canada Park, miss. We'll get there as soon as we pass the town of Modi'in and the Latrun Interchange. Just behind that, there's the park."

The guide went back to her papers, her gaze wandering over them until she settled on one page in particular, trying to summon her confidence.

"Shortly, we will take a tour of the National Park of Israel, proudly established in 1975 with funds from our people living in Canada."

When the passengers returned from their tour of the park, they found Dawit sitting in his spot near the window, as if he'd never left. He greeted them with a lukewarm smile before nodding in response to the guide's question about whether he'd enjoyed the park.

Time had passed slowly for Dawit in Canada Park. He chose to sit on a wooden bench not far from the bus, while the other passengers spread out joyfully throughout the park. The whole time he sat, he remained still among the greenery that surrounded him, his mind trying to anticipate what would happen next. He'd been worn out by the endless anticipation. From Asmara to Endabaguna to Tel Aviv, and now to Jerusalem. All of these places had tossed him to the surface, like foam, without allowing him into their depths.

As he was consumed by these exhausting thoughts, he passed a rough hand over the wooden bench with a monotonous movement, back and forth, as though his hand were echoing the thoughts racing back and forth in his mind. Then his fingers passed over the deep lines etched into the heart of the brown wood. He looked down and saw what looked like Arabic inscriptions. He adjusted his position and stared at them, finding something he didn't fully understand: "This isn't Canada Park. It's Imwas, Beit Nuba, and Yalu villages."

Back on the bus, the driver slowed down a little at the Sha'ar HaGai interchange, before continuing on through Neve Ilan and the Shoresh

Interchange, and then Mount Herzl. As soon as the bus went by the mountain, the guide stood back up. Until now, she had been satisfied with reeling off the names of landmarks into the microphone without paying any attention to the passengers.

"This is the Israeli National Cemetery, named for our founder. I think you'll have an opportunity to visit it soon. And now we can say that you've finally reached Jerusalem."

Here, Dawit came to attention, opening the window to breathe in the city's air. The entrances to cities usually don't lie—either they embrace you from the start or they shun you forever. He should have observed things like that all along, from the very first moment he had left Asmara. But now, even though he knew what to look for, the entrance to Jerusalem offered no clear answers. At noon, its streets seemed confusingly full of life, and fleets of cars and green buses moved in both directions without pause, separated by a gray train that ran through the center of the street. Tall buildings with gleaming marble facades faced each other on either side of the road, as though they might pounce on traffic at any moment.

As they waited for the green light, Dawit noticed a woman in a convertible swaying to a melody that sounded Arab, strands of her hair flying around so that it covered her face. As soon as the song ended, a Hebrew one started without dampening the girl's mood. When the light changed, Dawit spotted the Israeli flag on the back of the girl's seat, side by side with the Yemeni one.

"Now we're passing Jaffa Street, which means that we're leaving the western part of the city and entering the east. That's where you'll find the Pisgat Ze'ev settlement, which is where you'll be living."

The guide's voice took on a serious tone, as if this wasn't information but a warning. Dawit noticed that the city's features changed as soon as the bus crossed into the eastern side. The gray train disappeared, and the dark-green buses turned white with green stripes along their sides. Here, the buildings appeared as random protrusions, groaning under black water tanks that sat on their roofs. Meanwhile, the sidewalks were full of students heading home from school on foot. This picture added to Dawit's confusion. How could a city so completely change its face once you crossed from one half to the other? Which face fit it best? Which part looked more like its people?

A soldier stepped onto the bus, checking the passengers' documents, and Dawit emerged from his thoughts. It was only then that he noticed the bus was at the gate to the Pisgat Ze'ev settlement. After it passed through the gate, it went down a winding road that led it to the top of a hill where Pisgat Ze'ev stood. From there, the settlement overlooked the Beit Hanina neighborhood and Hizma village on one side, and the Shu'fat refugee camp on the other.

The passengers were taken in by the fancy-looking buildings scattered along both sides of wide and clean asphalt roads. The buildings were separated by neatly manicured rosebushes. They whispered to each other that they had finally reached their promised paradise. The driver went slowly, as if giving them the chance to enjoy the beauty of the place, but then he was forced to speed up in confusion as he tried to avoid the eggs that were now being hurled at the bus windows, followed by the insults of angry women. Dawit managed to close his window before he met the fate of the man sitting in front of him—an egg hit him, and his clothes were soaked.

Things calmed down a little when the bus passed into another square that looked less ritzy and a bit dirty. The people also changed, with light-skinned blondes shifting to a more wheat-colored tone. Dawit's gaze met that of a man whose braids dangled down over his dark cheeks. Dawit smiled, feeling a strange familiarity, but the man remained grim as he raised his middle finger and said something Dawit couldn't hear.

The bus turned into a new square, crowded with low-rise buildings, the roads full of trash. Here, the passengers got up from their seats to see their kin heading up and down the streets in all directions. It didn't take

much for Dawit to realize they had entered the Beta Israel neighborhood. The bus's path caught the attention of passersby. Some stopped,
curious, while others just cast a casual look and then continued on their
way. When they reached Square 22, the guide made a phone call to ask
the number of the building assigned to the passengers. Then she turned
to the driver and asked him to go to Building 7, just as the question
leaped up once more in Dawit's mind: Had he arrived at long last? Or
was his journey in search of a merciful salvation still a distant wish?

(18)

"I made sure I was up before the bell sounded. I got dressed and left the Revolution School with the last threads of night.

"At that time of day, Asmara's in its truest form: naked, empty, lonely, and with one single face. At that time of day, cities can't lie. They don't have the luxury of choosing between the many faces they wear during the rest of the day.

"The milkman passed me on a bicycle, announcing his wares by ringing his bell. This, too, happened only at this one time of day. What did he do with the rest of his day? Was he involved in other things in the city, or did he withdraw and wait for his moment? I felt jealous of him—at least he had one particular time of day when he was the master, when he was wanted.

"I passed the Bar Royal Café, where the staff were preparing for their day, and turned right. The street with the Central Hotel wasn't up yet, except for the laundromat, which didn't close its doors even on holidays. It was the envy of Asmara because its water was never cut off. I was walking with no destination. I was just killing time, revisiting the places I knew so I could discover their true faces. I avoided walking down Komochtato Street since I couldn't risk running into a security patrol. There was no way I'd be able to explain why I'd left the Revolution School at that hour.

"Once the sun had risen and people's footsteps thronged onto the streets, I went back to the steps of St. Joseph's Cathedral, where I watched passersby head to their destinations. They gave the city its many faces.

"'Hold out your hand.'

"I hadn't noticed Aisha until she'd settled down next to me, her smile filling the place.

"I gave her my right hand, and she reached into her small bag and pulled out a stylish woolen bracelet woven with black and white threads. She put it on my wrist.

"'Let's go.'

"That stylish bracelet, which she spent the whole night weaving, was just the start of my day with her, and she saved the big surprise she had promised for our journey to parts unknown. As we walked, she held my right hand, and I followed her from street to street. She took complete control, and my attention shifted between the softness of her hand and the bracelet that rubbed against my wrist with every step. Finally, we stopped in front of a sports complex on the east side of the city.

"'I'll beat you at bowling first, and then I'll tell you the promise I've made you.'

"I was too embarrassed to tell her I couldn't really bowl. But anyhow, she didn't give me a choice. The hall seemed empty except for the two of us and the staff. When we chose a lane to play on, a boy no older than seven came forward and crammed himself into the empty space between the white pins and the wall. I understood what he was doing only after Aisha threw her first ball and knocked over half of the pins. The boy clutched the iron ball and gave it back to us before arranging the pins for my throw.

"I took the ball, and its weight surprised me. Aisha asked me to throw it as hard as I could, and I thought about the boy, whose job it was to catch all that weight. I took a few stuttering steps and let go of the ball. It dithered this way and that until it shot off completely, settling into the gutter before it could reach the pins. Aisha gave a mocking laugh, and I felt relieved that I had spared the child the hassle of catching the iron ball. But the problem wasn't over, and I could now see Aisha's enthusiasm to hurl the ball. I thought about trying to direct her attention to the boy, but I was afraid it would spoil her fun. This time, all the pins fell, and my feelings were mixed between my girl's euphoria as she bounced up and down and the child who brought back the ball while inspecting a wounded finger.

"I ended my turn without hitting a single pin. Aisha got bored when she realized how useless I was at the game.

"'Let me show you the surprise.'

"We left the bowling alley through a side door and took a path that led us to a pool. I turned to Aisha in surprise, and she met my gaze with a mysterious smile.

"'Now you're going to pay me back for not letting me swim with you at the Massawa beach. Wait for me.'

"She disappeared down a nearby corridor before coming back and taking off her short blue dress, under which she was wearing a black swimsuit. Hesitantly, I took off my clothes as I stared at the roundness of her breasts, the curve of her waist.

"She didn't wait for me. She jumped into the water and set off a tsunami that led to a new charm: her short hair clinging to her neck as she reached out a hand and called to me.

"'Come on, jump in.'

"She'd barely finished saying it when all three of us were in the water: Aisha, her hair, and me. I had never felt so lucky as I did in that moment. Aisha cut a path through the water as I stood there, following her with my eyes. She turned and called to me, and I took the same path, savoring the water that flowed around me and which had just flowed around her. When I got close, she moved away, so I swam back in the other direction. When she noticed, she kept lapping me until she caught up with me at the end of the pool, where my chest and hand were resting against the edge as I panted. Aisha looped her arms around me from behind, pressing her chest against my back, and a delicious shudder moved through my body. I felt her breasts as she pressed harder against me. She kissed my neck, and I couldn't hold back anymore. I turned around, pulling myself free, and met her cloudy eyes. It felt like a siege.

"I moved closer and saw her slightly parted lips trembling. When she closed her eyes completely, it was my signal to slide into the unequal fight. I pulled her submissive lower lip between mine—but she confused me; her tongue darted into my mouth in a hit-and-run, and her hand gripped my chest so that her nails plunged into it. Her hair grazed my forehead, hanging down to block my vision, and her thigh rubbed against mine, igniting the primordial flame that never goes out. I was one defenseless individual facing the whole tribe of lust. In the end, I found no escape from defeat.

"When we got back to St. Joseph's Cathedral, the day was about to fade away and so was our meeting.

"Time slipped by as we moved from one street to another. Aisha preferred the quieter streets so she could be alone with me. I preferred the most crowded ones so I could delight in how she stood out from the crowd, how I could see no one but her. Time passed between Aisha and Aisha. Sometimes I would study her face, and other times I would remember the details from our morning in the water. When she was about to leave, she asked me about tomorrow, and I came back down to earth.

"I couldn't find an answer. I still didn't know what punishment was waiting for me at the Revolution School. But what I did know, with the fullness of my heart, was that I wouldn't regret meeting Aisha, whatever the consequences.

"'I'll be here.'

"I answered her with confidence, and her lips quickly landed on my mouth, then flew away.

"And oh, it was so *good* to be filled with kisses. You can take them home, hide them from the eyes of strangers, and plant them next to your window, so that they produce beautiful dreams throughout your whole life.

"But these fantasies melted as soon as I reached the outer gate of the Revolution School. The guard glared at me resentfully, ordering me to go straight to the duty officer. I realized the news of my absence had spread so far it had very nearly reached the world outside.

"The whole meeting took no more than a minute, and I was sent to solitary confinement.

"The officer asked why I'd been absent, and as soon as I started searching for an answer, he shouted at the soldier to take me away. I had known my fate in advance, and this softened the blow. But my lukewarm reaction increased the punishment from one week to ten days. Now, I felt trapped. I wanted to try again, plead with him, but he rebuked me, pride leaping into his eyes at last. Nothing irritated the executioner so much as his failure to humiliate a victim.

"In that dark room, I couldn't think about anything except Aisha, about what she was going to think and about all the obsessive worries that would live in her head for these ten days. I didn't notice until it was too late that the ceiling was so low I couldn't stand all the way up, and I couldn't lie on the floor except curled up. The only window was the one in the door, and it was so narrow it made me feel like I was suffocating."

"So the only times you left your lockup were to go to the toilet? Once a day? Or twice?"

David laughed at the European's questions. "The 'toilet' was just a small open hole at the end of the room."

The European put a hand to his nose with disgust, telling him to say no more about this matter, while the session secretary lowered his head to hide his laugh. David wanted to tell the European that Endabaguna was heaven compared to solitary confinement, but he held his tongue at the last moment.

"I didn't sleep my first night. I just waited for morning as if, somehow, I might still make my date with Aisha. I got lost in my imagination: taking a quick shower, putting on my best clothes, dabbing on some of the cologne that my girl had already complimented, and hurrying out to meet her. This time, I would be the one to give her a surprise. I would pay her back for yesterday's gift in the most beautiful way.

"I got there late, to the corner across from the Keren Hotel, where we had agreed to meet. I was relieved when I didn't find Aisha there already. I leaned against the wall, next to the photo studio, and I spent a little time watching passersby. A few minutes later, Aisha appeared with a smile as clear as the morning. She kissed me and asked when I'd gotten there. I would have said *just now*, except I wanted to seem more eager.

"'I didn't notice the time—maybe an hour or more. But it's nothing.'

"Aisha clapped a hand over her mouth. I tried to guess what she was laughing about, but she changed the topic, her features taking on a faint undertone of regret. When I insisted, I realized she had come to our meeting spot an hour ago, waiting so she could surprise me. When I was late, her desire had deflated. I was full of shame, my lies stripped bare. But Aisha pulled me out of my tangle, taking me by the hand and drawing me toward the photo studio.

"'Don't move. One, two, three.'

"As soon as the photographer took the first shot, Aisha decided to try a new pose. She told the man to focus his camera and leave the rest to her. She sat on the chair and asked me to stand right behind her, my hands resting on her shoulders. That photo was normal enough, both for me and for the photographer, but the second shot confused me a little and an obnoxious smile spread across the man's face.

"'Now you sit on the chair.'

"As soon as I followed her command, Aisha settled onto my lap, pulling my arms around her neck. In the third shot, she didn't change our positions but instead asked me to place my lips against her neck in a long kiss. For the fourth, we exchanged a long kiss; for the fifth, the kiss was unchanged while she hid our faces with her hair.

"While the photographer was getting our pictures ready, I changed my mind, deciding I wouldn't tell Aisha about the surprise I had for her, since it had now lost all meaning in the face of what she'd just done.

"Then the noises around me grew louder, and a thread of morning light began to creep into my cell. This shook me out of my fantasies. I realized that Aisha was waiting right at that moment, alone, at the corner across from the Keren Hotel.

"And she would be waiting for a long time."

(19)

The blue Peugeot turned onto a narrow lane. At the top of the street, there was a green sign that said "Nablus Road."

The driver slowed down, careful to avoid the cars parked on both sides of the road. There was barely space for a single car to drive through. Then the road narrowed even more, forcing the driver to turn left, where he headed through a gate that opened onto a huge, dusty two-story parking garage, where cars traveled up a spiraling path. He searched for a parking spot on the upper level. When he couldn't find one, he went to a larger lot, where he parked the car.

"This is as far as we can get by car."

As soon as she heard that, the guide got out. Two men followed, one fiddling ostentatiously with his watch while the other adjusted the collar of his blue-striped shirt. Dawit was last to get out.

This was the group Dawit had joined this morning, according to the teams that were created for new arrivals. They were supposed to visit the Old City in small groups as a safety precaution. The other two men were in his group only because they shared a bedroom with him in the three-bedroom unit that was Apartment 18, on the fifth floor of Building 7, in Group 22 of the Pisgat Ze'ev settlement.

On the day he'd arrived, Dawit had found his name posted at the entrance to the building with a note about which apartment he'd be staying in. The elevator wasn't working, so he had to carry his luggage up five full flights of stairs. He stood panting in front of the half-open door. Piled in front of him were men's and women's shoes of various sizes, and the walls were marred by drawings and Amharic graffiti. He edged forward slowly, trying to feel his way in, and came face to face with a girl holding a basket full of sodden and dripping underwear. Her hair was tied in a handkerchief, the lower half of her skirt folded up above her knees. She looked him up and down before moving past him to go up the stairs. Across the narrow hallway, he found a room. He wanted to open the door, but he pulled back and went into the next room, where he found three empty beds, traces of their occupants still visible. The final room was next to the kitchen, and it looked exactly like the one he'd just seen. He grew confused as he looked around for his spot, until finally a young man came out of the closed room. Before Dawit could even ask, he found himself directed to the middle room.

He set his bag to the side and looked at the three beds. Two appeared as if they'd been slept in, while scattered bags and clothes were piled on the third. He set the rest of his things on the floor, waiting for someone to come in and tell him which bed was his. He waited like that for a long time before he went out, no destination in mind.

At the door to the apartment, he met the girl again, heading down the stairs. This time, she didn't pay him any attention. It occurred to him that he, too, should go to the roof so he could see the area from the highest possible point. He climbed two floors to find himself facing a forest of clotheslines, electrical wires that ended in satellite dishes, rusty equipment, and broken tables. The roof seemed like a storehouse of things without end. Carefully, he picked his way to the edge of the roof, where he began to see with fresh eyes.

The settlement stretched out in a spiral that began on a high hill. The buildings in front were modern, but the rest were older. He saw silver trains heading down the street in both directions, dividing it in half. He looked farther and saw a high concrete barrier that separated the settlement from the foothills, and between that wall and the foothills, another concrete wall that rose up several meters. Below and behind the wall, there was another world swimming in poverty. From where he stood, he caught a glimpse of the congestion; narrow, dusty streets; and tightly packed buildings that seemed to have no clear pattern.

He went down seven flights to the street. Then he headed down the sidewalk toward a mall he'd caught sight of from the roof. He walked for a long time, taking in his surroundings. Two Black policemen in dark-blue uniforms passed him, each clutching a machine gun to the center of his chest. One looked at him narrowly. Dawit chose to go on walking, his head lowered.

"Atzor. Teudat Zehut."

He stopped when he was sure the policeman was speaking to him. He took out his card, and then he took it back after the two men checked it and walked away without a word. He went on, confused, until he got to a sign that read "Pisgat Ze'ev Center." He took a look at the center's marble facade, which was covered in bright-colored murals. He decided against going in, however, as soon as he noticed the people inside were watching him suspiciously. He seemed to be the only Black in the place. He turned around, wanting only to get home without coming to any harm.

When he got back to his room, he found someone in there, naked except for his boxers, flicking through the TV channels. The man introduced himself, then gestured toward the bed crowded with bags before he went back to staring at the screen.

◆ ◆ ◆

Now, the small group—him, the guide, and his two roommates—stepped out of the garage to find themselves standing in front of a colossal marble building. In front of it, there was a small green gate topped with a blue plaque that read "82 Nablus Road." At the very top of the building, there was an upside-down red triangle, and above it the phrase "Young Men's Christian Association—Jerusalem YMCA." They walked down the other side of the street, on a narrow sidewalk fenced in by iron bars. On a nearby wall, Dawit noticed plaques that marked other Christian institutions. They were overhung by trees, which shaded the group's path as they walked toward the Old City. His attention was caught by one sign that read "The Garden Tomb of Christ." It occurred to him to ask about it, but he was reluctant, since the rest of the group was more interested in the local food trucks parked at the side of the road. He passed another marble plaque embedded in the wall, its features marred by heavy gunfire. He struggled to read it, finally realizing it was a sign for Nablus Road in Arabic, Hebrew, and English. Next to it, someone had painted "Al-Quds Arabia." Jerusalem is Arab.

The road reached Sultan Suleiman Street. The group then turned to follow the signs to Damascus Gate, until the guide pointed out the entrance to the Old City.

Dawit felt unsettled. While the Old City made his soul feel light, the security presence certainly didn't. Although he had been trailing behind, now he put himself in the middle of the group, wanting to hide from the eyes of the security officers, who seemed to be watching him alone. He didn't feel comfortable until he had sunk into the crowd of people crossing in both directions through Damascus Gate. Here, finally, he was able to surrender himself to the place. He felt he was sinking into time, as if he were moving against the current of history. A sameness colored all the details: the cracked floor, the faces that appeared from a distant age, the ancient smells, the schoolchildren who looked like adults, and the vendors' voices that rose up without causing a clamor.

The guide greeted a colleague who was leading a group on their way out, and Dawit spotted the old woman who had one lonely pair of teeth in her upper jaw. He avoided her, pretending to be interested in a store selling chessboards. The old woman left with her group, but Dawit kept looking at the shop, impressed by how the owner had mastered the art of shaping pawns, sometimes making them look like candlesticks, other times like crosses, while a small group of pawns took the form of crescents. He smiled. This was like his life, switching from one religion to another in order to survive. He saw Dawit and David, and there was Dawoud off by himself in the distance. His small group moved on, walking past Bab Khan al-Zayt and the narrow passageway 'Aqabat al-Tout, as well as the Spice Market, before reaching the Butcher's Market.

The road ended at the entrance to Bayt al-Maqdis, the al-Aqsa Mosque Compound. Soldiers were ringed around it with their fearsome weapons, and radios encircled their arms to rest on their shoulders.

"Unfortunately," the guide announced, "we can't go any farther."

Dawit's expression fell, and she gave him a consoling look. Girls in short skirts passed in front of them. The soldier asked if they were Muslim, and they nodded. He let them pass, and then the girls stopped at a group of Palestinian women who stood just past the soldiers. There, the girls took long robes, which they pulled on hurriedly, hiding everything except their faces, before they walked toward the mosque. Dawit felt a swell of curiosity, eager to cross the security barrier and see the mosque up close.

"Come on, I'll show you the Church of the Holy Sepulcher."

Dawit had to catch up to the group, which was already following the guide. He noticed a Palestinian clothing shop with T-shirts out front: one shirt glorified the Israeli army, another proudly stated Israel's independence, and a third featured large menorahs. Only at the far end of the store did he see a few white T-shirts that had "Palestine" and a V-for-victory sign printed on them.

He followed the group down Khan al-Zayt Street, past 'Aqabat al-Tekiya' passageway, to the stairs that led up to the Coptic monastery to the west. Dawit divided his attention between the guide—who was enthusiastically telling them about everything they passed—and the waves of tourists from around the world. The group veered slightly south, passing the Church of the Knights Templar and the Deir al-Sultan, about which the guide said in passing: "This monastery is being fought over by the Copts and the Ethiopian community." Dawit felt an urge to stop at this Ethiopian church, but he followed the group.

In the middle of the square that opened onto the Church of the Holy Sepulcher, the guide told them they could either choose to go with her or walk around on their own, but then they had to come back without delay. Spirituality, she added, sometimes required solitude. Dawit immediately opted to wander on his own, while the two others stayed with her, looking at him in surprise. He felt a strong desire to get rid of any intermediary, anything that stood between him and this place. His eyes couldn't take in everything around him. He wanted to immerse every one of his senses in these details: the intense scent of incense mixed with the smell of wax candles lit in fulfillment of vows, the jagged walls made up of huge stone boulders of different ages, and a short wooden ladder at the center of the front of the church, attempting to connect a rocky ledge and a huge glass window.

This last scene filled him with nostalgia. The ladder couldn't reach the window, nor could the window reach down to the ladder. His amazement increased when he heard a nearby guide tell their group that the ladder had been in the same place for three hundred years.

◆ ◆ ◆

When Dawit went to take the last bag off his bed, he didn't notice it was open, and suddenly its contents were spilling out onto the floor. The half-naked man turned to him sharply before getting up and yanking his things off the floor. Dawit gave a confused apology as he carried his own bag over from the door. He wanted to cram it under his bed, but he found the space full of other bags.

He thought of asking the half-naked man about it, but he hesitated when he found the man's features tense. A little while later, another man entered, a towel wrapped around his waist. He seemed a little surprised at Dawit's presence, but he quickly pretended not to be fazed and started talking to the man in front of the TV. Both men ignored Dawit. For his part, he didn't try to get their attention. He understood the way things were, since he'd been through situations like this dozens of times. He liked his self-sufficiency, limited as it was. He turned it into a game, betting himself that they were *totally* thinking about him, and that they wouldn't be able to tolerate his indifference without itching with curiosity. Finally, as soon as he opened his bag and began to flip through its contents, it happened.

"Do you need help, uh . . . you didn't tell us your name, brother."

As he gave his name, Dawit thanked the half-naked man, who was unable to take his eyes off the bag. Then the two men circled the newcomer and his belongings, peppering him with questions. It wasn't so much that they were in search of answers as they wanted a reason to stay near the bag. The one with the towel noticed the watch with the shiny black metal frame, snatched it up, and took a step back, asking how much it cost and where to buy one. His friend leaned over him, but he wouldn't let him look at the watch as he measured it against his wrist. Then he went back to interrogating Dawit—the man's interest in the watch matched Dawit's loss of interest in it, so he cut the discussion short by gifting it to him.

Then the other man pounced, asking for something similar, and, without waiting for an answer, he dumped out the bag and pulled out the shirt Saba had given Dawit. At that, Dawit tried to object, to give him something else in its place, but it seemed the half-naked man wanted to get revenge for his bad luck. Since he had missed out on the watch, he wanted to take something dear to its owner. He left Dawit and examined the shirt while stealing annoyed glances at the watch with its shiny metal frame, which now adorned his friend's wrist.

It wasn't long before their voices rose as they traded insults, each describing the other as a thief. Only then did Dawit learn their names: Mehari was the one who had gotten the watch, while it was Aaron who had reluctantly accepted the shirt. At the end of the evening, before they went to sleep in preparation for their long day in the Old City, Dawit tucked his money into a pocket in his underpants and lay on his stomach, in order to protect the only valuable thing he had left.

◆　◆　◆

"It seems that separating the group was not a good idea."

Dawit lowered his head when he saw the guide's irritation. She had been waiting for him with Mehari and Aaron for a long time, just outside the Church of the Holy Sepulcher.

Dawit had sunk deep inside himself after he had touched something unfathomable in the Church of the Holy Sepulcher. It was only by entering the church that he had been able to tear his gaze away from the wooden ladder that was propped at the front of the church. It was as if Dawit were trying to grasp the ladder's essence, to understand the secret of its strength, its endless waiting.

Inside the church, he was taken in by the domes decorated with crosses and icons, the giant gold-and-silver chandeliers hanging above him. He could scarcely figure out where to put his feet, and yet he felt at one with the spirit of this place, which gave him a mysterious sense of spaciousness. To his left, people were gathered around an altar in which they were planting candles. In front of him were women who wet their robes and bags with the blessed water that flowed through the cracks in a rectangular piece of marble.

He pushed forward with difficulty, until he found a long, spiraling line of people that ended at a small room with a low door. This, he knew, was the shrine of Jesus. For a moment, he was aware that people were marring the splendor of the place by clinging to their usual tourist rituals: making loud noises, snapping photos, wearing shorts and giant round hats. All this felt like the climate of tourism in Gondar—the heavy traffic that moved over the surface of things without paying any attention to their depths. The tourists didn't pause. Or, if they did, they did it with considerable anxiety, as if they were only concerned with gathering evidence that they'd passed through a place. The tourists didn't give the place anything of their soul, and they rarely took anything from it, even though they'd think the opposite. Dawit wished he could be left alone in the Church of the Holy Sepulcher, to listen reverently to the sounds coming through the cracks and to wipe his hands on the weeping rectangle of marble—not because he wanted to be blessed, but to console the church for its alienation. Because the people had definitely changed even if the place had remained the same.

He looked for a way to get upstairs to the window, under which the short wooden ladder was resting. He was told that he couldn't. His sense of the ladder's pain deepened. Perhaps there were many before him who had tried to extend aid, and they, too, had faced this stern refusal. Looking around, he found an iron fence that separated a hall filled with carvings from the rest of the building. At the end, there was a niche that opened onto a stone spiral staircase. That *must* go up to the window that overlooked the ladder. He looked around, and when he didn't see anyone watching him, he sneaked lightly across the alcove toward the spiral staircase. Then he paused for a moment, reaching down to the stones beneath him, wiping a palm over them. He felt they were surprised, but not resentful. He stepped on them gently, fearing it might hurt, as the rocks might have forgotten how to adapt to human behavior. When he reached the entrance to the room that overlooked the outdoor courtyard, the large window sat humbly in front of him.

He approached. When the window didn't object, he stepped even closer, until he was almost pressed against it. He tilted his head down, and the wooden ladder raised its own head, pleadingly. When it saw Dawit, it trembled and let out a muffled groan. Like the ladder, the window, too, was asking this sudden visitor to end its long, exhausting wait, to bridge the distance between them, to either lower the window or raise the ladder. To do *something*, even if the distance between them grew larger. It occurred to Dawit that the ladder was grieved more by this stillness than by its inability to reach the window.

But what if he did it? What if he really opened the window and reached down to pull up this ladder that had waited for so long? He almost did, but then he was afraid of the people down below. He was afraid that their habits would be disturbed—the habits they had formed around this unjust distance—until they were more concerned about these habits than they were with the ladder joining the window.

He took a step back and felt the window almost crying. He turned around and left her behind. Her wailing rose.

Now, he decided to be the savior, even if he ended up crucified. He turned and opened the window, which made a loud *squeak*. He looked from her to the crowd, which was gazing up at him, clamoring as they saw him reach a hand toward the short wooden ladder.

He shifted his gaze between the growing crowd beneath the window and the ladder that was approaching the moment of its salvation. He leaned his body down even farther to bridge the distance, but he was fighting alone. He felt the ladder shrink away every time he nearly touched it. Had it given up on its goal, satisfying itself with the unjust distance? Was its goal real, or was it just a reason to stay there?

The noise below him swelled. Dawit felt confused, and the window took advantage, pushing him out until he fell on his head in the middle of the stony square. People laughed, and the window shared in their laughter. A loud chuckle rang out from the short wooden ladder, which was swallowed up by the rest of the sounds.

Dawit stepped on an elderly woman's foot, and her shouts drove him out of his imagination, and out of the church.

He walked toward the group's meeting point, keeping his back to the wooden ladder hanging below the glass window. He avoided looking back at it, as though his extravagant fantasies might have become reality, and the ladder might really be walking on two feet. An idea flickered through his mind, and it took a moment before he could grasp it: There was a spiritual distinction between the church's exterior and the world inside it. Its rocky exterior rained an avalanche of spirituality onto each visitor, which stayed with them until they left the church courtyard. The interior, however, didn't have the same effect: he wasn't taken in by the ceiling domes decorated with crosses and icons, not by the giant gold-and-silver chandeliers. Instead, he held on to the first feeling that the stone exterior had cast into his heart.

Then, he'd spotted a hunchbacked Ethiopian priest stepping into a neglected-looking building. Dawit's curiosity was roused.

He followed the priest and stood in front of the low door, wavering a little. Just a few steps away, he saw an iron fence that had been painted green. His curiosity surged, as though he were in front of an abandoned cave. He took a step in and found the priest on his right, sitting on a wooden chair in baggy black clothes. His eyes were closed, and his head was propped on one hand while the other held a long brown rosary. In front of him, there was a small bowl filled with coins. Dawit didn't want to disturb the man, so he let his gaze drift around the narrow room.

The vaulted ceiling had been eroded and from it hung a plain chandelier. In front of him, there was what looked like a fenced-off room full of candles and icons of Christ. At the edge of the room, there were dark stone steps. That was it—it took Dawit only a moment to see everything inside the Ethiopian chapel.

He turned to leave with the same caution he'd used when entering. This time, on his way out, he noticed the wooden church door with an iron knocker in the middle. It was stained black, as often happened with doors that had been knocked on many times—except no one was knocking at the door of this small, run-down chapel.

The stark irony elicited a smile from Dawit as he went to join the group at the entrance to the stone plaza.

(20)

"When I stood in front of the officer a second time, after the end of my solitary confinement, he stared at me narrowly, as if examining the effect of those ten days. I must have grown paler and skinnier, since I'd shocked one of the soldiers who knew me when I passed him on my way to see the officer.

"'Will you do it again?'

"He looked me straight in the eye as he waited for my answer. His question took me back to the cramped cell, to the long nights and tedious days. It took me back to Aisha, who had never left me in my lonely days, and to my painful questions: Had she forgotten me? How long had it taken before she went back to her normal life? Had she forgotten me right away, or had she waited a long time? Was she resigned to my absence, or did she hate me now?

"My eyes filled with tears, and the officer's gaze relaxed. His smile broadened, as though he considered that enough of an answer. He gestured that I should go back to my room to prepare for the day, and his features took on a fake fatherly look.

"It was the middle of the day when the movements in the school slowed down a little. This was the time of day when soldiers snatched a little rest before returning to their busy schedules.

"Taking advantage of this quiet moment, I spilled my suitcase out onto the bed and set it on the edge, where it would be clearly visible. Hopefully this way, people would believe I had stepped out only briefly. Then I walked off with confident steps. As I walked, I greeted everyone who passed. I answered the ones who stopped me, giving them brief answers about the cruelty of solitary confinement, before I continued on my path with the same steady pace. At the gate, the guard gave me a suspicious look. I put my right hand up straight, palm facing him, and put my left flat in front of it. He nodded, understanding that I meant to buy a box of tobacco for an officer. My face brightened, and I passed through the gate before I noticed his look. I quickly put back my mask of dejection, more appropriate to someone who had just left solitary.

"When I got a little ways away, I started to run. I ran with all my might and without looking back. It was less like I was running *away* from the Revolution School, and more like I was running *to* Aisha.

"I stopped only when I reached the sidewalk across from her mother's place, since that was where she usually was at this time of day. While I waited for her to appear, I realized I hadn't prepared a story about where I'd been. The task of putting together something persuasive was hugely daunting, and it exhausted me. I thought that maybe, the moment she saw me, she would forget to ask. But sooner or later we would come back to it.

"While I was in the middle of my confused thoughts, Aisha appeared on the opposite sidewalk, walking toward the restaurant with her head bowed. Her heavy footsteps pressed deep into my heart. I knew that when Aisha grieved, she did it with her whole heart—nothing but grief stood before her. I wanted to call out to her, to stop her before she went inside. But at that moment, I felt I wasn't ready to receive all her sadness, all at once. So I let her go in, since I needed to invent good reasons for why I'd been gone. But even more than needing to invent good reasons for my absence, I needed reasons that could block this flow of sorrow or divert its course until it had streamed far away.

"I spent a long time waiting for her to reappear, and I felt calmer as I caught the end of a thread that led me to an elaborate tale. I would do two things: lie with every fiber of my being and also say everything that had happened to me, exactly as it had truly been. I would simply exchange one final detail for another so that the story went in a different direction from reality. I would tell her the story of solitary confinement, of how I had suffered in it without her face, of the deprivations that had struck my soul, then my body. But as to the reason for this punishment, let it be that I'd assaulted a soldier who had harassed me on the street. This simple switch wouldn't tarnish the honesty I'd use for my lie.

"Still, Aisha didn't show.

"From where I was standing, I could see people moving inside the restaurant. The mother reappeared. So did the staff. But it was as if Aisha had been swallowed up, disappearing into some deep hole inside the building. I couldn't stop myself from creeping closer, despite my fear of her mother. I crossed to the other sidewalk and passed by the restaurant, trying to peek in, but I turned my face away as soon as the mother noticed someone near the door. I waited for a while, thinking maybe Aisha would go out, but she didn't. So I went back to the other side of the street, this time with greater focus. It helped that the mother was absorbed in her notebooks.

"And there was Aisha, sitting at a corner table, gazing absentmind-edly at the opposite wall. She put her head down on her arms, which were resting on the table. I waited for her to raise her head as I shifted my gaze between her and her mother, who was sitting at the front of the restaurant. Aisha heaved herself up into her previous sitting position, this time looking around with a seeming weariness, until her gaze bumped into me.

"Everything happened very slowly—her head lifting up, her back slouching back against the chair, her eyes moving around. Only the collision was thunderous, as if it were separate from all that slow motion. Her eyes widened in astonishment. Mine did the same, even though I had been waiting for her eyes to finally land on me. I don't know how much time passed until I realized I was standing across from her. She was still in the restaurant, and I was on the street, but there she was, sitting directly in front of me. Slowly, her stunned expression subsided, replaced by an angry one. Her eyes narrowed, and her pointed look intensified. But she didn't stay that way for long either, and sadness surged through her body. I saw Aisha collapse right where she was, her body falling and striking rock bottom, even though she hadn't moved from her spot. I was the only one who saw as she slipped into sadness without any outward sign. She shook her head, then turned her face away from me. I waited for her to turn back, but she didn't.

"I didn't even know what was happening—but then I was storming the restaurant, heading right for her. Her mother raised her head in shock, and so did the patrons and staff. Only Aisha remained unchanged. I fell to my knees in front of her. I put a hand on her knee and looked up into her face, but it stayed the same. I craned my head until I met her eyes, and she swept her face the other way. I grabbed her shoulders and yanked her toward me. Here, I heard her mother shout at me to *leave her daughter alone*, while one of the staff walked up to shoo me away.

"'What do you want?'

"As soon as Aisha looked at them with her tear-filled eyes and stony features, her mother stopped shouting, and the employee froze. I couldn't find an answer. I just stared at her angry, sad face. She wasn't really expecting an answer—she just wanted to have my face in front of her, so she could have a long, silent conversation with it. I gave it to her, backing off. She reached out and took my face. I could see her getting angry, then calming down a little, then filling up with affection before she fixed her features to reveal a look of spite. She let go of my face and turned away.

"My anxiety returned, and it spiked when I saw her turn back with a cold, neutral expression. She stood up in front of me, looking like someone who was preparing for a long kiss. My facial muscles relaxed, and I felt that the storm had passed. My smile grew, but before it could reach its fullness, she slapped me hard, setting off a buzz that moved from the center of the slap, on my left cheek, all the way to the deepest part of my brain.

"There was a confused silence. Everyone was looking at me, and I saw Aisha staring at me, a smile of relief clearly spreading across her face.

"'Now you can tell me whatever lies you like.'

"She took me by the hand and pulled me outside, telling her mother she might be a little late and ignoring her mother's pleas not to go. I walked behind her, still not fully recovered from the slap. When she was far away from the restaurant, she turned down a side street, pushed me up against a wall and stood opposite me, waiting for me to start talking. I didn't know what to do, since I felt completely naked in front of her, and my lies died before they could emerge to collide with her watchful gaze. I failed at all attempts to regain my resolve, so instead I turned to silence while the anger grew inside me. I wished I could tell her that I was one of the Free Gadli. I wished I could leave the tiny corner that I had been crammed into, which always made me the bad guy, the liar. I didn't even want to think about what would happen if Aisha knew I was cut off from family and ancestors, and that everything I knew about mothers and fathers had come from the revolution.

"'Dawoud, that slap was because you didn't keep your promise. If you disappear again, there won't be a way to fix it.'

"'I won't. I promise you, from the bottom of my heart.'

"I didn't recognize my own voice, which sounded like I hadn't used it in ages. But my soul was pushing out those words, insisting on them. Maybe that was why the Aisha I knew returned, smiling affectionately before she hugged me, crying. We replayed our first reunion scene: we cried, and we told each other about the bitter taste of absence, before we got lost in a long kiss that mixed the light saltiness of tears with Aisha's saliva. It gave us back a sense of security after the shakiness of the days that had come before."

David fell silent. It was as if he had traveled back in time in order to carefully study what had happened. The session's secretary lifted a hand and sighed, massaging his fingers, which had grown sore from writing the young man's story. Only the European was asking for more, expressing annoyance at any break in the thread of the tale. After David was recharged by the interest clear on the European's face, he went back to his story.

"When night fell, I had to persuade Aisha to go, so she wouldn't worry her mother. When she left me, she took one promise after another that I wouldn't disappear.

"I walked Asmara's streets blindly. Half of me was excited to be back with Aisha, and the other half was busy thinking about what would happen when my escape was discovered. Life in the city began to fade, little by little, but without one half of me or the other winning out. I thought about going back to the Revolution School—I could slip in at the last possible moment before the new day began. The urgency of this idea grew as I remembered my harsh days in solitary confinement. But it weakened again, overwhelmed by the thought that I might lose Aisha forever. On the road that led to the Revolution School, the two ideas clashed even more fiercely, as if two ends of a rope were pulling me sharply in opposite directions, until I almost snapped in two. But, in the end, I chose to turn my back on the school, and I headed off toward the unknown.

"My feet led me to the home of a friend's father. I hesitated a few moments as I cooked up a lie that would buy me a little time, allowing me to stay here until I could take care of a few things. I knocked on the door. It opened, and a look of amazement filled the man's face. It didn't take much effort to convince him that I had gotten leave in exchange for certain services for an officer. I let him understand that the officer had insisted this was not a matter to be broadcast publicly, and that my fellow soldiers couldn't know.

"When I laid my head down on a bed the man had quickly gotten ready, contradictory thoughts struck me all over again. The sound of the clock's ticking grew louder in my ears, as though it were shouting the countdown to when I would become a fugitive from military service at the Revolution School. I tried to catch hold of a plan, a decision I could settle on and then rest. But under the pressure of time, thoughts faded and scattered, growing hard to pin down. I wished I could fit the two pieces together: having Aisha and avoiding punishment. I wished I could choose between them without one of them considering me a criminal.

"So what would you have done? If you were in my shoes?"

The European looked surprised by David's question. It took him a moment to realize he had emerged from the story, only to be dragged right back in. He almost answered—and really, he would've liked to give an answer. But after a moment, he realized his dilemma. He had the choice to come closer, but after that, he wouldn't have a chance to back out. Stories have one door through which we can enter, after which we spin in their world forever. No matter what we think, there's no escape from the stories in which we become entangled.

"No, no. I'd prefer to just hear it from you."

David smiled as he saw the European lift his foot from the trapdoor David had prepared, sidestepping it in spite of his curiosity. And so he returned to his story:

"I don't know when I fell asleep, but it seemed as if only a moment passed before I woke up in terror to the sound of a loud knock at the door. Light had slipped into the room, and the clock showed nine. I tried to catch the owner of the house before he opened the door, but he got there first. Security forces stormed in, pushing past the stunned man before they grabbed me and left in a hurry. I had been expecting something like that, but I hadn't thought it would happen so fast. I sat in the Jeep, handcuffed, next to two policemen, with a third opposite me. No one hurt me or even talked to me. They just glowered at me.

"Regret started to creep up on me, getting bigger and bigger. If I had gone back to the Revolution School before dawn, I could have avoided this fate. Yet here I was, being led to a punishment for I-didn't-know-how-long, without even getting Aisha. It was as if the cost had been doubled. Well, that's what happens when we want to have it all—it's inevitable that we lose out.

"Then it dawned on me that too much time had passed, and we hadn't reached the Revolution School. I looked out and realized we were going in a different direction. I thought maybe they were doing other raids before returning us to the officer as a good catch, but then the police vehicle turned away from the city and headed toward the outskirts. With all the politeness I could manage, I asked the soldier where we were going. He laughed as he told the others that I didn't know we were going to the Blue Valley.

"The name pierced my chest and settled into my heart like a burning coal. I covered my face with my hands and pressed my head against my legs, imagining the fate to which these men were leading me. I hadn't realized that, as punishment for my absence from the Revolution School, I could be thrown into the very cruelest of prison camps. I had thought that the choice was between Aisha and solitary confinement. Entering the Blue Valley was worse than anything. I wanted to cry, to scream, to beg the soldiers to leave me by the side of the road. Now I understood the secret of their calm, why they hadn't bothered talking to me. Nothing beat my destination of pain and torture. They must have been surprised by my complacency, by how I'd come with them so easily.

"I started to remember the stories that soldiers at the front told about the place, and how they'd been afraid to pass through it. I remembered how the revolution had sent traitors and thugs to the Blue Valley before their execution, and how they had shined up its reputation for scattered limbs, curses, and excruciating screams of pain. Whenever I'd hear the name *Blue Valley*, dread coursed through my body. But that had been the fear of distant things, of things that happen to other people. It was the kind of story that stirred up your fear and disgust, sure, but you never imagined it would happen to you. The Blue Valley was like a monster that everyone talked about, but nobody ever saw. I had never known anyone who came back from it. Maybe no one ever did.

"I turned back toward the soldier, but this time I spoke in a louder voice, a voice that was miserable and held a note of protest. My voice was angry, and it was searching for a way to survive at any cost. 'Why me? What did I do? Is the Blue Valley now the punishment for skipping out on a day at the Revolution School?'

"The soldier looked over at his comrades, then turned back to me, speaking in a tone that seemed to appreciate my panic. 'We're just following orders, you know. We don't get into the reasons. Once we get there, you can ask them.'

"I pressed my head back down against my legs, damning my poor judgment.

"I thought about Aisha, and I damned her too. I damned her family, the moment when she'd shown up in the crowd, the moment I'd followed her, the moment I'd talked to her; I damned liking her, her liking me, loving her, her loving me. I damned all those moments and wished the balance of them had been slightly different so that I could have survived.

"What if I hadn't gotten down from the truck during the independence celebrations? What if I hadn't tried to get the man to carry me on his shoulders and dance with me through the crowd? What if I had let her disappear from view? What if I hadn't caught up with her again and again, until she had no way out?

"What if I'd stayed angry with her after I saw her with that other guy? What if I thought about how her mother showered me with insults every time she saw me? What if I'd given in to the officer's threats and stayed committed to my training at the Revolution School? What if I hadn't gotten trapped inside her sleepy eyes, her pillowy lower lip, the beauty mark at the base of her neck, her soft fingers and short black hair?

"What if? What if only one thing in this long series of things had changed? I would have survived, no doubt about it. One link in the chain would have done the job, diverting the course of my fate. Then I would have been taken somewhere else, somewhere other than the Blue Valley. Now it was all useless.

"The soldier's words kept ringing in my ears, and I watched as the vehicle slowed down to enter a side dirt road, as the soldiers got ready to leap out."

Now, David pressed his palms against his face and tucked his head between his legs, as if he were acting out the last part of his story. The European asked if he needed a moment, but he shook his head. He took a sip of water and went on.

(21)

On the way back, the guide turned to Dawit, Mehari, and Aaron to ask them which of the three sites had made the biggest impression. The other two answered without hesitation: "Kotel."

Dawit would've liked to say the Church of the Holy Sepulcher. But even before that, he would have liked to correct her, to say that they hadn't even visited the al-Aqsa Mosque, they'd only gone near it. But when he found the other three waiting for him to speak, he quickly echoed his companions' answer, since he'd noticed it made the guide happy: "The Western Wall."

The Western Wall didn't have the same effect on him as on his companions. Maybe because he had come to it drained by the Church of the Holy Sepulcher, or maybe because the visit was quick and collective, with no time for reflection. He didn't know, but the visit had been so rote. They had left the church's stone courtyard and headed toward the western area near al-Aqsa Mosque, where they found the huge rock wall that stood between the Mughrabi Gate to the south and al-Tankaziyyah School to the north.

The place had been nearly empty, except for a few small, scattered groups of worshipers and tourists. Dawit didn't feel in harmony with the place; he felt the twenty meters between the ground and the top of the wall were like a spiritual barrier, and he couldn't understand why. Maybe he didn't want anything to revere. Instead, he was searching for affectionate walls nearby, like the one he'd found in the Church of the Holy Sepulcher.

At the Western Wall, the guide reminded them of the rituals, and the three immediately set off to cling to the wall and shed tears at all that remained of Solomon's Temple, mourning its destruction. Before they left, each of them wrote his prayers and wishes on a piece of paper and tucked it between the wall's cracks. This moment changed how Dawit felt about the wall, at least a little. His heart softened toward these cracks, which were endlessly receiving people's wishes and prayers.

Back at Apartment 18, on the fifth floor, in the seventh building of the twenty-second square in the settlement at Pisgat Ze'ev, Mehari urged his two companions to tell him what wishes they had written. He started by telling his own: "I begged God for a lot of money and a good wife, one who'd make me forget your sour faces."

Aaron repeated the same wish, in slightly different words, although he lingered over the specifications for his desired wife: "Actually, I didn't ask God for her to be a good wife, since we've got plenty of those. I just want her to make me happy in the you-know-what department. Other than that, she can be *good* for her parents."

They burst out laughing, and then the two of them turned to Dawit, who tried to avoid the question by telling them that the prayers slipped into the cracks were between a person and their Creator, and that secrecy ensured these prayers would reach Him without any mix-up. But all his attempts at evasion failed in the face of their insistence, especially since they had noticed he spent a long time writing his prayer. Finally, he had to say something:

"I divided my wishes between the ones for me and the ones for our people. I asked God to extend my life and grant me health, to make up for the lost years that I spent far from the Promised Land. I also called on Him to write a positive future for this nation and to gather up its scattered peoples after their long years of suffering. So, are you happy now?"

Mehari and Aaron seemed moved; in front of them was a man who might be younger than them, but his heart was not so narrow as to hold only his own wishes.

As they stared at him, Dawit remembered the blank sheet of paper he had pretended to write on for so long, before looking around him and shoving it deep into a lonely crevice. In the end, he had finally written only one word that summed up all his wishes: survival.

When they were all lying in their beds, Dawit stared up at the ceiling, thinking back on their long morning. The Church of the Holy Sepulcher had planted seeds in his soul. He marveled at how attached he felt to a religious relic—he, who'd never practiced any religion in his life. But his astonishment eased when he told himself that he had been captivated by the place—by its ancient smells and by the spirit that dwelled within it—and not by what it meant to others.

This thought led him to contemplate his generally neutral feelings toward religions: he neither loved nor hated them. They stayed on the sidelines of his life. Even the names he chose for himself, which were each aligned with a particular religion, didn't inspire any affinity. Down in his deepest core, he was still Adal, the young man who belonged to the mountains and the valleys, to the places that were cut off from any origin, despite the sadness and self-pity this aroused in him. He didn't know if it was good or bad. All he knew was that he'd been made this way, and that he had no hand in it. He felt it was too late to belong. Belonging was something that had to do with the way your heart was made at the very beginning.

Now, his curiosity returned, and he wanted to see inside al-Aqsa Mosque. The fence around it had given him a strange feeling of longing. But he didn't know how to do it—how could he ask the guide to get him in?

Even if he went alone, how could he claim to be Muslim without arousing the suspicions of the guards, who were everywhere? He pushed down the idea for a little while, but then it sprang back, even more urgently. He got out of bed, overwhelmed by the idea. He put on his clothes quietly, trying not to make any noise that might wake his two companions from their siestas. He went to the bus station and discovered that all of the buses had the number 44. He was a little confused until he asked a passerby and learned they were all going to the Old City, and that the number meant the bus would make a return trip to Pisgat Ze'ev.

It was two in the afternoon when Dawit got off at the central bus station near Sultan Suleiman Street, which was buzzing with pedestrians headed in every direction. He didn't need to ask for help, since the sign right in front of him pointed to his destination.

Once again, he stood in front of Damascus Gate. This time, he noticed its towering ornate walls, which looked like the remnants of a fortress. He stepped through the gate, telling himself to look natural, as there were soldiers scattered everywhere. He made an effort to keep his head up and look one of the soldiers in the eye, and when he passed by without any trouble, he lifted his chin, puffed out his chest, and slowed his pace. Now, he felt on firmer ground.

He took al-Wad Street, after seeing a sign that said it led to al-Aqsa Mosque. It looked a lot like the route he had taken that morning with the group. He wasn't sure whether it was the same or different; the road was narrow, crowded with shops and people and canopies that created shade for passersby. He walked past an Ethiopian soldier, which rattled him a little, but Dawit quickly regained his composure as he nodded at the soldier, who answered with a similar greeting, but with a stern expression.

By the time he neared the end of the winding road, he had prepared himself for the guard's question about his religion at the gate to al-Aqsa. But then he was stopped by a tender melody that pierced through all the noise, reaching out to him from a shop selling musical instruments. From where he stood, he could see a girl with her back to the entrance, holding an oud. He walked up, not knowing whether it was the music that attracted him or the girl's short charcoal-colored hair. He hesitated a few moments, then stepped into the shop. The shopkeeper, who was facing the girl, raised his head and then went back to taking in the song.

This indifference encouraged Dawit to move closer, as if he were invisible. He, too, could play this game—walking around and looking at the wooden and brass instruments crowded together on the walls—without turning toward the girl. When he reached the corner, he turned around so that he was facing the musician.

Here, he filled his eyes with her features, taking advantage of her focus on the oud. She was in her early thirties, with a white face that was a bit long, framed by wavy hair. Her sharp eyes were almost fierce, topped with thick eyebrows, and she wore circular glasses that seemed to be so much a part of her face, he couldn't imagine her without them. Dawit looked down at her hand, at the graceful movements that would have seemed silly if not for the flowing melody they produced.

Dawit's eyes remained on the girl until he noticed the shopkeeper staring at him in surprise. This coincided with the end of the music, and the girl lifted her head to see the newcomer. Their gazes were trained on him and so he left, confused, without saying a word. At the door, he turned to steal another glance, and he found her smiling as she followed him with her eyes.

He was close to the guard of al-Aqsa now and so he retreated, giving himself a moment to shake off his confusion. But when he saw a group crossing toward the mosque, he slipped in among them and avoided the question he feared. As soon as he passed the guard, he parted ways with the others; they stopped at a group of Palestinians who were making sure the women had the right clothes for the place.

Dawit passed a plaque that said this was the tomb of the Mamluk prince Alaa' al-Deen al-Busiri, which was under the auspices of the Palestinian Department of Waqf Endowments. Then he found himself in the heart of a large courtyard that was divided into stone pathways surrounded by shrubs and small domes—al-Aqsa Compound. Behind them, his gaze caught on the towering golden dome.

Dawit walked toward the Dome of the Rock with quick, nervous steps, climbing the stone stairs that led him to the square that lay directly in front of the dome. He paused and looked at her: she seemed so *arrogant*, so brimming with her own brilliance as she looked down at everything from above. He had to force his head up to look at her, and he didn't like this excessive bowing and scraping. This dome knew she was beautiful, that she was lofty, and she made her living off it. He wished he'd known this before coming, and he would have ignored her; he would have ignored this game she played with the rays of the sun, using it to highlight her beauty. He would have ignored how she looked down at each newcomer, just to fill them with astonishment and respect. He would have passed by her, staring at the small stone domes before approaching their peeling paint, brushing against it with all the affection he could offer. Only this sort of move might make the Golden Dome step back from her naked ego.

But it was too late.

He moved closer. All along the walls, there were small, scattered groups of women sitting in the shady spots, passing the time in humdrum chatter. Dawit walked around the Dome of the Rock until he reached its entrance. There, he saw Palestinian guards. He noticed that they had beards and that, actually, they looked a lot like their Israeli counterparts, except they didn't have weapons. They had the same haircut that left hair only on top, their sleeves rolled up to show off their muscular arms, and they had the radios that perched on their shoulders and wrapped around their arms, as well as the dark police sunglasses hiding their eyes.

From where he stood, he looked into the Dome of the Rock and saw only women there as well, with female guards among them, wearing brown jackets with an image of the golden dome at the center.

And so the dome chased him wherever he went.

He found another entrance and turned in, but it was full of even more women. Here, they gathered around stone steps that led down to what looked like a stone vault. He was curious to find out what was going on down there, but it seemed like this place was only for women.

He turned his back on the Dome of the Rock and followed a sign that pointed him to al-Aqsa Mosque. Now, from where he stood, he saw something different. It was an elegant, unassuming stone structure, topped with a silver dome. When he reached the entrance, he took off his shoes and stepped in without hesitation. He walked over the red carpet with yellow patterns. It wasn't new, but it was clean.

In front of him, the mosque stretched out for about fifty meters before reaching the mihrab. Brass chandeliers hung from its ceiling, decorated with Quranic verses, and at the tops of its columns were black electric fans with the brand name Venta. He walked in farther and found a fenced-in brown niche with a warning on the front: NO CLIMBING. This mihrab seemed just right for the mosque: imposing, but without arrogance; old, but standing on its feet; humble, and without pretense. A feeling of reverence settled into his soul. He felt as though he might cry, and he had an impulse to stay here forever, to embrace the mosque, to protect and cherish it, and at the same time enjoy its protection, its tenderness toward him.

He loved this reciprocal relationship. He loved that this mosque didn't erase his presence. It looked at him and *understood* his presence. It was as if it were telling him, out loud, that it wanted and needed him too.

It occurred to him to pray, and this was the first time such a thought had visited him. But his complete ignorance of how to do it drove the idea from his mind.

He left, and he walked most of the way to Damascus Gate while still looking back at al-Aqsa Mosque. He didn't turn his face from it until he was forced to.

Just before he came out of the compound, he leaned against a solitary tree, kissed it, scooped up some of the dirt into which the tree's roots were sunk, and tucked the dirt into his pocket.

He returned to the noise of the people on the narrow road. He would have liked to keep his raw, wet soul away from others, to guard it so it wouldn't dry out again. He wished he could see his face because it felt wet, too, and he deliberately didn't look at anything in particular. He went on like that, feeling his way along like a blind man, using his spirit as a stick that carefully tapped the ground, avoiding collisions with people and objects.

But this blindness suddenly disappeared when he passed the musical-instrument store. His eyes didn't see it, but his raw, wet soul raised its head and turned toward it, as if some incomprehensible force had tapped it gently and left.

He moved toward the shop carefully, so that he wouldn't be in the shopkeeper's line of sight. He found the shopkeeper playing for a few tourists, but he didn't see the girl. The playing sounded very elaborate and yet also dry and predictable. He was able to see, without much effort, the direction the music would take, and it rose and fell without capturing his heart. The music leaped here and there, but his feelings stayed fixed in place. It didn't make him feel like crying or even laughing.

He left, lest *all* his reverence leak away. He walked quickly even though, by moving forward, he was leaving the things he loved behind. When he reached the end of the road, his heart pricked him. He felt the trick that Damascus Gate was playing on him, intending to hand him over to some other place that had no link to al-Aqsa. He felt the taste of the name for the first time. How could "al-Aqsa" take over his feelings like this, dwelling in the depths of his being, clinging to him? But the mosque was far away now, and it would wither away as soon as he crossed into the noise of Sultan Suleiman Street.

On the stone steps of Damascus Gate, he saw the Ethiopian soldier again. This time, he looked fearlessly into the man's eyes, without greeting him. The soldier, for his part, only glanced at Dawit before leaning in toward another soldier and engaging in some kind of banter. Dawit climbed the stairs lightly—before coming to a sudden stop. The girl from the music store was sitting on the steps, fiddling with her phone. Next to her, the oud was stretched out, wearing a dark leather case.

He didn't know why he felt that he had gone right back to the heart of al-Aqsa. The raw wetness returned to wipe even more gently at his face and heart. He didn't know what to do. He couldn't leave, and he couldn't find a way to approach her. He stayed where he was, cursing the distance that separated them. If only he'd paid more attention when he was near her; if only he'd bumped into her, stumbled over the oud. If only he didn't need to go forward any farther; if only he'd made it all the way there before he noticed her. Which was worse: to notice something too early or to see it too late? He didn't understand why the passersby didn't take note of her, why all the thoughtless movement around her didn't stop. For the first time, he would have tolerated—even welcomed—attention, for it would single him out from every other person.

It was as if he had found a coin in the middle of the road that thousands of others had passed by before him without giving it even a glance. He didn't know who had schemed to make this happen, but in any case, he felt grateful.

The girl tucked her phone into the pocket of her skinny jeans and raised her head, wearily, playing with her curly hair and tugging it back, only to notice Dawit frozen there, staring at her. Her eyes narrowed as she stared at him, as if she was checking whether she knew him. It all happened very slowly, but that didn't stop him from being exposed in front of her. Confusion flooded through his body, which he tried to hide as he averted his eyes, but his feet remained right where they were, as if daring to stand against him. He looked back at her and found that her stare had eased, and a bewildering half smile had taken over her face.

She stood up and adjusted her white shirt, after having revealed a little of her skin, and he caught a clear look at the bra beneath. She picked up the oud and headed for him, her smile widening. He nearly retreated, nearly ran away. She was doing what he couldn't, bridging the cursed distance between them. But what he wanted the most was also what he now feared the most.

"Are you Sudanese?"

Her question surprised him, as though she'd suddenly fallen out of the sky and landed in front of him; as if he hadn't seen her first, while she was fiddling with her mobile; as if she hadn't raised her head, wearily, and turned to him with a confusing half smile; as if she hadn't risen from where she was sitting, hefting up her oud and heading toward him. As if it hadn't all happened slowly enough for him to take hold of each moment and anticipate the next.

Confused by his silence, she shifted her question into English: "Are you Eritrean?"

He nodded before reversing course and denying it just as quickly. Confusion crossed her face before he answered in a tone that he meant to sound confident: "I'm from Beta Israel."

She pursed her lips as she apologized and turned to leave. He felt surprised. He didn't want this meeting to end so quickly. He didn't know what to do except stop her with a quick lie, which he made sure to do in Arabic:

"But I've lived in Eritrea and Sudan, and I have lots of friends from there."

"Hmm. Actually, I'm looking for refugees from Eritrea and Sudan for my PhD research. Could you help me find someone?"

His lie left him with an unexpected dilemma. It occurred to him to introduce her to Yaqub, to keep the connection, but he didn't want to be a bridge between her and anyone else. He wanted to be the only path, the only destination.

It occurred to him to backpedal and tell her he was Eritrean, that he was perfectly suited to her research, which he hoped would be long and complicated. But he was afraid to squander his secret like this, without any guarantees. "I can, but I don't know if they'd be willing to cooperate. You know how refugees are. Suspicious of strangers."

This lie seemed more precise than the last one, and he saw the girl's face go cheerful as she pulled a white card from her pants pocket and handed it to him: "Everything will be done confidentially, and they'll remain anonymous. This is my phone number. I hope to hear from you soon."

The girl then left as slowly as she had come. Dawit felt surprised by this too. He held on to the card until she had disappeared from sight. The place was empty of people, empty of noise. He was alone on the threshold of Damascus Gate. His soul returned to a state of reverence, yet a harsher one. This reverence, which he had asked for, now gnawed at him on its way to his deepest point.

In his bed that night, he was still cradling the card: feeling it, studying it, holding it up close to his nose. He wanted to involve as many of his senses as possible. And, before he had fully shut his eyes, he repeated the name that was engraved on the front of it with a delight that didn't lessen with repetition: "Sarah . . . Sarah . . . Sarah."

(22)

"The soldiers got out, but I stayed where I was. Someone shouted at me. I followed them as I looked around—it was a barren land, surrounded by mountains and strewed with metal containers that were piled up on top of each other among the rutted tracks in the ground. A soldier signed a piece of paper and handed me over. He slapped cuffs on my wrists and my ankles and then looped a rusty chain around my neck and pulled me by that, in a promise of dark days to come. I made no sound. I felt far away from this place, deep inside myself. Things around me grew dark, and hazy spots blurred my vision. My emotions roiled inside me—growing and shrinking, moving in all directions—but then died away before they reached my face.

"A young man passed near me, dragging a cart with a huge rock in it. Whenever he stopped to steal a few moments of rest, a soldier who stood some distance away would throw rocks at him. I emerged from my fugue state and stopped, following the young man with my gaze. This provoked the soldier who was walking with me, and he gave my chain a painful yank, his face twisting with a devilish smile. But the pain in my neck felt like a slight tingling, and the trace of it quickly passed from my face. The soldier seemed distressed by my condition, and he tried cursing me, kicking me, tightening the chain again, but nothing changed. I couldn't feel pain. I wished I could have given him what he wanted—to scream or cry, to beg him for mercy. But it was all beyond me.

"The soldier then lowered me into a pit. The mouth of it seemed wide, but it got narrower and narrower the deeper I went, until I settled into a hollow where I almost needed to crawl. I was kept in—"

Irritably, the European interrupted David: "Yes, yes, I know all the details of the Blue Valley. I know them by heart from everything I've heard here. Skip past these ugly bits, if you don't have anything different to say."

David wanted to defend his account, to say it was totally different. He wanted to tell this man how the Blue Valley had broken him, shattering his certainty in everything around him. How he had spent nights wishing for the salvation of death. He wanted to say that he remembered it clearly now: he'd seen Yohannes smirk at him as David groaned in agony—*how could he have forgotten?*—and that he hadn't understood the reason for the other man's happiness. He still didn't. Maybe Yohannes liked to watch people suffer; maybe another's suffering meant he wouldn't have to. David wanted to talk and talk, emptying his story out onto the table, but he satisfied himself with two words: "That's it."

The European sighed and turned to his coworkers. He was silent for a moment, as if gathering his thoughts.

"Well," the European said. "I must confess that you're the best storyteller in all of Endabaguna. I have never enjoyed an entertaining tale so much. I have spent many a day impatiently chewing over these ridiculous stories that the refugees pass on to me, without even *once* thinking that they should come up with something new or just change them around a bit. But you are cut from a different cloth! I salute you for this. Your unique story has made my day. I truly do not know how to reward you. First, I'll recommend you be exempted from deportation to Eritrea. And not only *that*, but I will ask for better conditions while you stay here in the camp. I'll have them serve you better food, and maybe we can get you a tent near the clinic. And you'll have priority if you need to apply again for resettlement in a third country, as stories like yours cannot be missed. But don't repeat the same one. I want a different story every time."

The European handed David's file to him after having stamped it with the red seal of rejection, wishing him success in his life here at Endabaguna. As he left, David spotted the strangely pleased smiles on the faces of the translator and the session secretary. He emerged with his head bowed, and those waiting behind him didn't need to ask the result.

When he'd reached the door, he heard them call for the next person, and the others craned their necks in that direction, leaving David alone.

(23)

Two days had passed since his visit to the Old City, and Dawit still hadn't gotten used to the noise that Mehari and Aaron made in their shared room. Sometimes, it was comments on some rerun of a pro wrestling match; other times, it was them playing cards with two other people they brought in to form an opposing team, although that didn't stop them from squabbling over every point scored by the other team. Still other times, it was their ridiculous bets on any future event, starting with predictions about the next day's weather and the lunch that the catering company would send to the building, and not even ending with what color underwear the poor woman who lived in the next room would wear as she passed by, which was visible beneath her deliberately see-through clothes.

He could have joined them, at least to pass the time, if he hadn't been busy thinking about that oud player—remembering her features, her musical performance, and their brief conversation, which he had reenacted dozens of times, adding and amending until he had crafted a story without end. Each time, he would stop at a sticky point and restart the conversation from the beginning. He didn't understand the secret of his instant attraction to her. Perhaps it was her features—her short hair and round glasses—or maybe it was the condition he'd been in when he left the Old City, ready to cling to anything he stumbled across. Or maybe she was just a tempting subject to be summoned during his many solitary moments. Yet as soon as he threw himself into obsessing over her, he found something stopping that obsession.

It was only a matter of time before the whole thing backfired on him, turning into grief or anger. He had never in his life shared a safe sphere with a woman.

But did that mean he would back off? No, Dawit decided—he certainly would not.

It occurred to him that he might look for an African refugee and introduce him to her on the condition—he'd tell her—that the man wanted Dawit to come with him each time they met, since Dawit helped him feel safe. It seemed like a solid idea, except there were no guarantees: he didn't know whether she would accept the condition or whether the refugee himself would sell him out after the first meeting.

On the other hand, it wasn't easy for him to risk pulling off the cloak and revealing himself, and he didn't know whether she had been sincere in guaranteeing secrecy. But what he *did* know was that he couldn't resist the desire to be close to her, in whatever form, and that he couldn't resist taking the path that led to that closeness.

It wasn't so much that he was confused about whether to approach her—what he wanted was reassurance for his anxious soul. He definitely meant to approach her, but he wanted to risk the least damage possible. When he got tired of thinking it through, he wondered: If the path was full of thorns, would he back off? His answer was an emphatic *no*. He was powerless against the hidden force that drove him to meet her, and he could do nothing but surrender to it. He pulled out his phone and pressed the buttons with a speed that surprised him. He had stared at the white card so much, he'd memorized the number.

The call was answered in her voice, telling him she was busy now and asking him to leave a message, if one was necessary, after the beep. The sound buzzed inside him, and he felt it rush through his veins. He liked this. He called back again, and again, smiling as happily as a child with a new toy. He didn't know how many times he heard her invite him to leave a message, if one was necessary, after the beep. He liked her way of speaking to him—it was as if she were addressing him alone, inviting him alone. Her polite tone filled him with a rising lust. He imagined her inviting him to take her harder, to push her against a wall, to grab her short hair, and to plunge into her until she gave a muffled moan. The image came to life in front of him, and it very nearly swallowed him up. He picked up the phone and left for the bathroom. He called again, ready to get off at the sound of her voice. But, to his surprise, she answered on the first ring. He stammered, pulling up his pants as though she could see him. Making a huge effort to hide his turmoil, he told her he'd found what she was looking for. He didn't hear her answer; he just understood that she was happy, and he cut the call short and hung up. He was sweating profusely. Now the urge had fled, replaced by a sharp pain in his lower belly.

He got to Damascus Gate an hour early. As he sat on the stone steps, he realized how much these steps shared in the intrigues of lovers. They served, even more than as a gateway to places of worship, as seats overlooking a legendary theater of love. He'd made sure to dress well; the night before, without Aaron noticing, he'd taken back the blue-striped shirt Saba had given him.

She was still a ways off when he caught sight of her. He took advantage of being outside her field of vision to study the way she walked over the uneven ground. It was like the way she played the oud. Her feet had the same talent—they played over the stone steps with a grace he had come to know well.

She pulled out her phone, looking around. He let her call him. His need for her was voracious; he didn't even want to miss the sound of her voice before she came.

He answered her call and pretended to look for her, before waving to her as he watched her walking toward him. She reached out her hand, and he gripped it in his. She was surprised to see he was alone. She waited for him to explain, but he was too busy looking at her face. She asked him about the refugee, and then he remembered what she'd come for. Only he knew what *he'd* come for. He waited for her to sit down beside him. He missed the oud, and he missed her white shirt, which she had traded for a dark-blue one that didn't show her bra. He wished he could ask about the oud and the shirt. He searched his mind for the complete picture of the meeting he'd been waiting for.

"I've found just the right refugee, but he wants to be absolutely sure, one last time, that he'll be safe with you."

She assured him that yes, he could trust her, and her look grew sharp. He knew that was her way of showing she cared.

He straightened up, drew in a breath that filled his chest, and said, "I . . . I'm the African refugee you're looking for."

She seemed upset, and she told him she was looking for a *refugee*, not a Falasha immigrant.

He told her he was Eritrean and that he had pretended to be a Falasha Jew to survive the world he'd fled. He didn't mean to tell her everything, but he was drawn in by her features as she absorbed his words. He told his stories, and he felt a sense of pride that he had her face all to himself: her fierce eyes, her pursed lips, her eyebrows that moved up and down with every anecdote, and the hand that moved spontaneously to comb through her wavy hair, pushing it back.

When he'd finished, she gasped in surprise. "This is *exactly* what I want. You're a gift from God, and no amount of prayers would be enough to thank Him for you."

He smiled with a childlike glee. He considered going even further, adding spice to his story to make it more interesting. He loved how he had come to control her through his voice.

But before he could start, he found her breaking in: "Listen. We'll start right away. My research is about the impact of the sufferings of refugees in societies that have a hard time accepting them because of their sex lives, and I couldn't find a better person than you to test all the psychological hypotheses. I'm sure my paper will be the talk of the whole university."

Her words pulled him out of his state of ease and plunged him into a new pit. What sex life was she looking for? What would she ask him, and how would he answer?

Sensing his confusion, she reassured him that she would be the only one who knew his real name. She added that the research required it. These attempts to mollify him didn't work; his anxiety swelled, and he couldn't shake his dread of the subject. His sexual fantasies were the only place where he could be all of himself, where he was free to do whatever he liked to whomever he liked. It was the only part of his life he'd never shared with anyone, and that he didn't have to change, twist, fabricate, polish, or invent for someone else's benefit—it was all and only for him. He could revel in his sexual fantasies about Sarah whenever he was alone, but it was difficult to even think about sharing them with her.

But surely he would find a solution? Lie, maybe, or skirt the truth. He'd figure it out. The important thing was to be near her, talk to her, hear her voice. Everything else was just details.

"All right. I'm in."

It was hard to say the words. But he told himself that their conversation would truly stay anonymous, and she let him believe this obvious fraud. It was a collusion that couldn't have happened with anyone else, as the girl had some incomprehensible effect on him.

"Then let's go to my place, have a coffee, and talk."

He walked with her to where she'd parked, trying to hide the effect her invitation was having on him. All he wished for was her company, and now he was going alone to her house—to talk about his sex life.

He hoped that this whole scenario was just a way for her to seduce him. Or more like he'd be the one doing the seducing.

The whole way to the car, she apologized for having parked so far away, while he noticed that he kept overtaking her and had to slow down to walk beside her. She started telling him about her psychology studies at the Hebrew University, while he soaked up the pleasure of strolling alongside her, gazing at the passersby to see the effect of their relationship now that he had her all to himself.

And yes—many eyes were on him. Necks twisted to look back at them, and there were a few inaudible whispers. He started to feel uncomfortable, since they were getting more attention than he needed. He was only rescued when they got into her blue Citroën and drove north toward the Sheikh Jarrah neighborhood.

It wasn't far from the Old City to Sarah's house. When they passed by a wide building, she pointed out her university, then turned left onto side streets that grew narrower and narrower, until she came to a street that took them up a hill, where she stopped the car. Dawit cast an eye around the place, which overlooked large sections of the neighborhood. He asked about the apparent disparity in the buildings.

"This is an old Arab neighborhood, but it's surrounded by Israeli settlements. The Hebrew University is to the east, like you saw, and to the north is the settlement of Ramat Eshkol. If it weren't for Mount Scopus, the neighborhood would be even more surrounded. Maybe you noticed the black water cisterns on the roofs—they're to make up for the water shortage. You'll find them only on Palestinian homes, unlike the Jewish ones that get enough."

Her mobile rang. As she answered, she motioned for Dawit to follow her. At the door to the old white house, she bent down to stroke a kitten as she looked for her key, apologizing to whomever she was speaking with for not coming, since she was busy with her studies. She ended the call as they walked in, repeating, "Habibi, habibi." The cat followed them, nosing around the place in a familiar way.

Inside, the house looked different. There was a spacious living room with sturdy white walls that had blue trim and recessed windows. Paintings, photos, and maps of Palestine filled the walls with an intentional overabundance. Dawit sat on a sofa embroidered in red and black; it stood in front of an antique table with legs carved into the forms of ancient faces. Meanwhile, Sarah stepped into the kitchen, asking him about how he took his coffee. The oud lay in its leather case on the sofa across from him. Her voice drifted to him from the kitchen, singing a melody, but he couldn't make out the words. He rose from his seat and walked to a glassed-in cabinet filled with memorabilia and wooden sculptures. She asked if he wanted to have his coffee where he was now, in the living room, or where she was sitting in the kitchen.

He crossed the narrow corridor that separated the living room from the kitchen and sat down at a small round table. The kitchen was messy, crammed with cooking utensils, pots, and pans. She presented him his bitter coffee and sat down across from him. He felt confused all over again, sensing that the task he'd been avoiding had begun. But, contrary to his expectations, she started to talk about other things. She told him about her house, where she lived alone, and how she rented it from a Palestinian abroad who was afraid he would lose it if he left it closed up. She told him about the neighborhood, the edges of which were being eroded by settlements that aimed to link the east and west sides of the city.

But each time he felt like he was in harmony with the conversation, he felt a pang of fear that her next sentence would launch into her research.

Once they'd finished their coffee, they moved back into the living room. Here, as if sensing his turmoil, she pulled off the oud's leather case, as if to strip away the seriousness of the moment. She asked if he'd like to hear her play. She began tuning the oud's strings as she embraced it with a remarkable tenderness. Then suddenly she lifted her head and asked: "By the way, which of your names would you like me to call you?"

The question threw him into confusion. Should he say Dawoud, with all the defeats and losses that old name carried? Or should he choose David, a newer name, yet with as many bitter experiences? Or should he stick with the infant Dawit, without knowing for sure whether it was any different from its predecessors?

He couldn't get rid of these names and everything they carried. Each one was a weight that dragged behind him, like a cupboard full of memories, and he couldn't seem to pass by any bit of anguish without storing it inside them.

He didn't know if *he* gave each name its wretched shape and features or whether it was the other way around. What he *did* know was that his many names were a lot like him, a good fit for him and his amputated life. These names, which he had wanted to save him, had instead become a burden. It occurred to him that, even if he continued to switch between all the names, it wouldn't change his fate. Thus, he felt a little more charitable toward the names since the jinx was part of his destiny. Names were just rags, after all; they couldn't hide his fate. He surfaced from his confusion and told her to call him whatever she wanted.

"Okay. Then I'll switch between them, until we settle on one."

She started to play. Dawit relaxed, succumbing to the melodies as he followed the movements of her fingers. His gaze shifted between the oud and her face. He didn't know whether she was playing with her fingers or with her features, which reacted to every melodic phrase. Her fingers seemed to be driven by her sharp gaze at times and at others by her pursed lips, or perhaps by the whorls of hair that followed the movements of her head like a dancer, her every movement at one with the music.

When she finished, she raised her head to give him a shy smile. He asked about the secret to her mastery of the instrument, and she talked for a long time about how she'd grown up in a musical family and how her father, a musician, passed on his passion before leaving too soon, which made music her forever-after bond with him. She talked about how she didn't want to be a professional musician, because she knew how it could consume a person and take them away from their family and friends. She wanted to stay at the sidelines of this passion so that its obsessive zeal would pass by her, harmless. The distance she kept made it her decision, and she would advance toward it when she wanted and retreat when she wanted. She told him that music was selfish and that it accepted no partner; when it held a person in its grip, it would pluck any opponents from their heart one by one.

He began to understand her way of speaking, the way she saw things. He loved the wisdom hidden beneath her beauty, with its strange humility. If he were in her place, he would flaunt his storytelling skills, instructing everyone on how to describe things well and imbue them with personal insights . . . so, well, he probably wouldn't be humble like her. He retreated into himself, annoyed.

"Where do you think we should start?"

And so, suddenly, he decided to take a step toward his fear. Was it because the music had relaxed him or because he'd heard those confident words coming out of Sarah's mouth? Or was it because she hadn't been in a hurry to get what she wanted, making him feel like a close friend rather than a means to an end? Either way, he decided to answer her questions truthfully.

Sarah got out her lined yellow papers and a small tape recorder, which she placed in front of her on the table.

"All right. Let's agree on a few things before we begin. First, I want you to sign this acknowledgment of your consent to participate in the research. Right here, you can see there's a paragraph that says you responded to an advertisement looking for volunteers. It's a routine thing, so just check yes. And one last thing, I don't want anyone to know this interview took place at my house. Are we clear?"

Dawit nodded, and Sarah immediately pressed record and waited for him to speak. He didn't know how to begin. He asked her, and she told him that to start with, he could talk about anything, anything about himself. When she noticed his confusion, she narrowed the topic: "Let's say, for example . . . What does 'love' mean to you?"

He was about to start, but then he felt the weight of the question.

What could he say? How could he describe something he knew so well but had failed to make a reality? But as he decided to push his way forward, experimentally, he started to feel a strange excitement.

"Well, I don't know the right answer, so I'll just say what comes to mind, and you stop me if I'm getting too far from the question.

"I haven't stopped thinking about this feeling for even a moment. I think about love all the time, looking for it in every pair of eyes I see. I'm often disappointed—I feel a bit broken; I curse my luck—but the weird thing is that I've never lost hope. I know love pretty well: what it looks like, what it tastes like, and even its negative qualities. It's so close that, if I stretched out a hand, I could touch it. But it's also so far away that it will take me a lifetime to reach it.

"I've often asked myself what I'm missing, what I have to do to find this love. I've realized a few things, and I've made some changes in myself. But nothing's changed. So, in the end, I was led to pleasuring myself . . ."

He was silent for a moment, regretting that last confession.

"You can move past this point if you like."

He cleared his throat, considering her comment before he decided to continue. "When I couldn't find someone who would accept me, I took revenge in my own way. Every girl I liked, I'd bring her into my private world, strip her down, and then take pleasure in making her submit to my desires. And over time, this has become even more enjoyable than if it were real—and less expensive than real life too. All it takes is one peek at a pretty face, or a round ass, or full lips, or . . . or a full bust to put the whole thing together in my mind. I've done it with lots of women: soldiers, students, waitresses, bus drivers."

Dawit remembered the singer from the bar in Ethiopia—Deborah. He recalled the teacher at the Gondar camp, the nurse at the medical center, his counselor in Tel Aviv . . .

"I don't know why it gives me even more pleasure when she's beyond my reach, or rude, or arrogant. It started with great beauties, and then my circle expanded to include the old and the ugly. It's often occurred to me that if women knew what was happening with me and them, they'd like it. I'm sure of it. In the end, it's more than they could've ever wished for."

Sarah was leaning over her yellow papers: taking notes, drawing circles and other shapes, making arrows. Dawit stopped to take a peek at them before he spoke again.

"They'd love it. Because with me, they'd be their very best. They're close to perfect with me. They become princesses, which is not something that happens to them in real life."

Sarah raised her head suddenly, surprising him with a question: "Has this happened with me?"

He stammered a little as he looked into her eyes, at her hand holding the pencil, her lips, her short charcoal-colored hair, her round glasses. Then he categorically denied it. She gave him a mysterious smile, and he didn't know whether it was the answer she had wanted or not. Then she asked him: "Do they all look alike? I mean, do they all take one shape for you?"

This was the first time he'd thought about it. They all had short hair, round glasses, a round ass, and—most importantly—big breasts. This last observation made him feel giddy. He could have told her, but he realized that, if he did, it would be describing her exactly. So he decided to camouflage his answer.

"Oh, it happens that way sometimes, sure. But it might be just down to my mood in the moment. Don't you think that, if they were all exactly the same, I'd get bored, and it would take away from the pleasure? The world's too big to have just one shape to fall asleep and wake up to."

Despite his intentions, Sarah took a long time to jot down her notes. She was writing and putting circles around some of the words. He wished he could see what she'd written from where he was sitting. But while she was close enough to hear her clearly, she was too far away for him to read her notes. When she stopped, she looked up at the ceiling before turning to him with a new question:

"What about names? I suppose you wouldn't have known their real names. So did you give your mistresses names, or were you content with their bodies?"

"I hadn't thought about that before. It wasn't just about the body. We'd talk—sometimes before, sometimes after. There's a lot of pleasure when it seems difficult at first, before I reach my goal. So it happens that I call them names when we're talking, but I don't remember them after."

"Have you ever met someone again, after you've lived with them in this way? I mean, how do you feel about the woman after?"

"At first, I try to avoid her. But then it occurs to me that *she's* the one who ought to avoid *me*, and then I look straight into her eyes with great confidence, and I study her body straight on, which I now know so very well. I don't go back to wanting her, though, or being obsessed with whether or not she's interested. I can see surprise in her face, and I leave her like that. That's a victory, and those details double my pleasure. I want those kinds of things to be the last things I remember."

Sarah fiddled with the pencil she was holding, quickly glancing at her sketches before she turned back to Dawit, remembering something. "Let's go back a little. I asked you about *love*, but mostly you've been talking about *sex*. Doesn't that seem odd? I mean, why don't you fantasize about having the girl as your girlfriend, if it started that way, as you say?"

The question seized Dawit, catching him off guard, and he searched for an answer that would get him out of this trap. For a moment, he put himself in the opposite chair, her chair, and looked at himself through her eyes, so he could understand why she saw things this way.

He was silent for a long time before he said, simply: "I don't know. I don't know."

"All right then, let me put it differently. If you found the love of your life, would you do with her all the things you hoped for in your fantasies?"

"No. Definitely not."

He didn't hear what Sarah said after that. His categorical denial echoed inside him and then, when it began to fade, he found the question still sitting in front of him. He didn't know whether he was driving these fantasies or whether they were driving him, and he didn't know whether these details were his way of expressing love or revenge—or maybe he wanted love in order to get revenge? When Sarah noticed his distraction, she set aside her yellow pages. She turned off the tape recorder and got up to make him a fresh cup.

The memory of what he'd said surged back. What puzzled him most was the neutral expression with which she had listened to everything he said. Except for her scribblings on the paper, she hadn't reacted at all. He didn't know whether she liked what he said or hated it. She was just swallowing his words. He felt as if he were headed toward some unknown destination. He was used to quickly adapting his words based on what he read in the faces of his listeners, but now this skill of his was completely useless. He didn't want these confessions, in the end, to take him away from his true intention—he didn't want to be hated or scorned by this girl.

She brought back two cups of coffee and asked if he wanted to keep going or take a break.

"Let's keep going."

As he spoke these words, the game reached its climax. Fear gave everything a strange thrill. We usually avoid fear, yet at the same time it gives us pleasure to take risks, to approach the edge of things, the fatal limit. There is joy in staying close to danger, although only as long as we are hopeful of surviving it, which was how Dawit felt now.

"When did you first hear the words 'penis' or 'sex,' and how did you feel about them?"

The danger level rose, and he felt he had gone so far that he had almost no hope of surviving. He felt the pleasure ebbing away, even though this risk-taking was his ultimate goal. He thought of repeating the story he'd made up for the counselor in Tel Aviv about his mother and the neighbors, but he changed his mind, feeling the story's naivete, told and retold to serve a variety of uses.

He wanted to tell her about the battlefront, where they passed their spare time talking about sex, about the women soldiers who fought with their wombs, about the soldiers who made up for a day's lost battle at night, with night's cheap victories. But instead, he resorted to his everlasting savior, to memory, from which he could pick and choose what he wanted.

"I don't really remember. It feels like they've always been with me. So when exactly, I don't know."

This answer seemed to frustrate her a little, and now she said that they would stop, not asking his opinion. He took this opportunity to suggest she play him the song he had first heard in the music store. She held the oud less passionately now, trying to recall it before she started to play. Meanwhile, Dawit headed off into his fantasies—he pushed her up against the wall, gripping her short hair. Then he ordered her to put on her round glasses and took pleasure in hearing her muffled groans.

(24)

As Yohannes waited for David, he was eaten up by anxiety.

"Hey, so, help me out here. How did the interview go? Why are you so late? Tell me, did my story help you out?"

David tried to keep it together. He wished he could tell Yohannes about the disappointment he'd felt in there, about the tremendous feeling of getting so very, very close, only to find himself facing a huge wall right at the end. He wanted to tell Yohannes about the story that he'd dredged up from his depths, although its origins hadn't stopped him from adding or subtracting from it. It had been about his ideal self as he wanted to be, and about Aisha, who had appeared just like she was: shy, honest, and pure. She had appeared just as he wanted her to be: strong and attached to their story. And she had also appeared as the European wanted to see her: bold, slutty, and easy.

Aisha's image had come together in his mind from all of that, until he no longer knew exactly which parts of their story had happened, and which parts had come from his imagination and desire, and which parts had come from pure fear and nerves. He didn't know if she would be angry about what he'd done.

By now, he wasn't even sure whether she was real enough to be angry with him, or if she was so totally false that he should feel sorry for putting himself through all that pain when he'd already had more than his fair share of it.

Now, David felt the grief of a tale brought to life by its teller in such a way that its dimensions disappear, and it dissolves and vanishes so that he no longer knows whether this tale was something that came from him or whether it was an invading body that came in and went, leaving him behind.

Aisha . . . he felt the authenticity of this name, in all its details, and also the aura that surrounded it. But he didn't know if it was real or if it was just an illusion that had escaped his safe zone of sex and taken him up the difficult and thorny path of love, nearly killing him.

He would have liked to say all this to Yohannes, but now he looked into his friend's face and saw it was full of evil. He remembered how Yohannes had convinced him to use a worn-out anecdote. He realized now that Yohannes must have already tried that same anecdote with the European, to no avail. He remembered his gloating, malicious face from the Blue Valley. He wanted to punch him, to get out some of his anger. But instead, he just shook his head sadly.

"I forgot some of the important details you told me. Otherwise, I'm sure I would have gotten a resettlement decision. It's my fault."

Surprise appeared on Yohannes's face before he rearranged it into sadness, and then he began to console his friend with artificial sympathy.

David, on his mattress, stared at the roof of the tent, ignoring his friend, who insisted that David tell him everything that had happened. David promised to do it as soon as he got over his exhaustion. His mind was filled with warring thoughts: Would he spend the rest of his life in Endabaguna? And what of it, as long as he was safe and could eat and sleep? But what if the European didn't keep his promise and decided to return him to Eritrea? The world grew dark around him. There were no options; he just had to wait for his destiny to lead him where it willed.

"I'll tell you a secret if you promise to keep it."

He paid no attention to what Yohannes was saying. He didn't even notice him. He was still drifting along on his own thoughts.

"I'm leaving Endabaguna soon. I'm going to join the last group of Falasha Jews being transferred to Israel."

David turned his head toward his friend, his pupils dilated. Yohannes, apparently sensing that he'd caught David's attention, began to speak in a slow, provocative tone. "I found a smuggler who'll take me to Gondar, where I can be registered as a Jew for ten thousand birr. I wish we could go together, but I know you don't have that much cash right now."

David didn't sleep that night as he turned the idea over and over in his head. He didn't know why, but it seemed like it had been sent just for him. He felt a path had opened up for him to try and escape the camp. Yet, on the other hand, he didn't have any of this huge amount of money—both ten thousand birr to pay the camp for entry and more money to pay the smuggler—nor did he know how to get it. An idea occurred to him, and immediately he woke up Yohannes.

"Listen, I have an idea. What do you say you forget about the smuggler, and we go to Gondar together? And once I'm there, I'll try to persuade them to accept me some way or another."

Before he went back to sleep, Yohannes rolled over, telling David he couldn't go without the smuggler, not on such a rough and unsafe road.

David repeated his attempts in the days that followed; whenever a new idea came to him, he would quickly bring it to Yohannes, begging him to accept it. But his friend refused him every time, taking pleasure in his own indifference.

By the eve of Yohannes's departure, David had stopped asking. He'd accepted his fate graciously, and was even helping his friend with all the arrangements. He knew all the details: the smuggler's name, where Yohannes would meet him, the route they would take. He learned facts about Gondar and its people, about Beta Israel and their promised salvation.

And so, on the day, even before the appointed time of departure, David was on his way to Gondar with Yohannes's money. He'd hit his friend with a stick, knocking him to the ground and struggling with his huge body. A swell of strength helped him overtake the man, despite his slender build, and then he'd tied Yohannes to the tree under which he had been hiding his treasure.

All the way there, he felt sorry for what he'd done. But then he quickly gathered up all Yohannes's evil deeds in front of him, and his feelings faded before disappearing entirely when he told himself he had no choice: either he had to survive or return to that hell in Eritrea. This was a convenient method, and he used it every time he felt the guilt return.

It seemed like going without a guide was a big risk, but David wanted to keep all the birr he had so he could register his name in Gondar. It occurred to him that the smuggler wouldn't be interested in *who* he was smuggling so much as the money, and that he would accept David instead of his friend—but he also remembered how Yohannes talked about the smuggler as if he knew him. Maybe it was just one of his boasts, or maybe this time it really was true. David couldn't take the risk.

So he settled on going alone. As he walked, he couldn't stop checking the place in his underwear where he'd hidden the money. He kept passing his hand over its warmth to feel as if he was nearing salvation. He got a lot of help from the shepherds he met on his way, and they pointed him toward his destination until he knew—from the last shepherd he'd asked—that he was on the outskirts of Gondar city. He was here! And so close to his dream of salvation. He felt an ecstatic joy unlike anything he'd ever felt before.

But his high soon evaporated. He fell into the hands of bandits, who took everything he had, sparing only his life.

And so, he was as he had been: destitute.

(25)

As soon as they saw him, Mehari and Aaron showered him with questions.

It seemed strange to them that he had been gone from Pisgat Ze'ev for hours and hours, since he was just a newcomer to Jerusalem. And that wasn't the only reason. He'd been distant when he returned, and they couldn't tell whether he was happy or sad. He wasn't sure how he felt either. It was a mix—this and that. All the way back to the settlement, he'd been waiting to be alone, since he'd found the 44 bus full of the noise and laughter of those returning from the Old City. He'd been disappointed when he found his two roommates waiting for him, their curiosity nearly killing them. He hadn't yet realized that simply sharing a room with them meant they had a right to know everything. He evaded their questions as best he could, but in the end, he was forced to submit and tell them a few stories that had roots in the truth, although the details were invented.

He told them that he'd gone back to the Old City because he wanted to visit the holy sites alone, so he could spend a good long time there without being under the watchful eye of a tour guide. He told them he hadn't even made it past Damascus Gate when a soldier had stopped to ask him for his identity papers, which he had forgotten back at the apartment, and he had been detained for several hours, and, if not for his command of Hebrew and his precise description of his building in Pisgat Ze'ev, things really could have gotten hairy.

Mehari and Aaron listened intently, asking for details, stopping the flow of his narration to get him to add in the minutiae. Each time, he got deeper into the construction of his story, making many unnecessary embellishments. He usually didn't like this method since this way he wasn't the owner and master of the story. Instead, it became the property of his listeners. Storytelling was a dangerous game, and the tale could slip from your hands at just the moment you thought it was fully yours. Still, he felt this was a good test of his ability to narrate, or rather to fabricate. After all, narration was fabrication. Anything else was just a poor imitation, merely passing on a story made up by someone else.

He began to challenge himself, responding to every twist and turn of the questions. He quit fidgeting and immersed himself in the game that had been set out for him, until he took ownership, turning it into his favorite game.

When he was finished, he was exhausted and waiting to be left alone, although this wish was thwarted when Aaron started to chide him for taking his blue-striped shirt. He seemed serious as he scolded Dawit for not asking permission, and Dawit had no choice but to apologize again and again, vowing never to do it again.

He couldn't escape this siege except by pretending to be asleep, and then he dove into his memories of what had happened at Sarah's house, where she had finished with the tune he'd requested, which had evoked such sweet fantasies. He came back to himself only when she put aside the oud, studying his reaction. With difficulty, he abandoned his inner state to express his admiration for what he had heard. He pressed his legs together so that his body wouldn't reveal the distance he had traveled in his imagination.

She had returned to her yellow papers, jotting down a few words. At first, Dawit thought she'd discovered something in his admiration for her music, but then he panicked at the thought that she might have noticed where he'd really gone.

He was only freed from his confusion when she asked: "Before you discovered this latest substitute of yours, what were you looking for exactly? Did you want to love, or did you want to be loved?"

Dawit had never paid such precise attention to his desires. He thought for a while, but was unable to untangle the two, and so instead of answering, he asked her, "And what's the difference? I think it's the same, to love means to be loved. No?"

Sarah switched off the tape recorder, so Dawit knew that she was breaking her research rules by speaking at last.

"Not always . . . sometimes, we want to be loved more than anything else, so we might look for love just so we can receive this gift. But let me go further—I'll say that we might think we're overflowing with love for others, when really, we're just receiving it. And if we start to distinguish between the two, then we can help control our chaotic ways of loving and figure out exactly what we want."

The words settled in his mind, scattering his thoughts, and he began to dig through his feelings, searching for his true desire. It wasn't easy. He tried to search for the thread that would separate the two, loving and being loved, but could not. When she realized he was lost, she tried to help him. But this time, it was after switching on her recorder:

"Try to visualize with me: You like a girl, and somehow, you've expressed your feelings to her. Would it be enough for you to just tell her, or is it very important to find out whether she feels the same?"

"I don't know. I might find some pleasure in just showing how I feel about her, but there will always be something missing. Yeah, now I can say that just expressing my love isn't enough, and that I'd be waiting for something in return. But at the same time, I've never tried it that way, to see if it's enough or not. I might need to think about it harder, in order to pull them apart."

Sarah went back to her notes before setting down her pen, as if leaving space for an urgent idea.

"All right then, what about your fantasies? In them, are the women admiring you, or are you the one who takes the first step?"

Dawit paused for a moment, then seized hold of the end of the thread. He wanted to express his surprise at these questions, which gnawed at him, drawing out things he'd never noticed, but he went back to focusing on what came to mind:

"I don't just play around with their features—I always give myself a different look. I'm handsome, I'm confident, my skin's a lighter brown. Now I can remember that I always wished I was lighter. It starts with an admiring look from them, which I answer with some pleasant nonchalance, and then I leave room for them to come to me before I finally respond. I feed off their constant praise about my looks, my manliness. I don't think even one of them passed me by without showering me with compliments."

Sarah smiled as she took down a few notes, as if she'd gotten what she wanted, before telling him that today's session was over and that they could meet tomorrow if that worked for him.

He nodded, increasingly curious to read all her notes, or at least the last few words.

"So what did you get out of all that?"

"As I'd expected, it was a very useful session, no doubt about it. Thank you very much, and I'm sorry if I wore you out."

It wasn't the answer he'd been looking for. He wanted to know her opinion of him. He wasn't sure if she'd misunderstood him or if she was just being evasive to freeze him out of her conclusions. It felt strange that he needed *her* so he could learn all these things about himself. He thought about how the soul was down deeper inside us than we could reach, to yank off its covers. He felt so wrapped up in the layers of himself that the more he peeled away, the more he discovered even thicker ones.

Now, on his bed, listening to the snoring of his two roommates, he thought about the layers under which their souls were hidden. He wondered whether they even knew it. He closed his eyes, determined to struggle his way to the bottom. He felt a mixture of curiosity and need and, above all, rage at the veils that separated him from himself.

He woke with difficulty to Aaron's shouting, telling him to hurry up so they wouldn't miss the tour of the National Cemetery. He felt as if he hadn't slept at all—that he'd closed his eyes for a few seconds before opening them again. Still, he'd been able to catch a faint trace of a dream he would have totally immersed himself in if it hadn't been for this rude awakening.

He remembered that he'd been walking alone in an endless land, and that he was busy searching for a destination that he could no longer remember. He got to a place that was like an oasis, with thick bushes surrounding a small stream.

He'd walked up to it, thirsty. But his steps betrayed him, and, as he struggled to lift his foot, he felt the ground beneath him sink its hooks into his legs. When he reached the creek, he had no strength left. He got down on his knees and lowered his head, but he came up against sand. All at once, the water had disappeared. He plunged his hand in and began to dig in the sand. It was pliable and flowing, layer after layer, but there was no water. The sand looked like identical pieces of fabric laid one on top of the other, with each piece pulled away to reveal the next, yet without any real change.

He didn't know what happened next—he didn't know if he made it to the water or if his quest was interrupted by Aaron's shouts. He got dressed in a hurry, hoping the tour wouldn't take too long.

The bus took them, in a long line of buses, to the top of Mount Herzl, which stood just to the west of Jerusalem. Dawit sat next to his two roommates, even though he had tried to avoid them at first. The noise of the other passengers died down as soon as the guide started explaining the schedule for their visit. He noticed how Aaron and Mehari showed exaggerated appreciation for every word that came out of the guide's mouth, as he spoke with reverence about the services rendered by those who were buried in Israel's National Cemetery. All this was repeated as they walked around the marble tombs that were now covered with a layer of grass. Dawit found himself copying his roommates' admiration whenever the guide's gaze fell on him. He felt the organizers were watching to see the tour's effect on the participants, so he decided to give them what they wanted to prevent any unintended consequences. For the same reason, he hid the question that popped into his mind about the identities of the leaders who lay on Mount Herzl, since he noticed the place looked like a family cemetery.

On the way back to the bus, he stuck close to his roommates. The cemetery's exit was thronged with visitors, and then all movement suddenly stopped. He shifted his gaze to the right—only to look straight into the eyes of the old woman who had a single pair of teeth in the middle of her upper jaw. She gave the same mean laugh. When his attempts to escape her failed, he resorted to pretending he didn't know her.

The tour ended on schedule, but he was still wound up tightly, since hiding his plans from his roommates was draining his energy, and he was in danger of missing his appointment. He was already late. The bus had moved only a little while the driver waited for the guide, who seemed to be involved in some kind of serious conversation.

Dawit's eyes flicked between this scene and the clock on the windscreen, hoping the conversation would end quickly. The guide and his friend finally boarded the bus, staring at Dawit before whispering to each other and giving the driver a signal to go. He felt a little bewildered, and he was anxious to understand their looks. He tried to convince himself that he was being delusional, but his roommates disabused him of that, asking what he'd done to draw this much attention.

As soon as the bus stopped, he jumped off, telling Aaron and Mehari that he'd be back soon. He ignored their questions and headed for the bus stop. He couldn't shake that last scene. He searched his memory of the day but couldn't find anything to warrant such looks and whispering.

Bus 44 took him to the Old City, and from there he took Bus 37, getting off at the entrance to the Hebrew University. He crossed the street, heading west, walking through the buildings with his eye on the top of the hill where Sarah's house stood. He wasn't too late, but he was afraid to miss even one minute of his appointment. If he hadn't been going to Sarah's, he would have made a lot of stops along these winding roads, as each one handed him over to the next. He felt the neighborhood's warm intimacy enveloping him. And, this way, he'd learned something new about himself—he liked narrow streets that went up or down. He didn't like straight ones, which were like a lifetime of walking with no end.

When he found the blue Citroën parked in front of the door, he exhaled with relief. He snatched a look at himself in the car's side mirror, adjusted his clothes, and headed toward the door, only to be surprised to see it open before he knocked.

"You like the car?"

He was too confused to say anything—he hadn't noticed that she could see the whole area beside the house through a recessed window. He waited for her to invite him in, but instead she came out, telling him they were going somewhere before they went back to work. He got in the passenger seat, not understanding anything. She set off, asking him questions without turning to look at him: his opinion of yesterday's session, how he'd spent his morning, whether he was excited to meet today. He started to answer the questions seriously, before losing steam when he noticed she was either busy with her phone or else glancing at her yellow papers, which she'd brought with her, although he didn't understand why.

She drove out to the main street, but a police car was blocking access. She turned the other way, where she found another vehicle blocking the road. The soldier told her that all roads leading to the Knesset building in Giv'at Ram were closed to cars. She parked, picked up her yellow papers, and told Dawit to hurry up and get out. Now, she finally started to explain things to him, as he tried to catch up with her unusually fast pace.

"We're going to see a demonstration. It's some African refugees protesting the government's decision to deport a bunch of them back to their countries. I want you to stay calm. Don't talk to anyone, especially the refugees. And if security asks you anything, just show them your ID papers."

Dawit's face shifted with anxiety. He wished she'd told him, so he could have waited at her house until she came back. But she reassured him that this was all normal, and that her instructions were just a precaution.

They got to the square that faced a yellow building with huge marble columns along the front. The square was packed with people. Dawit's eyes immediately fell on his own country's flag, and pictures of his president covered in red spots. Meanwhile, in other photos, the president seemed to have a noose around his neck. Then he noticed signs calling on the government to reconsider its decision. Sarah was trying to get as close as possible to the protesters, while Dawit wanted to keep watching them from a distance. She didn't stop until she was right next to the soldiers who had surrounded the demonstrators.

From where he stood, Dawit could see it all clearly. The faces he knew so well, the chants that had sat in his throat so often he couldn't get them out: "Death to the dictatorship . . . death to the dictatorship . . ." The scene brought him back to the square where he'd grown up, to Komochtato, to the Revolution School, to the Blue Valley. Heat singed his heart, sending him back into all the torments he had thought were buried so deep he could forget them.

In front of him stood a soldier from Beta Israel, holding his machine gun. He passed the time cursing the Eritrean motherfuckers who had followed him to Israel, wishing that the government would send them back to their miserable fucking country, while his blond fellow soldier laughed at his outrageous insults.

Sarah was busy scribbling down notes. He tried and failed to avoid the soldier's endless stream of comments, until she drew him out of his thoughts by asking, "What do you see in the faces of the refugees, the Eritreans in particular? Are they angry or disappointed?"

He couldn't find the exact answer. He studied the faces he knew so well, struggling to see what lay behind them. An idea he had often entertained popped back into his mind—that Eritreans didn't know anger, that they only grieved and were broken and withdrew, while never losing their temper. For the oppressed, anger was a luxury, and between them and anger there stood a fence of humiliation and oppression. Anger was an act of will, and the oppressed had no will and no ability to make decisions. He wanted to explain all of that to her, but instead he could only say: "It's both."

Sarah took photos of the demonstrators, particularly the people's faces, while Dawit went back to listening to the conversation between the Ethiopian soldier and his blond colleague. He dared to get a little closer, since all the noise meant he couldn't hear them clearly. The soldier gave him a suspicious look before turning back to his friend.

A demonstrator approached the security fence, and the soldier pointed the butt of his machine gun at him.

The man retreated, giving a muffled curse, as though he were muttering to himself. The man noticed Dawit and channeled his frustration with the soldier into flipping Dawit his middle finger before disappearing into the crowd.

After that, the Ethiopian soldier relaxed, failing to notice that a white officer had appeared beside him. The blond soldier gave a smiling salute before he went back to watching the crowd, but, for his comrade, it was already too late. The officer poked the Ethiopian soldier in the shoulder, wordlessly, and he stiffened in a panic, caught between raising his head in a military salute and lowering it to show respect for the officer.

The officer moved on, but the soldier kept watching him anxiously out of the corner of his eye. Dawit was delighted to see the Ethiopian sweat. It eased some of the anger he felt at the insult flung at him.

Sarah turned and asked Dawit to follow her. He walked for a while before turning back to the soldier, who was distracted, muttering a curse to himself. He went on following Sarah, but then he suddenly stopped, remembering something. He made sure the Ethiopian was focused on his colleague, and then he closed his fist and straightened the middle finger, briefly pointing it at the man before he continued on his way, fully satisfied.

Back at Sarah's house, he sat in the same chair while she went to change her clothes, coming back with two cups of coffee. He waited for her to finish looking at the photos she had taken and to jot down her quick notes. She looked more serious today: the way she sat, her facial expression. He missed the easy way she'd been with him before, her warm introductions that had melted away his confusion. He longed for her to play for him, but considering her demeanor, such a request seemed out of the question.

Once she had finished, she lifted her head and looked at him. She let out a sigh of relief and smiled as she asked his impression of the previous session. He stifled his anger as he told her that, actually, he had answered that question in the car, but then he backed off.

"I've come back with more questions than answers. I don't know. Maybe it's because I'm entering a totally unfamiliar world. I thought about it a lot, but basically: Why did you choose to research the sex lives of refugees? Is that the best shortcut to understanding their psychology?"

Sarah laughed, saying it was a good question. "I can see significant progress. In and of itself, this question means that you're starting to engage with our dialogue in a positive way. Still, I don't want you to get too caught up in the particulars. Just answer me, and that will be enough to help us reach the goal."

He wanted to ask her what *goal* she had in mind, and he wanted to remind her of his question, which she had said was a good one, but she shrugged all of that off, switched on the recorder, and started asking questions.

"Okay. Let's imagine you were one of the participants in today's demonstration. Would you be more likely to insult the government for its decision, or would you appeal to them to reverse it?"

Dawit felt a surge of irritation, since this was more or less a repetition of her question about the refugees' facial expressions, while she'd just ignored *his* questions. Now, he decided to start toying with her.

"I don't know if I'd take part in the demonstration at all. But if I did, I might do both. Maybe I'd just walk silently in the crowd. Maybe I'd hold some sign, maybe not. I don't know exactly."

Sarah thought for a while, holding her pen. She wrote something, then went back to cross it out, and Dawit watched her with delight. If only he had done this right from the beginning; he wished he hadn't gotten carried away and revealed his innermost thoughts, if this was the way she was going to treat him. When she got tired of trying to seize hold of something in what he'd said, she tried again from another angle.

"Okay then . . . let's make it more specific. If you had just finished with one of your fantasies, and you went out to a demonstration like this, would you be more inclined to shout and curse or would you be relaxed, and then you'd make your demands more calmly?"

"Is there some relationship between sex and the way I express myself? I mean, I just want to understand so I can answer."

Dawit tossed this out, then leaned back in his chair. He had started playing her game. He would give her as much as she gave him. Sarah heaved a tight sigh before she stopped the recording and answered him curtly. "Yes. There are people who experience some or all of their emotions through the lens of their repressed sexuality. That is, to the extent that we aren't able to express our sexuality, our other emotions will become confused or exaggerated."

Dawit smiled, pleased to see that she was the one answering to *him*, before going back to play his part in the game. "In all likelihood, I wouldn't participate in the protest. I would be so relaxed I couldn't do something like that, and if I did go out—"

Sarah's phone rang, interrupting Dawit midthought. She went to another room to answer the call. Dawit picked up his own phone and found several calls from Aaron and Mehari, since only *he* had to silence his phone. Sarah came back to her chair, asking Dawit to go on. She didn't apologize. This was the first thought that came to his mind, and he told her that he'd finished his answer.

It took some time for her to recover before she went on: "Right now, regardless of how you expressed yourself at the demonstration . . . let's suppose you were holding a sign or a picture. Would you have taken it home, or would you have tossed it away?"

Dawit didn't understand the point of this question. By now, every time she asked a question, he would pause before answering and ask himself: *What does she want with this question?* This particular question seemed vague and pointless. He wanted to ask for clarity, but he avoided provoking her anger and went with the first answer that came to mind.

"I'd take it home with me. Maybe it would give me a good feeling every time I saw it."

Sarah gave a mean smile, as if her hook had come back with a good catch. Dawit spotted it and felt a wave of anxiety, replaying the question in his mind.

"Have you also been keeping things from the girls, the ones your imagination feeds on?"

Here, Dawit finally noticed the trap into which Sarah had led him. He returned to his fantasies and found that, yes, the most vivid ones were associated with things he had taken from the girls: a handkerchief, a pen, an earring, a ring, stockings, and glasses. They were associated with whatever he could get hold of by theft and fraud. He remembered how just seeing the object in front of him would make him feel aroused in the extreme, and that he would touch it only when he'd reached the heights of his cravings. He collected all these images in his mind, but he didn't want to put his feet into the trap of his own volition. Instead, he chose an answer that was far off the mark, as he avoided looking at Sarah's face.

"Absolutely not."

If Sarah had been as kind to him as she had been on that first day, he would have told her everything plainly: collecting women's things was his greatest pleasure. Collecting these objects was like filling a huge hole in his soul. He collected and collected, and it was never enough. Collecting women's possessions was the best way he had of feeling safe. Although only one of these objects could get him to climax fast: the round glasses. He had managed to steal a pair and always kept it in his stash. Whenever he imagined a girl wearing those glasses, she would come back to him, full of a drowsy lust.

"What comes to mind if I ask about your mother's life story? How would you describe her to me?"

Once again, Sarah had stepped into a dark place. Where was this mother to say anything about, or to describe his feelings for? He wished he knew *something* about her. No. He didn't want to know anything. This was how he'd spent his whole life, and this was how he would go on with it. Perhaps it was just curiosity that had led him to search for his mother among all the women who had cared for him. Now, he wished his mother had been the most tender and sympathetic among the women soldiers, the one who had hugged him tightly, whose chest he'd pressed himself up against, inhaling her scent, before she had decided to ignore him for no good reason and go off to care for others, even though he'd tried so hard to connect with her. The woman with short black hair and round glasses. He didn't imagine any mother but her, and he didn't want any other mother, despite how angry he felt with her.

When Sarah repeated her question, Dawit left it all behind—that tender and tough soldier whom he both loved and hated. He let go of the bosom that had held him so tightly before it had abandoned him forever. He left behind the scent that had never left him, her round glasses, her prominent chest, her big buttocks. He left it all, and started to tell a story about an imaginary mother, giving her many qualities but without feeling any affection for her. When the meeting was over, Sarah walked him to the door, thanking him mechanically as he struggled to shake off his confusion. He avoided looking her in the eye, hoping their goodbyes would end as quickly as possible.

As soon as she closed the door behind him, he felt a high as he took out the round glasses from his pocket. He had managed—without their owner noticing—to slip them from their place on the table. He was filled with a joy he knew well. There was a hole in the depths of his soul that had been filled with a new object.

(26)

On his way back to Pisgat Ze'ev, Dawit tried to get ahold of his roommates, but they didn't answer.

He guessed that their incessant messages must mean that they were
curious about where he'd gone, nothing more. He returned to his day
with Sarah, to her carefully calculated questions about the things that
he had spent a lifetime hiding from the people around him, and before
that, hidden from himself. These might be things he made up or things
that actually happened. He was now able to put a dividing line between
the two realms, between what had really happened and what was imaginary, but he didn't want to go any further in separating the two. There
was a comfort in having fuzzy boundaries, as it gave him the chance to
choose the side he liked.

Once again, the elevators were out of service, so he took the stairs
up all five flights, hoping that, when he arrived exhausted, he would
not find his friends waiting for a thorough explanation of what he'd
been doing all this long day. He passed by the people who lived in an
apartment on the second floor, who were about to go out. He greeted
them, but they didn't respond. Instead, they just gave him looks that
he didn't understand.

He got to his apartment. He paused to catch his breath before
walking in through the always-open door and heading for his room.
He ran into the unattractive woman who lived in the room next to his,
who deliberately wore see-through clothes. But instead of finding some

meaningless topic of discussion, like she usually did, she walked right past as if she hadn't seen him.

When he got to the closed door of his room, he didn't hear anything, even though it was usually loud at this time of day. It seemed strange that his two friends would have gone to sleep so early, but he didn't want an explanation; he just felt pleased. When he opened the door, he found Aaron and Mehari whispering intently, their expressions troubled. As soon as he stepped in, they fell silent. He said hi and quickly threw himself onto the bed, hoping that the night would pass without any trouble. When they didn't say anything, he slowly lifted his head to see what was going on. They had been staring at him, but they averted their eyes when he looked up.

He sat up in bed, asking if there was something going on, but neither of them answered. He repeated the question, and Aaron told him to ask *himself*. He knew that his disappearances had annoyed them, but this time, things seemed different. He started to apologize, weaving together a new story that he hoped would shake off their surprised looks and make them forget their anger. But he didn't get the reaction he was expecting, and they spent a moment trading glances before Mehari interrupted:

"You can cut it out. We know everything."

As Dawit asked what he meant, he was already growing anxious. He begged Mehari to tell him, then turned toward Aaron. He got up out of bed and sat between them on the floor. Mehari was the one who finally spoke: "We know that you're a traitor living among us, and that you have nothing to do with Beta Israel. Unfortunately, we trusted you. We thought of you as a brother."

These words shook Dawit, and he went silent, waiting for anything to appear that could cancel out the truth of what was happening. For example, maybe he'd fallen asleep, and this was nothing but a nasty dream. Maybe he just had to wake up; maybe he was living out one of his fantasies, which he'd gotten used to being in the realm of truth. He wanted anything except what he was hearing now.

When nothing like that happened, he asked, hoarsely, if the news had spread to everyone or if they were the only ones who knew. He didn't know why he didn't ask anything else, like: How did they know? Who had told them? Why did they believe them? In fact, he didn't know why he hadn't just denied the accusation from the start.

They told him that this was the sole topic of discussion in their building, and that the news might not have stopped at just their square. The message reached Dawit loud and clear. He went back to his bed and started to collect his things. Aaron interrupted him, cruelly advising him to flee with only a few things and leave them the problem of the suitcase. He saw it as a small price to pay for their silence. As he left the apartment, it wasn't clear whether the elevator was working again. He leaped down the stairs, floor by floor, until he found himself back out in the street. There, he ran for the bus stop, hoping no one would stop him until he got out of Pisgat Ze'ev. He settled in by the window in the last seat on Bus 44, concealing his features sometimes with his hand, other times with his shirt collar. It began to feel like an astonishing echo—his journey to Israel had been so similar to this escape. Was he destined to move from country to country, with no homeland ever in sight?

The partially empty bus drove out of the settlement on its way to the main stop in the Old City. Meanwhile, since evening was falling, most buses were going in the opposite direction. Here he began to rack his brain: Who had seen and reported him? His old neighbor from Gondar, who had only one lonely pair of teeth in the middle of her upper jaw—the woman who had seen him that very morning at the National Cemetery?

But she hadn't done it before, and she had known he'd come with her to Israel. Had it been Yaqub, overcome by envy and the desire not to be a lonely loser? Or would it be a surprise? Maybe it was Sarah who had spread the news about him, now that she no longer needed him? He didn't know. He felt his head swirling with possibilities, each of which had some grounding in reality.

He switched to Bus 37 and got off at the Hebrew University. From there, he cut through the winding streets. He felt the streets were empty of everything that, before, had filled them up, and he no longer liked the narrow streets that rose and fell. Instead, he wished for straight, monotonous streets in which there was nothing to stop him.

He gave the door a sharp rap. He hadn't looked into the Citroën mirror to adjust his collar. When Sarah opened up, she looked at him in surprise. He walked in without waiting for permission, and, as he told her what had happened, he watched her expressions. She was surprised, but not as surprised as he'd expected; she was sad, but less than he'd hoped. She started to search for a solution, but in a way that seemed almost relaxed.

He couldn't really tell what was going on with her. Nothing proved that she had done it, but, at the same time, nothing proved she hadn't. In the end, he was compelled to tell her about his doubts. She scoffed at him, saying he was crazy. She asked why she would do such a thing when she still wasn't finished with her research, and she reminded him of their agreement. He withdrew, bowing his head and apologizing, trying to justify his offense. She sat on the couch. She lit a cigarette and began, anxiously, to smoke. He sat across from her and repeated his apology. She waved a hand at him, and he was silent. She looked overwhelmed. He had hoped she would find a solution for him, that she would offer to let him hide at her place. He didn't know whether she had another idea.

He dismissed all these thoughts and began to listen attentively as soon as she started to speak:

"I never expected such a thing to happen, otherwise I would have compressed things into a shorter period. It's true that I've finished with the most important parts, but still, what remains is not insignificant."

Dawit didn't know what she was talking about, and he searched her words for something about him, about the place he could find shelter, for a solution that would mean he didn't have to go back to being on the run. After a brief silence, she spoke again:

"Anyhow, I'll definitely find a solution."

She stood up and left the room, leaving Dawit with a ray of hope. Finally, she was taking his problem seriously. He cursed the hour when he had doubted her and thought her the snitch, and he cursed himself for being so reckless as to tell her his doubts.

She came back and, without sitting, handed him a wad of cash. "Don't worry. I'll find a way to finish the research, however difficult it might be. Thank you so much for all your cooperation. It's really helped me a lot."

Dawit stood up, stunned. He nodded as he walked slowly toward the door. There were no words that would fit this scene. Only the silence was fitting. Silence was always the right size for such moments, when it took only a word to turn things upside down.

When he reached the door, he turned toward her, stretching his lips as far up as they would go, forcing a smile. In that moment, he had a strange desire to hear one last thing, to leave with something other than the five hundred shekels she had put in his hand.

He asked if he could know her opinion of him—if she would tell him what conclusions she'd drawn about his personality. He asked for just one word, but her smile faded while her eyes grew sharper. She pursed her lips and pushed back wisps of her curly black hair. These were all the things he loved about her, and she did them to perfection, although now he didn't find them seductive or attractive. He didn't know where his desire for her had first started—in his mind and heart, or in all these mannerisms that had now lost all meaning.

She closed the door behind him, excusing herself for not giving an answer. She told him her work was for the purpose of research, not for treatment.

It had a purpose, in any case. He repeated this as he wandered through the streets of Jerusalem. He was surprised to hear this word so starkly and wished she had used some hazier word, one that had a lot of meanings, to soften the blow. He remembered the European, who had listened so intently to his story in Endabaguna before brushing it aside. He remembered Saba, who had helped him just as much as it had been useful to her, and now Sarah had put him in the same box: he was only for a purpose. The worst was when our stories led us to something other than what we wanted; the worst was when they gushed out until the udder was dry, and we found ourselves—we, the owner of these stories—completely empty. So Dawit was like his stories: solely for a purpose, an object that was not afforded the luxury of survival after it had been used.

His feet carried him down the only road he knew until he ended up at Damascus Gate. The area was almost empty, and the shops at the edges were about to close. He avoided meeting the security guards' gazes as he walked down the narrow road, while the few remaining tourists headed back in the other direction. He wasn't sure why he kept going down this road, whether he was headed for al-Aqsa Mosque, or the Church of the Holy Sepulcher, or the Wailing Wall. Was he going to be Dawoud, or David, or Dawit? All he knew was that he was empty inside and looking for something to lean on.

He saw security ask the few who remained in the Church of the Holy Sepulcher to leave, and he saw it was the same at the Wall, while the road leading to al-Aqsa Mosque was already empty and blocked off. Even places of worship needed to rest and take care of themselves after a long and arduous day of wooing itinerant flocks.

Everything around him seemed tired: the faces, the shops, the buildings. Yet all of them had reached their time of rest. All of them could escape from the troubles of the day, everything except him—he was still on a long, exhausting journey. Or, to be more precise, he was at the start of it.

He passed a Black man in his fifties who was closing the doors to his shop. The man looked at him, studying his features, before asking him in Arabic if he was Eritrean. Astonishment flooded Dawit's face, and he wasn't sure how to answer. The man gave a proud laugh. "Nobody beats me in picking out the faces of Africans. Now come on, tell me, did you come from Massawa or Agordat or Assab? Your features aren't saying Asmara."

Dawit nodded in agreement, although he avoided choosing one of these Eritrean cities, which the man had listed with such knowledge. He'd never felt that he belonged to any city in his country, and he knew only the field where he'd been born and raised. But the man came back to it, insisting, and Dawit found he had no choice: "Assab."

He said it, not knowing what difference it would make to the man.

The man looked pleased, telling Dawit that he'd known he was speaking to a Muslim, and then the man started to explain how reading faces led him to a knowledge of their owners' religions, before he stopped, as if he'd just remembered something. "You don't like the Israelis . . . right?"

Dawit nodded, unthinkingly, and it seemed the man wasn't waiting for any other answer. The man grew even more pleased as he asked his name.

"Dawoud."

He let the man praise this name, and he almost smiled at the game life had thrust him into. Here he was, going back to the first name he'd chosen, as if he had gone full circle, yet without reaching his final destination. How many circles would destiny take him through before he reached the end of all these exhausting turns?

"My name is Muhammad Ali. Or you can call me Mariel for short. Come visit my store whenever you like."

The man finished closing up his shop, and he would have left, except that Dawoud stayed right where he was, confused. The man asked if he could help him with anything, but his question was met with silence.

"HaKol BeSeder?" Mariel asked. Then he repeated his question in Arabic, as it seemed the Hebrew had inadvertently slipped from his tongue. When he learned that Dawoud was homeless, he insisted that Dawoud come with him, reminding him that "Muslims are like the bricks of a building—they support one another." He walked, and Dawoud followed.

They took al-Wad Street, and from there they turned onto Alaa' al-Deen Street, walking until they reached a building that bore a plaque that read, "African Community Association—Holy Jerusalem," but its doors were locked. Mariel paused for a moment, muttering, "We didn't catch them," before asking his companion to follow him. Dawoud was confused: Mariel seemed completely African, and yet he spoke Arabic with a pure Jerusalem accent, and he used Hebrew words as if he had mastered that language.

A few steps from the community association building, they came to a large plaza. There were two odd-looking low-rise buildings on either side that met in the middle, while crowded at the edges of the square were shops that looked totally African. Mariel stood and called out to a child who was playing football with some other kids, while Dawoud's gaze wandered around.

There were women in hijab, pictures of the Kaaba, several murals that extolled trips to Mecca, and posters that congratulated those who had returned from the hajj. He saw Arabic calligraphy that looked beautiful, although he couldn't totally understand what was written. A skinny girl in leggings leaned against the wall, sharing a laugh with a good-looking young guy with braids. When Dawoud lifted his gaze, he saw windows covered by iron bars, and it reminded him of how he'd felt in the Blue Valley.

The child said hello to Dawoud, as his father had instructed, and then he ran ahead of them to the house. Mariel had a brief chat with someone on the street before he walked his guest home. Dawoud passed through a dark hallway that ended at an open door that separated the rooms on the right from those on the left, and he went in and settled down in a narrow room. Scarcely any time had passed before a woman in a wide jilbab came in and began to set plates of food in front of him.

"Um Adam," Mariel said to his wife. "This is our son Dawoud, a Muslim from Eritrea."

The woman greeted Dawoud in stilted Arabic. She finished putting out the dishes and then hurried away. Adam came in, showing his skill with the ball until it nearly landed in the middle of the table.

"Dersus!"

His father shouted at him, and the boy fled. Dawoud didn't know what language Mariel was speaking. He invited his guest to eat, and Dawoud stretched out a hand to the African dishes as Mariel explained what each one was: "This is asida, and this is idam karkanji, and this one is madeeda. Don't be shy. You're at home."

Adam returned, peeking in at the door, and his father called out that he should come and share the food. He sat down right away, cutting off a large piece of the asida dough and dipping it in the ghee at the center.

Relief crept into Dawoud's heart. This was the first time he'd felt he was an honored guest just for being himself. Although he remembered that if he hadn't chosen a particular religion, he wouldn't have found all this. Had religions finally started to pay attention to him? Had they decided to save him after all this time?

It didn't matter. Here, he had found shelter, after he'd bounced from mattress to mattress with no end in sight. Now, he adjusted his pillow as he settled down in the corner of a smaller room. Around him were four of Mariel's sons, who had left him to sleep, promising to wake him at dawn for the Fajr prayer.

"Are you Israeli?"

He turned to Adam and said no.

"But ummi says you're a Falasha."

The child threw out this word and then pretended to be asleep. Anxiety came back to eat away at Dawoud's heart, just now, when he had finally moved to the column of the survivors.

(27)

At the first threads of morning light, Dawoud sat on a wooden chair in the narrow space crowded with misbaha prayer beads, in Mariel's shop near Damascus Gate. They had just finished the Fajr prayers. Dawoud had chosen a far-off water tap, and he had spent a long time in front of it, allowing his companion to go on ahead of him into al-Aqsa Mosque so that he wouldn't pray near him, and the man wouldn't notice his rank ignorance of the rituals of prayer.

Mariel was busy sweeping the dust off the shelves and the shop display as people began to walk past on the street. Once he'd finished, he handed Dawoud a string of brown misbaha beads.

"These are made of sandalwood. If you like them, they are my gift to you. Otherwise, choose what you like from the store."

Dawoud thanked the man, and he was about to put the beads around his neck when he realized that they were supposed to stay in his hand. He tried to mimic the quick movements Mariel used to flip through his beads.

It wasn't long before Dawoud got into the flow of the souq's moods and the movement that reached its climax just before noon. He went to fetch breakfast from a nearby shop, and then he handed Mariel the misbahas that the customers demanded, feeling proud when he was praised by the owner for his dedicated assistance.

They hadn't come to any agreement, and Dawoud took up these tasks without waiting for anything. He acted out of gratitude. When activity slowed in the afternoon, Mariel turned to his assistant, flustered, telling him that he would like to employ him, but the shop couldn't afford another worker's wages, and that he hoped the African Community Association would find him a solution. In the meantime, he would shelter him until God relieved him of this charge. For now, that was all Dawoud had hoped.

He walked toward al-Wad Street, and from there he turned onto Aladdin Street, carrying a message from Mariel to one of the center's employees. From the outside, the building didn't seem much different from its ancient surroundings, but inside it looked like a modern two-story, with floors made of a glossy inlaid marble and vaulted yellow ceilings that rested on stone pillars.

Dawoud waited for someone to appear so that he could deliver the message. He went through a room with "Sewing Workshop" written above it and passed a music corner. He stopped at a plaque on the history of Africans in Jerusalem. His curiosity was piqued after he discovered that Mariel was among the descendants of those immigrants who had come to Jerusalem a century before from Sudan, Chad, Nigeria, and Senegal. Next to the plaque, there was a photo of a young Black man carrying a rifle with a number of Palestinians gathered around him. Written under it was "Tareq the African, the hero of Jabal al-Mukaber, who defended the southern neighborhood."

"How may I help you?"

An employee's question cut off Dawoud's train of thought. Dawoud gave him Mariel's message, which the man read on the way to his office. By the time he had settled into his chair, he had finished reading.

He was silent for a moment before he asked Dawoud to wait a bit. Then he picked up his phone and left the room. When he pushed back his chair, it revealed what was written beneath the large portrait of the turbaned sheikh: "Hajj Amin al-Husseini, Mufti of Jerusalem, 1895–1974." The employee returned and told Dawoud that these were hard times for finding work or shelter and that the center's entire budget, which was insufficient for the needs of the community, had been spent. Dawoud rose and headed back to Damascus Gate, having been made a promise that his request would be considered as soon as there were sufficient funds available.

He had scarcely left the center when he ran into a young Black man who was dashing, terrified, inside. A little farther on, he came across a group of soldiers who were chasing him. Dawoud was filled with panic. His legs froze, and he couldn't calm down even after they had passed him, storming into the center after the young man.

He told Mariel what he'd seen as he tried to collect his wits, but Mariel wasn't surprised.

"We see such things every day. We'd be surprised if we didn't. But more importantly, what did they tell you?"

When he'd finished relaying the news, he found himself driven to know more about the Africans of Jerusalem, and he took advantage of the lack of customers to ask Mariel.

"It's a long story, and you'll hear it in time, but for now I can tell you that we came here for different reasons; some of us came to the neighborhood near al-Aqsa Mosque, and we're called al-Mujawirun, or 'the Near Ones.' Some came only to battle Israel as soon as the state was declared in 1948. There are older groups of Africans who were brought in by the British to build the railway lines, and when they returned to their countries, people were enthralled by their stories about Jerusalem. In any case, we are now Palestinians down to the marrow of our bones, and we will defend it heart and soul. The young man you saw being chased by the Israelis is one of those who protest every day against the Occupation, one way or another."

"Does that mean you have Palestinian IDs?"

Mariel laughed, and he put his misbaha beads back in their place before answering the question. "We are opponents of Israel, as I told you, but we are forced to use her blue IDs. The funny thing is that they wrote 'Jordanian' on my card in the field for nationality, since East Jerusalem was under Jordanian control before the Israeli occupation. But Jordan didn't give us their documents because it considered us immigrants. And because of that ill-fated Oslo agreement, the Palestinian Authority can't give the residents of Jerusalem Palestinian IDs either, so we have nothing but the documents of our adversaries."

A man about Mariel's age came in. Dawoud got up to ask the man what he needed, but the man just smiled as he came inside, pulled up a chair, and sat down.

"This is my twin brother, Muhammad Yassin," Mariel said. "There are three more, younger than us, who you'll also meet: Muhammad Mahmoud, Muhammad Is'haq, and Muhammad Jibril . . . this is our son Dawoud, from Eritrea."

After Yassin and Dawoud exchanged greetings, Mariel told his brother that he'd been giving his guest an introduction to their long presence in Jerusalem.

"And for sure you told him we're all strict religious prudes like you."

Dawoud was shocked by Yassin's language, but Mariel's laugh softened things, and he said, "No, I did not. And I didn't tell him we're all communists like you either."

The two burst into loud laughter, and Dawoud joined in, enjoying their camaraderie. Then Mariel said, "But you can't deny that the original reason for us coming here was religious. Also, the Mufti of Jerusalem, Hajj Amin al-Husseini, would not have made us guardians of al-Aqsa Mosque if we weren't all brothers of the faith."

"We're all Muslims, man. Don't make this young guy think badly of us. I'm just talking about strictness. Listen to this story, Dawoud, and judge for yourself."

Dawoud straightened up as he listened to Yassin.

"You know how they say someone is more Catholic than the Pope? It was like that for our fathers and grandfathers, who were more observant than any other Muslims. They only allowed Muslims to enter al-Aqsa Mosque, no matter what. Once, the Sultan wanted to fulfill the wishes of the Belgian Duke of Brabant and his Austrian wife, who wanted to see the insides of al-Aqsa. But the problem was—how to persuade the African guards to comply with the Sultan's order? They finally settled on a strange trickery; they granted leave to all the African guards of al-Aqsa Mosque on the day of the visit, and that way it went off smoothly."

Yassin's final words were twined with his laughter, and Mariel smiled, shaking his head. "That is not fanaticism. That is devotion in service to the sacred. You know what happened when Jibril Tahruri took a bullet meant for the Mufti. The Hajj rewarded us with the al-Mansouri and al-Basiri ribats."

"You mean Little Harlem? Man, those two buildings are nothing but Ottoman prisons, just like the life we live here. Why don't you tell Dawoud their real names? They were the Prison of Blood, for those sentenced to death, and the Prison of Bindings, for those serving more than ten years."

Now Dawoud understood what he'd felt when he saw the iron bars on the windows of those two buildings, and how they brought him back to his days in the Blue Valley. Yassin went on, but now in a more serious tone.

"But tell me, what reward did Fatima Bernawi get for being the first woman prisoner of the Occupation? And what about what Tareq al-Afriqi did, and Ali Jeddah, who spent seventeen years in detention, and Inam Qalambo, and so many others?"

"We are not expecting a reward from our homeland. We are Palestinians, and we do our part."

Yassin was about to respond when he noticed something grim in his brother's features that made him hold back. So he steered the conversation in another direction: "Tell me, Dawoud, what made you leave Eritrea? Were there people there who consider themselves Eritreans, while their countrymen can't bear to look at their faces?"

Dawoud didn't understand the question, but Yassin wasn't really looking for an answer. He rose, saying he was busy, and told Dawoud he'd like to meet up with him again.

"Yassin has a temper, as you see. He had a bitter time in detention after he tried to plant a bomb on a bus carrying Israelis, in response to the assassination of a prominent member of the PFLP. Our eternal disagreement is that I believe the homeland is not always obligated to meet us with immediate rewards. Yes, it's true, we have our problems. The Israelis are hostile because of the position we take on the Occupation, while some of our own people still can't accept the color of our skin. But no life is without problems. Isn't that so, Dawoud?"

Dawoud felt himself sinking into the paradox of the African Palestinians. He didn't know why he saw himself in them. It was the black foam all over again, floating to the surface despite all their attempts to become part of the heart of the place.

"Yep. There's no life without problems." Dawoud tossed off his answer, then rose to take care of a new customer.

(28)

Dawoud's first month as Mariel's guest came to an end. His relationship with the residents of Ribat al-Mansouri and al-Basiri grew stronger, and everyone called him Dawoud the Eritrean.

Instead of mastering the Jerusalem dialect, he improved his knowledge of the Chadian Gorani language that Mariel's family spoke, with some words from the languages of the Fallata and Balala peoples. Mariel came to depend on him in the shop, and he would leave Dawoud there on his own so that he could tend to his own affairs.

But one thing troubled Dawoud: he hadn't told anyone his real story. It particularly bothered him that he hadn't told Mariel that he was on the run from the scandal of impersonating a Falasha Jew. He often acted in ways that made no sense to the shopkeeper; he would leave suddenly, without saying anything, or he would turn away, showing the customers his back. Each time, he found a convincing excuse to ease Mariel's concerns—after all, what the man feared most was being fined for having an undocumented worker.

Dawoud hid because, once, he noticed Aaron loitering on the street near Damascus Gate. Another time, it was because Sarah had appeared, her oud slung across her back as she walked in a friendly way beside a young African man who seemed to be infatuated with her. The other times, he was attempting to avoid the security guards who never stopped walking up and down the street, giving him suspicious looks. He didn't know if they were really looking for him or if they just found it funny to intimidate him.

But aside from that, he was starting to get the hang of his new life. He was getting used to it, even accepting it. He was embracing the idea of black foam now and no longer trying to get past it. Let the surface be his place—what of it? He hadn't ever experienced settling into the depths of things. He hadn't gotten to the core of a place. He didn't know—maybe the core was bad, too, one way or another.

He wished he had gotten over this idea sooner so that he could have shortened his journey of suffering. But he had gone back to thinking that he had no choice in everything that had happened to him, since misfortunes chased him with a fury. He wasn't asking for much: he just wanted to survive, live a normal life, wake up, sleep, love and have children, and then die in his bed. He wasn't asking for more. Another time, he dismissed this idea and took up another—wasn't that the reason for his suffering, because he was looking for something cheap and ordinary? What if he'd raised his hopes a little? Would things have changed around him? Maybe the world always gave less than we asked of it, and since he had asked for the very rudiments of survival, it had given him nothing.

His days began to look monotonous. It didn't bother him, since living in this monotony had been his greatest wish. One day, he was sitting across from Mariel, who passed the time by reading an outdated newspaper since there were so few customers. Dawoud didn't have anything to do. He had finished cleaning the shop, arranging the prayer beads and rearranging them, until he sat, turning his gaze to those coming and going in front of him.

Suddenly the market surged with shouting and running in both directions, and it took a moment before Dawoud registered what was going on. He saw a large deployment of Israeli security forces. Quickly, Mariel closed up shop after learning that a young man had stabbed an Israeli soldier and fled the scene.

"Let's go. They're going to arrest anyone they suspect has any connection to this."

Security officials began closing the roads, and it was too late for them to get home. They went to the African Community Association, but found it closed. They wanted to go back to the shop and hide there, but the way back was no longer open. Mariel suggested that they separate so that they wouldn't arouse suspicion, and he told Dawoud to pretend to be a Jew: "If anyone asks, pick any Israeli name that comes to mind. And stay calm. The only thing that will save you is keeping a calm expression on your face."

Mariel headed off in the direction of the soldiers, while Dawoud stayed put, trying to keep it together as he searched himself for answers to whatever the soldiers might ask. He put a hand in his pocket and took out his Beta Israel ID card. He folded it and refolded it several times, then tossed it into a nearby landfill. He wouldn't dare show it and expose himself. Yet, at the same time, he couldn't find any name for himself other than Dawit. The familiarity of that name would make this reincarnation easier.

He took a few steps forward. The path seemed familiar, as if he had walked it thousands of times. He had gotten rid of his identity card, just as he had done back in Endabaguna. And he'd gone back to the Dawit he'd left behind. This was the same circle, and it did not stop whirling him around, toying with him.

He pushed through a crowd of confused soldiers without drawing their attention. The way they ignored him gave him a shot of confidence. He kept walking and found two soldiers running right at him, armed with automatic weapons. He froze in place, but they passed him, and he kept going. His fear began to fade as he approached the public square by Damascus Gate, which would take him onto broader streets, where he could free himself completely from the area that was sealed off. He had just barely started to feel a sense of relief when his anxiety surged back. Now, he walked up to another phalanx that surrounded the scene, blocking the road to the square.

He turned, trying to slip off down a side street.

"Atzor . . . Atzor."

The firm order came for him to stop. He stopped for a moment without turning back. He wasn't sure if the words had been directed at him. There was still movement headed in all directions, and the soldiers' shouts, telling people to stop, didn't stop them. He tried to walk again, and the voice grew sharper.

Then he found himself running. He ran with all his heart, without knowing where he was going, only wanting to get away, to save what was left of his body and soul. He was running with all his might, but with every step, he felt that some part of him was falling away. He didn't have the luxury of stopping to pick it up. It had been like this his whole life; he'd been content with so little, and now it would be enough for him to have just one foot, either his left or right hand—it didn't matter—half a face, a broken heart, a damaged lung. He would keep whatever it took to survive.

The bullet slammed into his chest, and he fell onto his back. Only now did he get a good look at what was behind him. The soldiers had caught a young man and begun to handcuff him. Then the order to stop *hadn't* been for him. But he had gotten used to the way Fate had of toying with him. It never missed the pleasure of dragging him into every tragedy, and there was no reason for it to be any different today.

The Ethiopian soldier who had shot him approached, realizing that he had hit the wrong man. The soldier held his head and asked him to identify himself, once in Hebrew and then in English before he tried the question in Amharic. Misery seized hold of his features as the rest of the soldiers ran toward him. The soldier repeated his question as he radioed for an ambulance. Dawoud didn't know why a strange sluggishness was taking over his body. The soldier's question very slowly echoed inside him. He saw the faces around him grow tense, but he still felt just as sluggish.

He tried to answer the man's question, but his tongue was growing too heavy. He wished he could have a conversation with the soldiers around him. Except now, he didn't want to answer them as much as he wanted to ask questions.

He wanted to ask them about his identity, whether his name was Dawoud or David or Dawit. He wanted to ask about his religion, whether he was Muslim, Christian, or Jew. About his nationality, too— whether he was Eritrean, Ethiopian, Israeli, or Palestinian.

He wished he could find the answer. He needed it now, right now, when people had finally turned to him, asking about the identity he had spent his life looking for. Then the noise around him began to subside. His body sank into a state of relaxation, and he felt the urge to sleep. He would sleep a little, and then he would wake up once all these people had found an answer to his question. He would leave them with this task, which had worn him out for so long.

He shut his eyes, and he could feel the foam of his spirit floating up to the surface. He left with a smile on his face, although he didn't know whether anyone would notice it.

(29)

One cold day toward the end of October, in 2015, a young Eritrean man was grinding through his monotonous day as he walked, feeling halfway secure, down one of the streets of Beersheba.

I don't know exactly what he was thinking in that moment, but if I wanted to make assumptions from the fact that he was Eritrean, I would say that he was dreaming big dreams. He wished, for instance, to find his three meals in an ordinary way, and he wished for all people to look on him with affection, except those few for whom he'd have liked to be invisible. These were the policemen, the border guards, the judges, the business owners, the sharp-tongued wives, the girls who could leave you first, the arrogant doctors, the guardians of important places, and, well, it was a list that never stopped getting longer because of injustice and arrogance, or maybe it was just because of the rising number of fools. I imagine that he would have smiled at my description and walked on without comment.

Suddenly, a noise shook his feeling of security.

The place swarmed with police cars and ambulances and panicked people running in every direction. It wasn't clear what was happening, and it wasn't his concern. He was just afraid the police would arrest him on charges of entering Israel illegally and send him back to his personal hell in Eritrea.

He tried to run, to save himself, but a bullet killed him.

The scene would have been filled with sadness, granting him his necessary glory, had it not been for the palpable relief from the Israeli police when they discovered their mistake was such a small one—he was only a refugee who had entered the country illegally. Meanwhile the Palestinians were busy wondering: Why did the Eritrean come to our country?

The young man couldn't answer. Perhaps he was focused on his place on the surface of things, a place he was in harmony with at last. Perhaps, before closing his eyes, he might have thought that he, too, would ask some questions of his own.

He might have.

No one knows.

He left with a smile on his face, unsure whether anyone would notice it.

—*In memory of the young Eritrean Habtom Ouldi Mikael Zaroum*

ABOUT THE AUTHOR

Haji Jabir is an Eritrean novelist who was born in the city of Massawa on the Red Sea Coast in 1976. He currently lives in Doha, Qatar, where he works as an Al Jazeera journalist. Jabir's creative aim is to shed light on Eritrea's past and present and to extricate his homeland from its cultural isolation. He is one of the most important Arabic-language authors of his time.

ABOUT THE TRANSLATORS

Sawad Hussain is a translator from the Arabic whose work has been recognized by English PEN, the Anglo-Omani Society, and the Saif Ghobash Banipal Prize for Arabic Literary Translation, among others. She is a judge for the Palestine Book Awards. Her recent translations include *Passage to the Plaza* by Sahar Khalifeh and *A Bed for the King's Daughter* by Shahla Ujayli. She has run workshops introducing translation to students and adults under the auspices of Shadow Heroes, the British Library, the Yiddish Book Center, the National Centre for Writing, Africa Writes, and the Shubbak Festival. She is the 2022 translator in residence at the British Centre for Literary Translation. She tweets at @sawadhussain.

Marcia Lynx Qualey is the founding editor of ArabLit, an online magazine and resource that won the 2017 "Literary Translation Initiative" award at the London Book Fair. She writes, edits, and translates for a variety of newspapers and magazines, teaches writing in Morocco, and also works with a number of Arabic literature projects, including Kitab Sawti and the Library of Arabic Literature.